Alternate Ending Publications Presents:

Twisted Fairy Tales

Anthology

Copyright

Rights

Printed proudly in the United States of America

CONTENTS

Dedication

The Twisted Fairy Tales Anthology was born of a dream and raised by some of the most amazing young talent to ever step foot in the indie publishing world. This project is dedicated to the writers who dared to dream and poured their hearts and souls into this collection, and to the countless authors, bloggers, publicists, and other support staff who donated their time, energy, and love of the written word to help make those dreams come true.

Handicapped Hearts

Faith Hays

True love.

The two words stare back at me from the white board in Ms. Shepherd's English class. She is somewhat of a hopeless romantic you could say. Judging by the pale circle that replaced the gorgeous engagement ring once glittering from her finger, she is ready to battle romance with a pitchfork and a torch.

"Class." She clears her throat and runs a hand through her limp, greasy hair. She really needs a shower. And some self-esteem. "These last few months of the semester we are going to be focused on a very important topic." She pauses briefly, her breath hitched in her throat. "True love."

Her red, puffy eyes are pinned on the floor. Whispers float around the room. A trembling frown makes its way to her face and she brushes away a fresh tear.

"This will be an out of class assignment," she further explains, clearing her throat. "You will search for it in every aspect of your life. Does it actually exist or did we simply make it up to help cope with our difficult reality?"

She exits the room without another word, leaving us stunned. Quiet sobbing echoes from behind the door. It takes us a second to process, but soon the room is filled with the sound of teenagers babbling about the scandalous breakup.

"Ugh," I sigh and dig through my book bag, searching for my latest novel.

I bury my nose in its pages and tune out the noise surrounding me. It's one of my favorites. I've read it so many times I've lost count, but that excited rush never fails to creep over me when I do.

"Your nose is always stuck in a book, isn't it Belle?" Leroy leans against the desk next to me.

"How long have you known me?" I ask, not looking up from my book. I hear him snicker and glance up to see a smile stretched across his charcoal face. I return to my book with a roll of my eyes.

"I wanted to talk to you about Gabriel."

I cringe. The mere mention of his name sends a grimy feeling creeping through my body.

"For the last time, no. I will not go on a date with him." I turn the page. *Why can't I just read in peace?*

"Just give him a chance," Leroy begs. "He's a lot better once you get to know him."

Leroy is blinded because he's Gabriel's best friend, but I see through his charming facade. Gabriel has been endlessly pursuing me for the past three months now. But I just can't. He is arrogant, entitled, and famous for breaking girls' hearts on a daily basis. I'm not giving him or any guy for that matter, that kind of power over me.

"No. It's not happening." I peer up at him with finality.

"Okay, okay. I tried." He sighs and turns on his heel. "But don't be surprised if he asks again."

"Thanks for the heads up." I mutter, more to myself, and shake my head.

The bell rings, I shove my book into my bag, and trudge off to my next class. The hallway is crowded and people walk incredibly too slow, making it impossible to pass through with ease. My hand tightens around my bag as I weave through the maze of bodies to my locker. A pink piece of paper is taped to it. I frown.

P-R-O-M.

The four letters are written in big, cursive font. According to the flier, the dance is only five weeks away. A ticket dangles from the bottom of the paper. I yank it off and turn it over in my hand. The words *pick you up at seven* are written on the back. I recognize the scribbled print from the numerous notes he's passed my way.

Gabriel.

I've turned him down every time he's asked me out. I've been more than clear how I feel about him, or rather how I *don't* feel, and somehow this boy still managed to convince himself that I'd go to the prom with him? He must be delusional.

"Watch where you're going freak!"

There's a loud crash to my left. I turn in time to see a stack of books scatter across the floor in front of a set of crutches wrapped around Aiden Peters' massive forearms. My eyes travel the length of them and land on his hard face. His jaw clenches as the jock yells at him, but he doesn't react. He stares straight ahead, emotionless. Letterman Jacket shoves himself into Aiden's shoulder as he stomps off, kicking a backpack out of his way.

The hall goes quiet with wide-eyed stares.

Aiden sighs and looks down at the mess at his feet. He maneuvers the crutches expertly around the pile of books as he repositions himself. Eyes burn holes in his head, but he ignores them, contemplating the situation.

Without thinking, I walk toward him. All eyes shift my way and heat rushes to my cheeks, but it's too late. I kneel on the floor and gather up each book carefully, keeping my eyes down. Whispers drift through the hallway as I slip the books into his backpack and come to my feet.

His hard, brown eyes meet mine before they flick down to my outstretched arm. The backpack hangs between us for a few seconds before he loosens his grip and snatches it from my hand.

"Thanks," he mumbles, shouldering his backpack. He takes hold of his crutches and swiftly moves past me. I study his retreating form. His back muscles are visible through his gray shirt as he works the crutches with ease.

The whispers continue. People gawk. I just helped Aiden Peters. Cripple Boy. My social suicide will be the talk of the school for the rest of the day.

I walk back to my locker, ignoring the stares, and rip off the prom flier. I dump it and Gabriel's pathetic proposal into the trash where they belong.

***

"The guillotine was created during the French Revolution." Madame Kristine explains in her thick accent. "It was used as an equalizing death measure for the classes. The whole revolution was based on this one concept. Freedom and equality."

My eyes wander to the dark head of hair two seats away. Aiden's crutches lay on the floor beside him, his legs tucked neatly beneath his desk. His head tilts toward me as he taps the end of his pencil. He brushes a stray lock of hair from his face, his eyes intense.

I can't help but be mesmerized.

His dark eyes narrow suddenly and flick towards me. I rip my gaze away and pretend to study the French flag that hangs behind Madame

Kristine. My heart picks up its pace as Aiden studies me. Eventually, he looks away and resumes his rhythmic tapping.

I don't know a lot about Aiden Peters. No one does, really. He pretty much keeps to himself and it seems as though he prefers it that way. He eats alone, studies alone, and doesn't participate in any extracurricular activities. People move away from him when they see those crutches coming. He's different and differences make people uneasy, I guess.

I shift my gaze back to the tapping pencil. He looks so normal just sitting there. Like any other high school boy trying to get through the day. I find myself wondering what he is really like.

"We will be pairing off on a project for the next few weeks." Madame Kristine says, drawing my attention back to the front of the room. "And before you ask, no, you cannot choose your partners."

The class grumbles in disappointment.

"Please choose a name." She smiles and drops a small basket filled with several slips of paper on the first desk. "Comprendre?"

The basket continues down each row and my nerves kick in as the basket gets closer. Why can't she just assign us a partner? That would be worlds easier. I subconsciously toy with the small sapphire dangling from my neck.

My name isn't picked by the time the basket plops on my desk. My heart pounds in my chest... the moment of truth. I choose a slip of paper and hold my breath.

"Aiden... Peters?"

The gasps come from all around. I look up to see his brown eyes pierce me as I try to gauge his reaction. He blinks a couple times, then shrugs and looks away. I pass the basket on and sink down in my seat.

This cannot be happening. First the hallway and now he's my partner for a French project? This day could not get any worse.

***

"At least I dodged Gabriel," I mutter to myself as I dig my stuff from my locker after final bell.

"There's my pretty baby."

And I spoke too soon.

Gabriel's croaky voice echoes from down the hall. A shiver runs up my spine. I clench my jaw and slam my locker shut, spinning to face him.

"Hey, babe." Gabriel waves me over.

I ignore him and turn in the opposite direction. Maybe I can still escape. Gabriel is the last person that I want to see right now. I spot Aiden at the end of the corridor and my nerves kick in. A few people scatter across the hall. He closes his locker and sighs, readjusting his crutches.

"Aiden?" I call out, turning my back on Gabriel. He pivots his head toward me; his hands tighten around his crutches. I give him a small wave. "Hi. I, um, I wanted talk to you about a good time to work on our project?"

He blinks a couple times, but doesn't say anything. I bite my lip as I step a little closer. This could not get any more awkward.

"You know, the French project?" I ask hesitantly. "We should probably figure out what we are going to do."

He looks down at the floor.

Please say something.

"It's Belle, right?" The way he says my name makes my heart speed up.

"Y – yeah," I stutter.

His brown eyes flick up to meet mine. They're hard and stern, and a pit forms in my stomach.

"Meet after school tomorrow," Aiden says flatly. "301 Grande."

"O – okay," I stutter.

"Okay." He bites his lip, turns away, and disappears around the corner.

My lungs scream at me as I finally exhale. My heart pounds in my ears. I get a few awkward glances around the hall. Still, I think that went well. At least he talked to me.

I smile and head to the parking lot.

When I get outside, I see him across the lot, talking to his mom beside a van. Her pencil skirt looks freshly ironed and her black blazer is pinched perfectly at the shoulders. She looks down at her watch as Aiden pulls himself up onto the front seat and drags his crutches in after him. He situates his legs then says something to her. Her brows crease into a frown as he slams the door shut. She checks her phone, shakes her head, and climbs into the van.

I open my door and plop down into the seat of my car, glancing at myself in the rearview mirror. My own mom's image resurfaces in my mind. She's probably on a beach somewhere getting a tan with her sleazy, loser of a boyfriend. I blink away a few tears and swallow back my anger before shifting my car into reverse.

***

When I get home, Dad is sitting at the dining room table tinkering with his latest invention. He's surrounded by tools and so focused he doesn't notice me come in. It makes me smile.

My dad works hard and does his best to support us. When I was a kid, he worked for a construction company. He hated the long hours, but he hated being told what to build even more. After mom left, he finally found the nerve to follow his dream. It makes him happy. He gets to be himself.

He sells a lot of great stuff on the internet, but mostly, our house is littered with all sorts of gadgets that only half-work. He once made me a cupcake-making robot for my seventh birthday. It worked once or twice before it started spitting cupcake mix everywhere.

"Hey dad." I drop my bag on the table, snapping him back to reality.

"Hey kiddo!" He stands and crushes me with a hug. I smile into his chest. "How was school?"

"It was," I pause. "Interesting."

He lets me go and knits his eyebrows together. "Oh yeah?"

He sits. With a sigh, I slump into a chair next to him. "Ms. Shepherds isn't engaged anymore."

He scoffs. "Little Miss Happily Ever After?"

"That's the one."

He picks up his screwdriver and meddles with the inside of an old clock.

"Well, I hate to say it, but sometimes the last rose petal falls too soon."

Okay then.

"Anyway, I have a project in French." I frown and fidget with my fingernail. "I got partnered with Aiden Peters."

He studies me. "What's wrong with that?"

"He's just..." I sigh. "Different."

"What's wrong with different?" He stretches his back. "I'm different."

"Not like Aiden," I say. "He walks with crutches and he's kind of strange. He doesn't really talk to anyone and people are always making fun of him. I helped him pick up his books from the floor today and he looked at me like I was the one who knocked them out of his hands in the first place."

His green eyes meet mine.

"Listen, Belle." He drops the screwdriver and reaches for my hand. "He's probably used to people treating him like an outcast. People don't handle imperfections very well. They tend to lash out at what they don't understand. It sounds like he's built up a wall because of how people treat him. You're on the outside with everyone else." He gives my hand a small squeeze. "But you've just been given an opportunity to scale that wall."

His words pierce me like bullets. I nod. Leave it to my dad to put things into perspective. My superhero and forever best friend.

"Thanks, dad." I stand and head for the stairs.

"Hey," he says, twirling a screwdriver between his fingers.

"Yeah?" I jerk my head toward him.

"I love you, Beauty."

I grin. "I love you too, old man."

***

I pull up to the huge gate and confusion hits hard. The sturdy black bars tower over me while I stare at the mansion behind them. I shift my gaze to the brick wall to my left. There's a small red button with a metal speaker beside it. A sign dangles above it. *301 Grande.* Yep. This is the place.

I roll down my window and my hand hovers in hesitation. This is seriously Aiden's house? I shake my head and press the button. A buzzing noise emits from the speaker.

"Hello?" I say, wringing my hands. I never in my wildest dreams would have thought I'd be in this situation. Visiting the house of a boy I hardly know.

"Yes? May I help you?" A woman's voice comes through the speaker. She has a slight British accent that takes me off guard.

"I'm Belle Rivers. Aiden and I have a French project to work on."

"One moment."

A click and here I am again. Just me and the giant, looming gate. Doubt squirms around in my brain the longer I wait. If we didn't have this stupid project, I would be curled up on the couch with a good book right now. My heart skips a beat and an uncomfortable feeling creeps over my body. I've hardly ever talked to Aiden. How am I supposed to get through a whole afternoon with him?

The large gate suddenly hums to life and slides open. The mansion looks even more massive without the bars in the way. My mouth gapes at the sight. Who is this guy?

The yard engulfs me as I curve around a large fountain that divides the path. Aiden's mom waves from the big wrap-around porch. Enormous pillars keep the roof in place and two white rocking chairs sit to her right. I notice one section of the house that spirals up to a point, reminding me somewhat of a castle. Amazing!

I get out of my car in awe.

"Hello, darling," the woman says, her British accent echoing off the pavement. She clicks down the front steps to meet me, a smile plastered on her face. "Belle is it? I'm Mrs. Potter. It's so great to meet you."

"So... you're not... Aiden's mom?"

"Oh no, darling." She chuckles and tosses her arm over my shoulders, leading me up the front steps. I smile at her welcoming attitude, easing my nerves. "I do think of him as a son, though. I've known him since he was little bitty."

"Really?" I ask curiosity laced in my voice.

"Oh yes. Chubby cheeks and all. You know, I'm really glad you're here, Belle. Aiden doesn't get very many visitors." She gives me a small squeeze. "This will be good for him."

I smile and nod, not sure how to reply. Luckily, she changes the subject.

"I was just about to make some tea, would you like some?"

"I'd love some, thank you," I say as we cross the threshold.

Just inside, a grand staircase spirals up around a sparkling chandelier. An elevator sits in the wall to the left, a red arrow pointing up. The whole house is painted in blues and whites and finished off with polished wood floors.

"You can find Aiden in the game room," Mrs. Potter says, pointing down a long hallway. "Down this hall here, last door on the right."

"Thank you." I smile.

She gives me one last squeeze before turning in the opposite direction.

I take a steadying breath and tighten my grip on my bag. Maybe this won't be as awkward as I thought.

"Oh, come on!" A voice comes from down the hall. I follow it and slowly creak the door open. Aiden sits in a wheelchair, a video game controller in his hand and his eyes pinned to the TV screen. His jaw clenches in concentration and his fingers move rapidly. The room is painted a dark gray and a few beanbags litter the floor. When his character dies, he throws his arms up as the screen glows down at him.

I clear my throat and his head jerks toward me at the sound. I guess *someone* forgot I was coming today. His cold eyes pin me in place.

"Hey," I quip, all too eager to fill the silence.

He clicks off the TV and wheels himself toward me. "We can work in the day room. There's more space in there."

I frown. *Well, that was a warm welcome.*

He leads me back down the hall and toward the elevator.

"Laura, we're going to the day room," he yells over his shoulder as the doors open. "Don't bother us."

"Okay dear," I hear from somewhere behind me. "But I'll bring–"

The elevator closes on us before she's even finished her sentence. I toss Aiden a wary glance. He keeps his eyes on the silver doors.

The day room is full of windows that lead to a long balcony and the afternoon sun illuminates the whole place. There's a table directly in the center of this huge room and Aiden wheels himself to the end of it. I pull out the chair next to him and take a seat. The site outside the windows is breathtaking. The sky is edged with a beautiful shade of pink as the sun begins to set.

Aiden drums his fingers on the table, drawing my attention back to his brown eyes.

"If you're done admiring the view, can we just get started so I can get back to my game?" he growls. I narrow my eyes in confusion, but don't say anything. I dig through my book bag. His eyes never leave my face, making me feel uncomfortable. I lay the criterion sheet on the table between us along with a pencil.

"Okay," I sigh. "So basically, we have to make some kind of visual representation to show that we understand the French Revolution."

"Right." He leans his forearms on the table, his biceps flex. His stoic eyes stare at me in annoyance. I keep talking.

"We could probably build something. You know, like we could make the Bastille out of toothpicks?"

He throws me a look and my stomach twists.

"Too safe." He shakes his head. "Everyone will do that."

"Okay. Um," I look up at the ceiling in thought. "What if we tried to make a replica of the Palace at Versailles? We could make it out of clay."

"No, that'll take too long." He's clearly irritated. I stare at him in frustration. Is he seriously going to shoot down every single one of my ideas?

We get distracted by the sound of the elevator. Mrs. Potter comes in carrying a tray. There's a pot of tea and two teacups on top of it. She gently sets it on the table in between us.

"Do you take sugar or cream in your tea, Belle?"

"Neither, this is fine." I take the cup from her with a smile.

She holds the second cup out to Aiden, but he ignores her and grabs the criterion paper, studying it. Wow, why is he so rude to her? She's only known him his whole life. She bites her lip and her hand hovers for a minute. Then she plops it down in front of him and it splatters out onto the table.

"Hey!" Aiden jerks his head up, glaring at Mrs. Potter.

She folds her arms over her chest and gives him a pointed look. His shoulders sag and he lets out a sigh.

"Thank you." He definitely doesn't sound sincere.

"You're very welcome," she says with a grin. "You two have fun." She gives me a small nudge before exiting.

"Do you have pencil?" Aiden asks, flipping the paper over. I pick mine up and hand it to him. He sketches.

I concentrate on a chip in my teacup as I study the top of Aiden's dark hair, which slightly curls at the tips. His sharp jaw clenches in concentration and his fingers curl around my pencil, tightening with each stoke he makes. Curiosity swims in my brain as I try to figure him out. He is so passive and even more rude, but why? Is he so mad at the world that he can't even show an inch of kindness?

"No." He mumbles, erasing something. He flips the pencil back around and rolls it between his fingers in thought. I don't make a sound, deciding it's my smartest option. He draws again as an idea forms in his head. I watch him, fascinated by his tunnel vision.

Aiden finally studies his work then pushes the page toward me. I stare in surprise at a perfectly proportioned guillotine.

"Wow. This is really good," I say, looking over at him in shock.

"Thanks." He shrugs.

"Where did you learn to draw like this?"

"Oh, I just doodle sometimes," he dismisses with a wave of his hand. "So, what do you think? Do you want to do this?"

He waits for my response and I nod my head, looking back at the drawing.

"Your dad's an inventor right? Maybe you could ask him if we could use some of his tools."

My head jerks up. "How'd you know that?"

"I bought some stuff from him off the internet a few times," he explains.

"Oh." I study the sketch once more. "Yeah, I guess I could ask him."

He nods, then pulls away and wheels toward the elevator, leaving me at the table.

"Where are you going?" I turn and study his retreating back.

"We have weeks to work on this. We're done for today."

The elevator doors open. I grab my bag, stuffing the drawing inside, and hurry after him. Downstairs, Aiden heads back to his game without as much as a goodbye. I stand there for few minutes in shock. I guess he's kicking me out.

The front gate opens instantly this time. I glance back at the mansion in my rear view mirror. I think I know why people don't like Aiden. And it's not because of those crutches.

***

Day two. Yay.

Rain pounds against the day room windows. A series of equipment lies on the table in front of us.

"My dad said he would help us if we need–"

"No!" Aiden snaps, interrupting me. Startled, I drop a wrench, and the sound echoes through the room. He clenches his jaw. "This is our project." His voice is stern and final.

"Okay." I fumble with my necklace.

Aiden stacks the last empty box beside the table.

"So," I say, examining the tools spread out before us. "You are planning to tell me how exactly we're gonna build this thing, right?"

"No, I'm just gonna keep it a secret."

He keeps his steely expression. I stare at him, puzzled. His dark eyes meet mine.

"Relax, I'm joking." He rolls his eyes and shakes his head. "I actually found something in a book about it in my library."

"Wait," I perk up. He stops, halfway to the elevator doors. "You have a library? Here?"

"Yeah." He wheels into the elevator. "It's downstairs."

I stare at him, blinking a few times, trying to process this newfound information. He turns.

"Are you coming? Or are you just gonna stand there all day?"

He doesn't have to ask me twice.

The library is at the end of a hallway. Its big wooden doors stand like soldiers on guard. Aiden wheels to a stop right in front of them and presses a button on the arm of his wheelchair. The doors slide aside, revealing a huge room covered from ceiling to floor in shelves upon shelves of books. I turn in a circle, amazed.

Aiden disappears behind a shelf. My fingers trail along the spines as I pass. I pull out a small blue book and flip through a few pages, walking to a tiny sofa that sits in the middle of the library. Soon I'm flat on my back, consumed by the story.

I get about three chapters in before a cleared throat interrupts me. Aiden sits across from the sofa, his head cocked to one side, a few wisps of hair falling in his face. Surprisingly, an amused smile tugs at the corner of his mouth, and for a moment, his eyes dance.

"What?" I question, creasing my eyebrows. "Am I not supposed to touch the books?"

In response, he smiles. A real smile, dimples and all, which really freaks me out. I sit up, folding the book. He wheels a bit closer to the sofa, a clunky book in his lap.

"I'm guessing you finally found what you were looking for?" I ask. He glances down and nods.

"What were you reading?" He gestures to my book. I smile.

"*To Kill a Mockingbird*," I flip it open to my place.

"Good choice." His eyes stay pinned on me. Blushing, I read a few words to myself. "That's one of my favorite classics."

I glance up. "It is?"

He nods. A small smile spreads across his face, releasing a few butterflies to flutter around in my stomach. *Butterflies? What?*

"It'll never beat *Huckleberry Finn,* I'm afraid," he chuckles. I smile as his eyes twinkle up at me for the first time, the cold facade dissolving from them.

"I don't think anything could beat good old *Huckleberry Finn,*" I agree. "I've actually read this about a thousand times."

"Really?" He throws me an expression I can't quite place. "I didn't peg you for a re-reader."

"Yeah, well I'm usually not," I admit with a shrug. He nods.

"You must really like this one then." He runs a hand through his messy hair. I smile at him. Now this Aiden, I like.

"We should get working on the project." He heads toward the doors. I watch him go for a moment, still surprised by our first real conversation. He turns back and studies me, creasing his eyebrows. "You coming, Belle?"

I smile, leave the book behind, and follow him.

***

I go to Aiden's house every day for three weeks to watch *him* work on the project. Anytime I even go near it, he snaps at me, his eyes returning to their familiar cold state. But that's okay; it gives me more time to read all the books in his library.

He's actually pretty fun and strangely, I begin to look forward to our little afternoons in the day room. Books are our go-to conversations. If we ever run out of topics, we fall back on books. We both hate small talk, which makes things a thousand times easier. And if we have nothing to say, we sit in comfortable silence.

I discover that Aiden loves Cheetos with milk (he made me try it and it was actually surprisingly tasty), his favorite fantasy book is *The*

Hobbit, and he loves baseball. According to Mrs. Potter, his room is plastered with Rockies decor. But I wouldn't know because personally, I've never been to his room.

Today, Aiden sits across from me measuring long blocks of wood.

"Okay," he says. "Write this down." I click open my pen. Finally, I get to help. "Height: Seven and a half feet..."

My fingers fumble with my sapphire as I write. Aiden looks up at me, snatching up a marker.

"I like your necklace," he states. I look up at him, holding the sapphire between my fingers. "It matches your eyes."

He smiles at me faintly and I blink once in surprise.

"Oh," I glance down at it for a moment and return his smile. "Thanks." He rolls the marker between his fingers in thought.

"Where'd you get it?" He marks a bit of the wood. I lay the notebook aside and fold my hands in front of me.

"It was my mom's," I say, gulping down the lump in my throat. "She gave it to me for my birthday one year. It's kinda the only thing I have left of her." He glances at me, curiosity flooding his eyes.

"What happened to her?" He grabs the ruler but keeps his eyes on me.

"She left us." I study his face, looking for the familiar pity most people give me. Instead, he just nods a bit in understanding. "And then she came back." He creases his eyebrows. I shrug at him. "She did that a couple times. The last time was five years ago. I haven't seen her since."

"Abandoned by a parent," he sighs. "Sounds familiar." I furrow my brows. "My dad... he's gone." He nonchalantly waves his hand.

"What about your mom?" I ponder.

His jaw clenches as he measures and marks another section.

"She goes on business trips a lot. She's supposed to be back in two weeks though." His eyes light up as he speaks.

"That's great," I say. He nods, a smile painting itself across his face.

We sit in silence. My fingers drum on the table as he continues to mark the wood.

"So I guess I should give you a compliment now?" His eyes meet mine, softening. "You know, to even things up?"

"Well," he shrugs, a smile forming on his lips. "I wouldn't mind."

"Okay." I bring my finger to my lips in thought. "Let's see, what do I like about you?"

He throws me a look. "That's a real self-esteem booster."

I hold my hand up in protest. "I'm still thinking. Shut up."

He just shakes his head.

"Okay, I got it," I smirk. "You sure know how to drive that wheelchair."

"Gee, thanks," he laughs, launching the marker in my direction. It pecks me on the forehead before landing on the floor.

"No seriously," I giggle, rubbing my head. "I see a lot of strength in you. And I admire that."

He studies me. "You know, you're different."

The heat runs up to my cheeks at his words.

"I'm different?" I question, blinking at him.

"Yeah." He leans on his elbows. "You treat me differently than anyone I've ever known. You make me feel, I don't know, more human, I guess."

My heart pounds. Did Aiden Peters just give me a compliment? His brown eyes break away, and he fidgets with his hands.

"I've been meaning to ask you, and I mean, you don't have to say yes. I'm not exactly the ideal date for a dance, but–"

He stops mid-sentence. I raise my brows.

"Yes?"

"Would you maybe want to go to prom? You know, with me?"

His eyes drift up to meet mine, gauging my reaction and the butterflies erupt in my stomach. What is it with these butterflies?

"I'd love to," I hear myself say.

His eyes widen in surprise to match my own shocked emotion.

"Really?"

"Yes," I nod, grinning at him. I reach across the table, brushing my fingers over his. He automatically envelops them in his palm. There's that dimple, and my heart races.

"Okay," he sighs in relief. "It's a date."

Three weeks ago, I never would have said yes to Aiden Peters. But here we are. And I just did.

***

The final bell rings, I elbow my way through the crowd of students and stop at the water fountain. I should have kept walking.

"Hey there, Belle."

My eyes drift up to meet the sly smile of Gabriel Barnard. Oh boy.

"Hi Gabriel," I straighten, and give him a polite nod. He steps a little closer to me, sending spiders scurrying up my spine. His long, black hair meets at the base of his neck in a ponytail and small wisps frame his face.

"I haven't seen you around lately," he says, pretending to pout.

"Yeah, well I've been busy." I take a step away from him.

"Yeah, I figured." He leans on the wall staring at me with a smirk. "Have you picked out your prom dress yet?"

A knot forms in the pit of my stomach as he studies me.

"Well," I look down and avoid his gaze. "Not yet."

"You better get a move on," he presses. "It's only two weeks away and I need to make sure I can match your dress."

I bite my lip and glance up at him.

"Gabriel," I sigh. "I'm not going to prom with you."

His eyes distort in confusion.

"What do you mean you're not going to prom with me?" His voice rises with a hint of anger. Thankfully, most of the hallway has cleared out, leaving us without an audience.

"Someone else asked me," I say evenly, keeping eye contact. "And I said yes."

"What?" He takes a step closer. His breath tickles my nose; I cringe. "I asked you first, Belle!"

"Actually," I tilt my head up at him. "You didn't."

A dark scowl forms on his face. He grits his teeth.

"You taped a prom ticket to my locker." I cross my arms over my chest. "Besides, why would you want to take me? You know you're too good for me, Gabriel."

I shrug with a small smile. He glares at me in fury.

"Do you even know how many girls would die to go to prom with me?"

"Then you shouldn't have a problem finding a date." I smile.

He clenches his fists. "Who are you going with then?"

I look down at my shoes before letting the words fall out of my mouth.

"Aiden Peters."

Gabriel's face contorts with disgust.

"Cripple Boy?" he howls. "You're kidding me!"

"Why do you call him that?" I drop my arms in exasperation.

"Because he's a freak, Belle."

"If you would just give him a chance and try to see beyond the crutches, you would see that he's so much more than that."

"Do you even know how he got like that?" He juts his chin out and folds his arms. "It's an ugly story from what I've heard."

"Well, that's just it," I say pointedly. "It's something you heard. You don't know. And you don't know him at all."

"You're right, I don't," he snarls. "And I don't plan on it. He's a lowlife, and he's never gonna be anything more than that. And apparently you're too blind to see it. Have fun at the prom, Freak Lover!"

He turns on his heels and marches off. I stare at his ponytail, releasing the breath I've been holding. He insists on believing whatever people tell him, people who know nothing about Aiden. No one ever sees the Aiden I know. They will never understand.

***

The next day when I arrive at Aiden's house, he is not himself, and I don't know why.

He sits in front of the half-finished guillotine, gripping a hammer. A dark scowl lines his face.

"I need some more nails." His voice lacks any emotion. I look up from the book I plucked from the library.

"How many?" I ask, reaching for the box of nails across from me.

"Four," he states. "No, I mean five." He shakes his head in agitation.

I gather five nails and walk toward his tensed back. He looks up at me, his eyes hazy. As if his mind is somewhere else, out of reach.

"Here you go." It takes him a moment to hear me before he finally reaches up. I let go of them, but he fails to catch them. They clatter to the floor and scatter between us.

"Geez, Belle, you're such a klutz!" he growls.

I stare at him, stunned. Where did that come from?

"I'm sorry." I bend to pick up the nails. When I stand, I'm greeted with his cold eyes.

"You should be."

"Are you okay?" I ask, hesitantly.

"I'm fine." His jaw clenches in frustration.

"Okay," I lift my hands in defeat. I walk back to the table and flip through a few pages in my book before...

"Aren't you gonna help?" Aiden scowls. I jerk my head up.

"I will if you want me to," I say, getting to my feet. "You just haven't let me do anything."

He narrows his eyes. "Well why don't you just leave then," he sneers.

"Aiden, what is wrong?" I raise my voice.

"Nothing!" His voice climbs to match mine. "I told you I'm fine."

"No, you're not." I cross my arms over my chest.

"Just drop it, okay?" He rips his eyes from mine.

"Okay fine." I step toward him. "But you're being a jerk."

Anger plasters itself on his face.

"I've always been a jerk," he snaps. "I was a jerk when you met me, and I'm still a jerk. It's never changed."

"No, this is not you." I place my hand on his shoulder. He shrugs away.

"Don't touch me!"

I drop my hand and stare at him, puzzled.

"Just leave," he says sternly.

"Aiden, what is your problem?"

"The only reason you're here is because of this stupid project."

My eyes widen. "That might've been my only reason in the beginning," I admit. "But not anymore. I want to be here."

"No you don't. You've never wanted to be here. Eventually, you're gonna leave like everyone else. So why don't you just get it over with?"

"That's not true. Why are you being this way?"

"I've always been this way!"

"Not with me."

"Well, that was just a moment of weakness, okay? You make me weak." He jabs a finger at me in accusation and I can't help it, my lip trembles.

"I make you weak?" I yell in astonishment.

"Yeah! You're too nice! You care too much!"

My brain rattles around, making my head hurt. "What are you talking about?"

"I'm talking about this!" His hand motions between us. "I'm shouting at you, and you're just standing there taking it."

"Well then, what do you want?" I scream, throwing my arms in the air.

"I want you to leave!"

"I'm not leaving."

"Why not? I'm sure you learned plenty of times how to do it from your mother!"

Now that just ripped my heart wide open. His eyes of steel freeze me in place. My vision blurs; I clench my hands. I don't know whether to feel angry or broken, but I'm stuck somewhere in between. I tear my eyes from him, but not before I see one single slash of regret cross his face. I don't care. I grab my bag. I have to get out of here.

"Belle!" Aiden yells. His wheelchair lurches forward. "Wait!"

It's too late for that. I leap into the elevator and press the button.

Only then do the tears gush out of me like an overflowing river. I clutch my stomach.

The elevator doors open, and I fly out of the house. My heartbeat pounds in my ears, and my head spins. I dig for my keys in my bag.

"Belle!" Aiden yells from the balcony. "Wait, Belle! Please, I'm sorry. Please, just come back inside." His pleading nudges me to look up at him. I can see the regret on his face, but I'm done. I'm never going back.

I speed away without a second glance. But I only make it to an abandoned parking lot before I break down completely. My shaky hands make their way to my face and I sob.

Why would he do that? My mom? I shared that with him and he just turns and uses it against me. He knew right where to hurt me.

When the sobs end, silence fills the air. I sit and stare at my messy hair and red-rimmed eyes in the mirror. Something must have happened. And whatever it was hurt him. Why else would he explode into some kind of monster?

Sighing, I run my fingers through my hair. My stomach twists in uncomfortable directions, and my chest aches. Clenching the steering wheel, I lean my head against the seat.

Maybe I should go back. If he's hurting, he needs someone to be there for him. I don't care what he says; he needs to know I care. That I'll be there for him through everything. Even if he doesn't want me there.

But I don't want to go back.

Maybe I should just give him his space. Give him time to cool off.

I shake my head in aggravation. *No, Belle. He needs you.*

With a sigh, I crank the engine. I'm going back.

Because apparently... I'm too nice.

***

A dark blue BMW speeds past me as I turn onto Aiden's street. I watch it race by.

Was that – was that Gabriel? Fear climbs up my spine and I speed up. *Oh, please tell me that was just a coincidence.*

Mrs. Potter left to get groceries an hour ago. Aiden was alone.

When I get close enough to the house, I notice the gate is open. The gate is *never* open. My stomach forms a knot; something is terribly wrong.

My eyes widen in horror when I see Aiden sprawled across the concrete porch. He struggles, crawling with his forearms to get back to his wheelchair where it's flipped to one side a few feet away from him.

"Oh, my gosh! Aiden!" My voice shakes. I jump from the car, rushing up the steps. He looks up at me, face covered in blood and left eye already swelling shut. I kneel down beside him, pushing his hair away from his face.

"You–you came back?" he gasps.

"Of course, I came back." I sigh and cup his chin in my palm.

I sit his wheelchair upright and hoist him into it. His arm drapes over my shoulder as we work together. Head leaning to one side, he breathes out a sigh of relief.

In the kitchen, I snatch up a cloth from the cupboard and douse it in water. Carefully, I dab the cloth against his face. He winces.

"Ooh, Sorry." I push his hair away.

"S'okay." He blinks at me with his one good eye. His hand grips the arm of the chair in pain.

"What happened?" I wring out the cloth before blotting away the blood covering his forehead. I'm pretty sure I know the answer, but I ask anyway.

"Your friend Gabriel happened," he says through gritted teeth. I shake my head.

"He's not my friend," I clarify.

"Well whoever he is, he seemed pretty pissed off at me for asking you to prom."

His lip begins to swell from a small cut. My eyes lace with concern as I stare down at the bruises across his chin, a hand resting on his cheek. He gently reaches up and brushes it with his fingers.

"Belle," he croaks. "I'm so sorry about what I said. I didn't mean it. Any of it. There's just some stuff going on with my mom and I lashed out. You were conveniently here and so I took my anger out on you. And I shouldn't have done that." His eye softens as it looks into mine.

Mom stuff. That's something I completely understand. I nod.

"I forgive you, Aiden."

He does his best to smile. "Yeah. Because that's what you do."

I sink to my knees. "You can't just shut me out like that, okay? I'm here for you, no matter what. You got that?"

He nods.

"I know." He looks down at his bloody shirt and sighs. "You don't make me weak. Not in the way it sounded, anyway. You just make me feel things, Belle. Things that I haven't felt in a long time. And I don't like it. It makes me defenseless."

"You don't have to be strong all the time, Aiden." My fingers entangle with his. "At least not with me."

"I know that now," he says with a small smile. "It's just, I lied to you Belle."

I crease my brows. "About what?"

"I didn't tell you exactly what happened to my dad."

I blink a couple of times and tilt my head to the side.

"When I was ten." He swallows before continuing. "He was diagnosed with stage four lung cancer." A tear wells up in his eye and I give his hand a squeeze. "He loved me more than anyone in the entire world. When he died, my mom threw herself into her work. She hired Laura to raise me and then she just left. If I'm lucky, she'll show up for Christmas or Thanksgiving." He looks at me. "She's not coming back."

"She's not coming back?" I ask, concern consuming my voice. He fumbles with the hem of his shirt.

"Before you got here today, I got a call from her." His voice trembles as he speaks. "She just got a promotion. She's moving to London next week and I probably won't see her for months." He takes a few ragged breaths. "I shouldn't have been so mean to you. I just–I really miss my dad."

"Oh, Aiden." I place my fingers under his chin, prompting him to look at me. A small tear rolls down his cheek and I brush it away with my fingers.

I don't know what comes over me, but suddenly I lean in and press my lips to his. At first, he tenses, but then his lips softly melt into mine until...

"Ow!" he pulls away, pressing a finger to his swollen lip.

"Oh! I'm sorry!" I say in a hushed whisper. He chuckles and lifts his hand, brushing a few strands away from my face, then rests it on my cheek.

"You still want to go to prom with me, right?" he questions. A gleam of hope sparkles in his eye. "I understand if you don't."

"Of course, I do," I blush, smiling at him.

"Good." He breathes out.

We sit here in peaceful silence. Finally, we've connected. For real this time. And I know this might sound crazy, I mean, it is crazy, but there's something about his hand entwined with mine that feels so right.

***

I stare at my reflection in the mirror. Grinning, I put on my earrings.

"Beauty?" Dad calls from downstairs. "You almost ready, kiddo?"

"I'll be down in a second."

Sighing in satisfaction, I take in my completed look. My bright, yellow gown floats to the ground in a puffy ring around my feet. It's finally time!

I beam at Dad as I drift down the stairs. His eyes widen in amazement.

"Whoa," he says, blinking rapidly. "I'd say you look just like your mother –but I won't."

I tilt my head. "Thanks dad."

"Listen, I want to talk to you about something."

"Oh, please tell me we're not having 'the boy talk.'" I pause on the bottom step and cover my face with my hands. He chuckles.

"We're not," he says. When I peek at him uneasily between my fingers, he raises his hands in surrender. "I promise."

"Okay," I say slowly. "What is it, then?"

He shoves his hands in his pockets and smiles. "I'm so proud of you, Belle."

"For what?" I ask, puzzled.

"For staying true to yourself." A satisfied gleam flashes in his eyes. "You just kept being the sweet girl I know and look what happened? You broke down that wall. Kindness goes a long way and I'm glad that you let Aiden see that."

I grin at his wise words.

"Thank you, daddy."

His arms enclose me in a big hug and I treasure the warmth of it.

The doorbell rings, pulling us apart. My heart beats rapidly and the butterflies begin to flutter.

"I think that's for you," Dad whispers. He brushes a few hairs out of my face and smiles.

"You sure I look okay?"

"You're gonna be the most beautiful Belle at the ball."

"Dad," I sigh. "I'm gonna be the only Belle at the ball."

He chuckles and swings open the door. Aiden waits for me on the porch, a fading, blue bruise visibly outlines his eye. His sharp tuxedo is completed with a yellow bow tie that matches my dress. He beams at me.

"Wow!" he whispers. He reaches into his breast pocket and wraps his fingers around the stem of a single, red rose. He holds it out to me. I grin at him and take it.

"You look pretty 'wow' yourself." I step aside to let him in. Sniffing the beautiful rose, I meet my Dad's gaze. "Aiden, this is my dad. Dad, Aiden."

"It's very good to meet you, sir." Aiden lets go of his crutch and extends his hand. Dad takes it with a smile.

"You as well, Aiden."

"Is Mrs. Potter outside?" I see a long limousine on the drive.

"Not tonight."

Aiden smiles at me just before my dad's hand clamps onto his shoulder.

"Now Aiden," he begins in a stern tone. I cringe. Here we go. "Belle is my greatest treasure. You better treat her like one, you hear?"

Aiden's eyes widen and flick in my direction. I shrug with a smile of encouragement.

"Loud and clear, sir," Aiden nods.

Dad grins and turns toward me. "You kids go have fun then."

We move toward the door. I glance one last time at my dad.

"I like that kid," he whispers with a wink. I grin at him. "Dance the night away, kiddo."

He steps a bit closer, placing a kiss on my forehead. I squeeze the stem of my rose and let Aiden escort me to the waiting limo.

***

I link my arm with Aiden's, the rose dangling between us. We slowly make our way to the gym doors and my heart quickens.

"Are you sure you don't want to use your chair?" I ask with concern. "I don't mind."

"I'm sure, Belle." He gives me a small smile. "They've never seen me use a wheelchair and I'm not gonna give them that satisfaction."

"Okay then." I smile.

Pounding music greets us, but everything else fades into silence when we enter the gym, all eyes on us. Aiden gulps and I tighten my grip on his arm. We maneuver through the crowd toward the punch table and for a minute, people lose interest in us and begin to dance. I sigh and glance at him.

"Well, we survived that," I whisper.

He throws me an uneasy look.

"Are you sure this was a good idea? I don't feel welcome here."

I tilt my head.

"I'm sure, Aiden," I smile. "I wouldn't want to be here with anyone else."

"Thanks," he sighs with a nervous smile.

We stand there for a few minutes watching the couples sway on the dance floor. I find Gabriel across the room. He glares at me with his arms crossed. Emily McDowell hangs on his shoulder, visibly pleading with him to go dance with her. He shrugs her off with a huff, keeping his eyes pinned on me. I glance over at Aiden in thought.

"Do you want to dance?" I ask boldly. He creases his brows, his gaze dropping to his crutches.

"Belle, you're joking, right?"

One look at me and he knows I'm not.

"You don't even have to do anything," I promise. "Just stand there."

I blink at him a few times, gauging his response. He sighs, rolling his eyes.

"Okay, lead the way."

A smile spreads across my face and my heart picks up pace. The dance floor clears a small path as we step into the center. I gently wrap my arms around Aiden's neck. My rose dangles from my fingers and peeks out above his shoulder. He stares at me, his brown eyes full of nerves. We begin to sway back and forth to the soft pulse of the slow song. Everyone forms a small circle around us, watching intensely. I ignore them and give

Aiden an encouraging smile. He lets out a small sigh and begins to relax a little.

"Are they gonna stare at us all night?" I ask him with a small giggle.

"You get used to it after a while," he shrugs. "But I think tonight they're looking at you."

I blush all the way to my toes.

"Guess what?" he whispers.

"What?" I ask. My eyes sparkle with anticipation.

"I got our guillotine to work."

"I never doubted you."

"I thought that would be your reaction," he chuckles.

I tilt my head, teasingly. "Just... don't make me have to use it on you."

He laughs. "Never, because it really works."

And then I'm laughing too.

We dance a few more minutes. His eyes study me with a look I can't quite place.

"What?" I ask, curious.

"Thank you," he whispers with a smile.

"For what?" I crease my brows.

"For you." He sighs, collecting his thoughts. "You are the nicest and most beautiful girl I know." My heart melts at his words. "You were there for me even when I was terrible to you. No one has ever done something even remotely close to that for me. Ever. And – I guess what I'm trying to say is – you made me want to actually live again. Not just exist in a hole of pity. You made me feel like love was possible for me." He stops swaying and places a hand on my cheek with a smile. "So, thank you."

He gently leans down, pressing his lips to mine. I melt into the kiss, my heart pounds in my chest, and all the butterflies take flight at once. And for that one moment, everyone fades out of existence. It's just Aiden and me on top of the world.

He pulls away and traces the outline of my bottom lip with his thumb.

"What was that for?" My eyes search his face. He shrugs, placing his hand back around his crutch.

"I thought you deserved a proper kiss," he whispers. "And I've wanted to do that all night."

My smile reaches my eyes as we begin to sway once again. I barely even notice the sweet "awes" echoing around the room. I just see Aiden, smiling down at me.

A single petal falls from my rose landing at our feet. I glance down at it and then back at Aiden.

He loves me…

He loves me not.

He loves me.

Faith Hays
Author of Handicapped Hearts

Faith Hays is a typical high school girl who loves to hide out in her room. You'll often find her re-watching her favorite movies, blasting heavy metal through her stereo speakers, or curled up with a good book. She's a collector of band tees, wears high heels as often as she can, and has a passion for cross country running and snow skiing.

She's also a bit of a hopeless romantic. Although she's had little experience in the boyfriend department, she waits for the day that her knight in shining armor will come sweep her off her feet. Until then, she lives her life pursuing Christ knowing that He will send her a man who will love her as He does.

The Goldweaver

Alex Clark

Seventeen-year-old Eileen walked heavily down the street. In one hand, she carried a few bags of groceries. Her other scrolled diligently through her phone, catching up on social media and checking the activity in her online shop. Every few seconds her phone would *ding*, providing ample distraction via the avalanche of tags, compliments, and new custom order requests. Her online clothing business was booming and for the most part, had been met with great reviews.

Occasionally, Eileen would be forced to contend with some imbecile who chose her work as a new target at which to spew hate. They'd hide behind their keyboard to drop a random hateful comment on her site. Most of them were devoid of merit and as lacking in common sense as they were in correct spelling and punctuation. Today's pathetic attack was no different.

The comment popped up in red on her screen and she stopped in her tracks. This fool was calling her work "generic" and "unimpressive." She rolled her eyes, deleted the comment, and blocked the troll. The school day had been stressful enough without this random hater trying to bring her down. All she wanted was to get home and away from everything.

Her father was there waiting for her and the pride she saw in his eyes each day made any stress she'd faced melt away. He had been the one who'd pushed Eileen to share her talents with the world and open her online shop in the first place. He bragged to anyone who would listen about her artistry. He called her textile works "pieces of gold."

She loved her father more than anything in the world and spent most of her free time taking care of him. After the accident, her father was no longer able to work. His meager benefits were barely enough to pay the rent. Thankfully, her indie shop had taken off and the income it provided more than picked up the slack. Orders were rolling in every day with customers from all around the world. In addition to providing her little family with financial stability, sewing offered Eileen an escape from the dreadful, ever-continuing monotony of her everyday life.

Ding!

Eileen resumed her trek home, smiling down at the new custom order request that popped up on her screen. At this rate, she might be able to afford a car soon.

The soft shuffle of gravel shifting across asphalt pulled Eileen from her daydream. She kept walking but cocked her head to the side a bit to listen. Someone was behind her. She quickened her pace and the footfalls matched her own. Her face flushed and her mind raced, unable to decide if there was a threat or she was just being paranoid. Unsure, she walked even faster.

Heavy footsteps and ragged breathing.

Eileen broke into a sprint, the grocery bags bouncing against her moving legs. She looked over her shoulder. The man following her was close at her heels. She was faster, but not by much. The man was a bulky shadow against the dwindling light of day.

He was too close.

Her sharp eyes scanned the area in search of escape as her feet pounded against the sidewalk. There were two alleys. One was lit by a streetlamp, the other completely dark. On a hunch, she dashed for the darker of the two.

Halfway down the murky corridor, she ducked behind a dumpster stacked high with discarded debris. Once there, she backed against the wall, dropped her bags, and slid to the ground. She hugged her knees close to her heaving chest, her breath as loud as canon fire in her ears. She slapped a hand over her mouth, desperate to shield the sound from hungry ears.

The footsteps drew nearer and her heart climbed into her throat. The minutes felt like hours as the hulk of a man stalked through the alley, throwing things about and muttering to himself. The area looked like a thrift store drop off. It was littered with broken-down televisions, battered couches, and boxes and bags full to bursting with grungy clothing and trash. Frustrated by his fruitless search, he kicked the very dumpster behind which his prey was crouched, let out a string of curses, and stormed back the way he had come.

Eileen waited for what seemed like hours. When she was sure he wasn't coming back, she let out a long, jerky breath and slowly rose to her feet, brushing off her jeans. Sweat clung to her skin in a sheet. A shiver crawled across her skin, the adrenaline finally starting to dissipate.

Criminal activity wasn't very uncommon around her neighborhood, but she'd only experienced it personally a few times before—thugs and wannabe robbers, mostly. The whole ordeal had lasted mere minutes, but had felt like a lifetime. It was like one of those twisting, twirling roller coasters at the local theme park. The ride itself only lasts about eight seconds, but the sick feeling stays with you for much longer. She hated those things. And she hated this.

She opened the flashlight app on her phone and surveyed the damage to her groceries as she stuffed them back into the bags. Only one of the eggs was broken, but the yolk was smeared over almost everything.

"Of course." Eileen groaned.

She scooped up her bags, pocketed her phone, and continued toward home. She should be scared, but she refused. And there was no way she was telling her father about it either. She wouldn't give that thug the satisfaction of affecting her life in any way.

***

Sweat gathered on Aldaric's forehead as he wrung his hands together. His *Leiter* wasn't going to be happy with him. He'd found the girl, but she'd slipped through his hands. The man had zero tolerance for failure.

King raised a bushy brow, his mouth curled ever downward. Wrinkles battled for purchase against the scars on his face. The man kept his hair shorn close to the scalp. Massive scars extended across his skull and down side of his neck, straight through the middle of the ink on his neck. The tattoo, a simple, black 'x,' marked him as *Leiter*. He was the tenth in succession and none seemed willing to overthrow him.

Aldaric had known King nearly all his life. He remembered a time when the man was handsome and refined. His strong jaw and blazing eyes stood firm beneath a thick mane of jet-black hair. It seemed like ages since he'd seen that version of the man who stood before him, glaring into Aldaric's soul.

"*Leiter* King, t-the stores have…" Aldaric's voice trailed off.

"Yes?" King's eyes bore into him, his mouth set in a grim line.

"*Leiter*, our funds are dangerously low," Aldaric said, his eyes set on the floor. "Adine Kronf was our main source of business."

King's eyes darkened, but his face remained set in stone. "Am I to believe that the loss of one woman is driving us all into a hole?"

"Yes, *Leiter*." Aldaric swallowed hard. "Our members profited greatly from the information she had access to. With her death-"

Leiter King's fist slammed down onto the table and Aldaric flinched.

"Passed!" King stared at him with hatred in his eyes. "You will use *passed* when you speak of Adine's tragic departure. Is that clear, Aldaric?"

The temperature in the room dropped suddenly. Aldaric shrank in on himself and nodded. "Crystal, *Leiter*."

"Good." King kept his gaze steady as fire burned in his eyes. "Now, back to business."

He rose from his chair, cracking his knuckles together. The sound echoed throughout the otherwise silent room. Aldaric watched *Leiter* King pace around the dim space, a hand on his chin, waiting for whatever came next.

"Have you found a plausible solution?" King paused his pacing. "It must be quick. If our financial situation is as dire as you claim, we need to act now."

"Yes, as a matter of fact, *Leiter*." Aldaric's eyes lit up. "We've located a possible replacement, a young woman in Lichtenberg."

"Does she have family?" King's brows furrowed. "Will she be missed?"

"I'm told she lives alone with her father," Aldaric squared his shoulders. "Our intel says the man is a crippled shut-in. He never leaves the house. The girl supports them both with her small shop. Those who have commissioned her work speak very highly of her talents."

"Many people have talent, Aldaric." King looked unimpressed. "That doesn't mean this girl is the one who will save us from ruin."

"I believe she is the one, *Leiter*," Aldaric said firmly. "They call her the *Goldweaver*."

***

Eileen slid on her boots and checked herself over to make certain she hadn't forgotten anything. Book bag, lunch money, laptop, and phone...yeah, all set.

She set out her father's lunch for him, gave him a hug, and stepped out the front door. It was a cloudy day with a few dappled rays of sunshine finding the courage to peek through the mass of water vapor. She didn't mind the fog. It calmed her. She smiled as the cool air washed across her skin.

She checked her weather app as she made her way down the street towards the high school. It was going to rain tonight, but it didn't matter much. She'd be at her sewing machine most of the night anyway. If she ever wanted to go to college, she'd have to sew like there was no tomorrow.

In a week, she'd be eighteen. For most kids, that meant freedom.

For Eileen, it meant more time to stay home and take care of her father. More time dedicated to doctor's appointments, paying bills, and keeping the house clean and safe for him. She clenched a fist and shook her head. Was it selfish to want to live away from him?

She hated high school, hated having to be the one to run everything. She was tired of all the responsibility. She wanted more for herself but deep inside she knew she couldn't leave her father.

He'd get too lonely and it was far too dangerous to leave him to fend for himself. What if he had trouble with his lungs or heart again? As much of a nightmare as that crash had been for her, it had been far worse for her father. The man had lost everything.

She shook her head and pressed on toward school. She shouldn't be wasting energy on such things. Old losses. A tragic car accident. Sad, sad story. Such a stereotype for teen angst. Her life had become a cliché. Eileen hated clichés.

A familiar sound caught Eileen's attention. Feet shuffling across pavement again. A shiver ran down her spine as thoughts of the night before ran through her head. She should have run, but stubbornness gained the upper hand over common sense.

She convinced herself she was simply being paranoid. She squared her shoulders and pressed forward on her original path. She had just rounded the corner near her school when she felt herself being pulled backward. She cried out, but a large hand pressed against her face and everything went dark.

***

Eileen cracked open her eyes, her hand pressed against her swimming head. She was in a dim room. It was nearly empty save for a ceiling fan, a desk, a chair, and a fancy-looking sewing machine. She recognized nothing.

She began to panic. Eileen lumbered to her feet and dizzily wound her way over to the door. Her mind raced with a jumbled up mess of conclusions and suspicions.

The door was made of gleaming iron and adorned with a huge lock that appeared to take multiple keys. She pushed against it with all her might, but the door didn't give her the satisfaction of a single groan.

"Let me out of here!" She banged her fists on the hard surface.

She yelled at the top of her lungs until her voice had nearly given out. She hadn't expected to be answered. It wasn't as if someone would kidnap you and then answer your plea for aid...would they? She plunged her hands deep into her pockets. No phone, no lunch money. Nothing. Eileen finally began to tear up,

Three consecutive little *clicks* sounded and the door started to push against her. It opened slowly, screeching as it dragged across the hard floor.

Food. They're just bringing you food. Maybe chocolate, she told herself, pretending it calmed her down.

Eileen backed up against the wall. A young man with short brown hair, skin a tad darker than her own, and earthy brown eyes stumbled through the door. His eyes weren't focused on her—instead on the keys. He looked rushed and nervous. Eileen got the same expression when a teacher cut the time for an assignment in half after she'd already deemed it safe to procrastinate. That was the worst. Well, present predicament aside.

Eileen waited a moment, watching the anxious lackey through narrowed eyes as he fumbled. If possible, he seemed more frightened of the situation than Eileen was. He didn't seem like he belonged here.

She found herself wondering how much experience he had. He didn't seem like the type, but then again, there was no such thing in real life. This wasn't some storybook where bad guys looked like bad guys, was it? He may seem like a nice enough guy but he was here, a part of all this. That alone made him guilty.

Didn't it?

An older man walked in behind Brown Eyes. This one wasn't so approachable—his hair was transparent in its thinness and short length, and scars dotted his skin. He stood at least a foot over Eileen and seemed to stare right through her. His brows hung low over his murky eyes, like heavy clouds settling on the horizon for a late-night thunderstorm.

"Eileen Bobbin." His voice was gravelly and low. She could almost feel it scraping against the thick atmosphere of the room.

It hadn't been a question. He was challenging her. She scanned the room for a moment, hoping he would stand for the stalling. The room was bleak. Pale light filtered in from a window over the desk.

Should she lie?

They had obviously known exactly where to find her. If they found out she'd lied, the consequences would probably be worse than handing over whatever it was they wanted. Money, most likely. Always money. Well, they had better prepare for disappointment because she had none to give and she wasn't going to grovel. Her meager savings had been hard-fought and there was no way she'd shove her hard work into their greedy little hands. Cloud Brows crossed his arms and frowned.

Eileen nodded finally.

"Hmm." He smiled. It wasn't sincere or even satisfied, merely an acknowledgment that he had received her reply. "Refreshing. Honesty is a rare commodity these days."

"Let's skip the small talk. What do you want from me?" Her voice was clear, which shocked her a bit. She sounded a lot more confident than she felt.

"Bold girl." The tall man chuckled, his scars stretching into thin lines as they moved with his mouth. "I hear they call you Goldweaver. You are a talented tailor?"

His mouth set in a grim line, but his eyes glittered with greed. He towered over her, his shoulders set with arrogant calm. He reminded her of the evil king from her favorite childhood fairy tale.

Fairy tales didn't exist. Happy endings and magic and perfect heroes were nothing but nonsense.

Eileen's brows furrowed.

"Yes," She answered slowly, carefully sizing up the man before her.

Eileen's father had always taught her to read her opponent before engaging. This man was obviously used to making people feel small. She wasn't going to grant him that.

Analyze and think logically, then decide what was useful and what could wind you up in trouble. Her father's advice replayed in her mind. She knew his type. Cloud Brows wasn't too much of a threat provided she didn't openly defy him.

"Pieces of gold, we heard." The man didn't change his expression. "Any chance your clothes are made using Cloth of Gold? Chinese origins?"

She shook her head back and forth.

"Liar." The man stepped toward her. "My sources never deceive me. We are in need of your assistance and you will grant it to us."

"And if I refuse?" Eileen asked.

It was Brown Eyes who spoke next.

"I'd advise you to do as *Leiter* asks, Miss Bobbin. His methods of getting what he wants are..." He spoke the word hesitantly. "Harsh."

She looked up at the tall man, staring him dead in the eyes. Never let your enemies see your fear. That's what she'd always been taught.

She remembered her father when he was still strong and able to stand unaided. He was solid as a brick wall and unwavering in his confidence. His eyes seemed to glitter whilst telling tales of his training and marches under the *Bundeswehr* leaders. He spoke only of the glory.

It wasn't until after the crash, after Eileen's brother and mother both had died, that her father had disclosed to her all the darker parts of his story. She shuddered at the thought.

"If you refuse?" Cloud Brows spoke with an icy tone. "We'll take bets on how long you will last."

Eileen's jaw tightened and she gave a terse nod. The man raised a hand and gave a snap of the fingers. *Ugh.* Eileen flinched and bit her tongue at his arrogance. A well-dressed woman with a massive wart on the end of her nose entered the chamber, pushing a cart ahead of her. The top was laden with neatly folded stacks of shiny material, threads, buttons, and really, anything she could've asked for.

She stared at the fabric, stunned. She'd heard stories about the material and its frequent use in the Middle Ages, but had no idea it still existed. The woman wheeled the cart over to the desk, inclined her head, and took a swift leave. "I expect the fabric to be processed by the time I come back," he handed Eileen a long list of sizes, designs, and measurements, obviously drawn by a team of professionals.

"Seriously?" Eileen gaped at him.

"You have twenty-four hours." He nodded and walked toward the door. "Perhaps I'll set you free if you comply."

Aldaric stayed behind and she soon discovered he was an eager conversationalist. Or perhaps he was just lonely.

***

"This is impossible," Eileen groaned, ripping the thread from yet another jumbled stitch line.

She didn't know what she was doing or how to manipulate the gilded fabric. The cloth was *literally* gold thread interwoven with silk. Every time she tried to work with it, something went wrong,—a stitch would snag on something, a gold thread came apart from the others, or an entire seam would simply unravel.

She massaged her temples.

Screeech.

The door opened, causing Eileen to jolt. Aside from the wart lady, she'd only had two people enter her chambers since she arrived. Cloud Brows had already made his appearance and likely wouldn't be back until she had what he wanted. Brown Eyes had come hours ago to give her dinner and talk himself hoarse (despite Eileen's fervent insistence on ignoring him). Why then, was he back? She didn't have time for meaningless conversation or snacks, so she turned to send him away.

"I'm not hu—." Eileen's words fell short.

A short man strode through her door, closed it behind him, and leaned back against it, glancing around at the meager surroundings. He was squat and he sported a bushy moustache, a feature that sat in sharp contrast to his bald head. He looked up and studied her for a moment.

"Who are you?" Eileen narrowed her eyes at him. "Why have you come?"

He cleared his throat and held up a hand. How very confident he was, stomping in her room with his short, round self and holding his hand up like that.

"My name is not something I give freely young one," he said. "Call me Tailor, for now. And you are?"

Eileen was past the point of confusion, but she did her best to be cordial. Perhaps this was a test. If so, she had no intentions of failing. "Eileen."

The little man bowed politely and she raised a brow at him. He folded in on himself with dramatic flair. When he stood straight again Eileen found a gun pointed at her chest. She raised her hands in surrender, her eyes wide.

Whoa! That ups the interesting factor.

"I don't want to harm a lady, but orders are orders," he shrugged, the gun still trained on her. "You belong to this organization, yes?"

"*Nein, Meister,*" Eileen shook her head furiously. "I was kidnapped for labor. I have no part in any of this."

The man's gaze traveled over to her desk. His eyes widened and a twisted smile stretched across his face when he saw the stacks of gold.

"I see." He gave her a pointed look and in one swift motion, put the pistol back in its place. "And is this the labor you have been assigned?"

"It is." Eileen motioned to the worktable and the mangled mess atop it. "They want me to make gold clothes, but I'm afraid they've been misled. I've never seen this material with my own eyes, let alone worked with it. It's a pain in the neck."

"Aye." The little man nodded, scratching his paunch chin as he stared at mess around her sewing machine.

"You still haven't answered my question, *Tailor.*" Eileen stepped toward the little man, her hands on her hips. "Why are you here?"

"I've been sent to gather intel on this blasted place." He smiled, yellow blunt teeth showing. "I have a proposition for you, my dear."

"You and everyone else," Eileen blew a stray hair from her face.

"So it seems," Tailor huffed. "At any rate, I can see you're having a bit of trouble there and I just so happen to be quite skilled with such things. I'll trade my services for any information you may have."

Eileen glanced between the desk and Tailor. Anything he could do had to be better than her mutilating the precious fabric. This deal could actually get her out of her predicament.

"I accept your offer," she decided, backing away from the chair.

Tailor waddled over to the desk breathing hard from the effort. He was not exactly stealthy in his movements. Eileen shook her head and narrowed her eyes, wondering how he'd ever managed to get into the building.

"Here's the deal, Miss Eileen; you'll give me one piece of information about the organization for each workload." His eyes met hers. "It has to be something *useful*."

"The *Leiter*'s right-hand man's name is Aldaric Vrosk," she said, the short introduction returning to her. Brown Eyes had been incredibly open with her. "He is quite young, brown eyes, short brown hair."

Tailor nodded with a satisfied grin. He didn't speak another word, but sat hunched at the machine and worked the fabric with expert hands and mind-boggling speed. It went on for hours, and still he did not tire. When she could no longer keep her eyes open, Eileen lay down in the corner to sleep.

When she woke to the faint light of morning, he was gone.

***

Eileen flinched as the door opened, that familiar screeching setting her nerves on edge. Aldaric poked his head in along with a tray of food.

He stopped a moment to stare at the desk with all the glittering items on it and nearly dropped the tray. He cleared his throat and tore his gaze from the table to Eileen, who was too busy staring at the plate of warm sandwiches he carried to notice.

She'd never been a fan of sandwiches. When had they started smelling so good?

Aldaric smiled and handed Eileen her tray, then watched as she gobbled up its contents. The quiet stretched on for a while before Aldaric cleared his throat again to get her attention.

"Would you like to be escorted to the lavatory?"

Eileen looked up, swallowing the last of her meal, and nodded. Aldaric extended a hand. She took it, heaving herself up from the floor, and followed him outside the room. She was suddenly a little self-conscious. Was this all a part of the soon-to-be-daily routine or did he just notice that she was a little stale? Did he actually care or was this all part of his job description? She wouldn't put it past Cloud Brows to forget about her essential human needs.

The building was enormous. Hallways and doors branched off in all directions from the main hall. The twisting chaos reminded her of Berlin's alleys. The two stopped abruptly at one of the doors. Aldaric gestured grandly to it, taking a place to the right as if he were a sentry. She stifled a laugh and turned her back to him. She couldn't let Aldaric know she was beginning to warm up to him. That may have been exactly what he wanted.

Eileen tentatively stepped through the door. She was surprised by the sheer size of the room. Her entire house would fit into this lavatory. She shook her head and made her way to a massive shower. Someone had already provided her with hair care products, soaps, and even a set of clothes.

The garments were simple, but clean and that's all she really cared about. She was suddenly very aware of how long she'd been wearing her old clothes. She used the restroom and allowed herself a moment to indulge in the warm water of the shower. When she finally felt clean, she stood at the mirror.

Her body ached and her green eyes were dark and tired. Her dripping blonde hair hung around her like a shawl, reaching her shoulders. Aldaric had not rushed her so she took her time, brushing it thoroughly, and then slipped the little brush into her pocket, worrying it wouldn't be there next time.

Or if there would be a next time.

Aldaric was waiting to escort her back. He was, as ever, quite talkative. As they casually strolled the halls, his chatter bounced from topic to topic. Eventually he told her of the *Leiter*'s attitude and the struggles of keeping up with such complex business. Eileen didn't interrupt him. The information would be far too valuable to her if Tailor returned. Aldaric was more than forthcoming with his stresses. He seemed much too naive to have such a high position. When they arrived back at her room, he glanced around at it with a frown.

"I'm terribly sorry about the accommodations. Most people in this type of business are… rough around the edges, but this is unacceptable." He shook his head. "These conditions are not proper for a young lady like you. I'll call *Leiter* King down here as soon as possible and make sure the situation is rectified."

And with that, he left Eileen with her thoughts. She simmered and turned back to the desk, glaring at the little window. Did he seriously just call her young lady? He couldn't have been all that much older than she was. She sighed and plopped down in her chair. Pompous little boy.

***

"*Leiter*?" Aldaric cautiously stepped into the dark room.

He was surprised to find that King was turned around, facing the wall. As Aldaric drew closer, he saw an old picture in the man's hands. He was studying it so intensely that King didn't even hear him coming. Aldaric strained his eyes, trying to make out who was in the photo.

"Don't snoop, Vrosk." King spat.

"Sir...I," Aldaric jumped at the sudden words, stuttering to apologize.

"Have you come with news?" *Leiter* King turned to him, slipping the picture into a drawer in his desk. "I have." Aldaric nodded, his heart finally going back to its normal pace. He cleared his throat. "Miss Bobbin has finished with the work you've given her." King gave a grunt.

"You will refer to her as Prisoner X8." The man leaned forward. "If I didn't know better, Vrosk, I'd say you're becoming attached."

Aldaric blanched. "*Leiter*?"

"Don't plead ignorant to me. I know you, down to every movement you make, every word you utter. I'm giving you a warning: do not become close with Prisoner X8. Only call her by her name when in her vicinity." King's eyes glanced down to the drawer for a moment before returning to Aldaric. "Attachment does not aid, but hinder."

Aldaric stared for a long while before nodding. "Understood, *Leiter*."

"Oh, I don't doubt that you understand. Do you agree? That is the question." King grinned down at him, but it was an empty expression. "It would do you well to remember where your loyalties lie, Vrosk. You would not be alive without me."

Aldaric's gaze turned hostile. "And *Adine*."

King shot up, his eyes blazing.

"You will not mention Miss Kronf again." King's nostrils flared. "If you do, I will see to it that you yourself will administer Prisoner X8's consequences should she fail to meet my expectations."

A wave of dread ran through Aldaric.

King smirked victoriously and cleared his throat. "Now, let us go see how our little Goldweaver is doing."

***

Eileen glared maliciously at King as he strode into her room, but that scarred tower of a man walked to the table, dismissing her completely. *Proud son of a donkey.* He held up each garment, one after the other, giving little grunts of approval. Eileen's toes curled in anticipation as he turned to her.

"Your work is...satisfactory." He looked unimpressed but Eileen could see past his stoicism. He hadn't expected the work to be complete, let alone skillfully done. "The next bunch will be just as good, if not better, or you will not see the light of day."

"No." Eileen blanched. "You said you'd let me go!"

The man offered a crooked smile. "I lied."

He snapped his fingers and the wart-nosed woman rolled a new cart of cloth into the room.

"I'll reconsider your request upon the arrival of our next shipment."

Aldaric gave her an apologetic smile. His gaze lingered for a moment before he followed behind King, flipping through the notes on his clipboard as he went. Eileen stared after them until the final lock clicked into place.

She glanced down at the cart, pondering for a moment if she could make an escape with those scissors.

"Ugh!" Eileen pressed her hands against her eyes.

No, be smart. Be logical. They had weapons of their own and were no doubt prepared for something of that nature from a peeved captive. She was stuck, in every sense of the word. With a huff, she settled in her seat at the sewing machine.

Suddenly, school sounded so appealing.

***

Night came soon enough and Eileen still hadn't figured out how to avoid splintering the golden threads. Tailor had made it look so easy. He twirled and twisted the threads together as if it were the simplest thing in the world. Eileen was about to rip her hair out. She should have asked questions when Tailor had been there before, but her pride had gotten in the way. Eileen sighed and looked over at the ornate locks on her door, wondering if Tailor would make another appearance.

She turned back to the fabric, running her fingers along it. Dim light from the scented candle on her desk cast a warm orange glow that rippled across the surface. Though impossible to work with, the cloth was quite beautiful. A screech and scratchy, labored breaths announced Tailor's arrival. Eileen smiled and he turned to him gratefully.

"Salutations, Miss Eileen," Tailor greeted. "I trust that you have more work to do today?"

"Unfortunately." Eileen nodded, abandoning her chair. "Have at it." He took her place at the sewing table and looked up at her expectantly.

Oh, right. He wanted information. She searched through all that Aldaric had told her that day.

"The *Leiter*'s name is King," she declared, smiling. Giving Tailor the man's name made Eileen feel victorious. It wasn't as she was loyal to anyone here. "He has a tattoo on his neck of a big black X."

"Wonderful!" Tailor gave a little grin and waved her off. "That narrows it down. My thanks."

He started doing her work again, fingers moving with practiced expertise. When Eileen crawled back into her corner to go to sleep, she felt a small pang of guilt. Aldaric had left her a soft woolen blanket and a small parcel of food. He was probably the one who had left her the soaps and warm clothes in the lavatory too. He was being so kind to her and had no idea Eileen had already sold him out.

***

Morning was stressful. The little man that never seemed to tire had fallen asleep at the machine that night. She'd had to shake him back to reality and stand guard by the door as he worked away at his task. He had attempted friendly conversation, but Eileen was a little too annoyed at that point to say much of anything.

It wouldn't do for Brown Eyes to come in, smiling that little smile of his. He'd see Tailor and run off to tell his *Leiter* all about their pact.

"So girl, how did you attract those ruffians' attention?" He tried again to engage her in polite small talk. His fingers were flying, threading the needle, and firing out stitches with lightning speed.

"I don't know." She rolled her eyes and listened at the heavy door. "How did you get so good at sewing? And so *fast*?"

The hum of the sewing machine halted. The little man heaved himself up from the chair and cracked his back. His potbelly and the lack of height made him look unbalanced. Tailor smirked.

"Same way magicians make their living," he said.

Without a second glance, he walked over to the door, opened it effortlessly, and strode through it. She rushed to the door, curiosity taking over. Eileen's mouth dropped open and she could almost feel her brain melting from all her questions. Just what kind of a little troll was this guy?

The door was always locked...from the *outside*.

***

"Miss Eileen?" Aldaric's muffled voice came from beyond her door.

She glanced at the slit of light coming through the sorry excuse of a window over her desk. The sky was the unmistakably bright, optimistic yellow of a crisp Berlin morning. Aldaric was going off his normal schedule.

She wondered how her father was doing, if he was worried about her. Who was taking care of him?

She immediately pushed away the thought. She couldn't focus on the gnawing guilt in her chest while she was in here. If she let something like that happen, she'd get emotional and possibly killed. Without Eileen, who would be there to give her father a reason to keep going, to keep fighting? He'd refuse his medicine and the cancer surgery he needed if he lost his only daughter. She had to make it through this.

Stay smart, stay strong.

"Still here," she said flatly.

The door unlocked and screamed in protest as Aldaric pushed it open. He walked over to the table, holding up one of Tailor's dresses. He smiled approvingly.

"You're a very good *schneider*," he said, folding it up and setting it back onto the desk. He stared out her measly window and smiled. "Beautiful day, isn't it?"

Eileen looked at him for a minute, trying to read his expression. Then she realized he'd left the door ajar. He wasn't armed and there was no guard outside her room. What's more, he was talking to her as if they were good acquaintances.

Something didn't seem right.

"Are you well, Miss Bobbin?" he asked, a playful smile on his lips.

She looked from the door to Aldaric but didn't reply. What was his plan? What was he playing at? Aldaric stared into her eyes, willing her to speak. His smile faded and his shoulders fell. He looked genuinely sad.

"What is your game?" Eileen glared at him.

"I just…" He let out a breath and looked her in the eyes. "I'm trying to make you more cheerful. This isn't right and I know a lot about doing things that aren't right. I just wanted to give you a moment of happiness, Miss Eileen."

"Why?" Eileen looked him over. He was either a traitor or trickster. "Why bother at this point?"

"Redemption, I suppose." Aldaric shrugged sadly and strode toward the door. "I'll inform *Leiter* King of your task's completion."

***

When the scarred man made his third appearance, Eileen barely heard a word he said. She found herself drawn more to Aldaric. His brown eyes, sad but steady, never left hers.

Trusting him was probably stupid, but her gut told her otherwise. Those eyes of his had good in them. She believed in him, somehow.

"It's a good offer," King said, snapping Eileen back to reality. "Finish this last bit and you'll earn a permanent position. Good day, Miss Bobbin."

Permanent position.

Not freedom.

What a wonderful birthday present.

How in the world was she supposed to keep a stream of information flowing? What was the information for and what would happen when Tailor finally put it all to use? Staying home all the time with her father was outright freedom compared to the "reward" she'd been promised. And what about her father? He must be worried sick by now!

Eileen banged her head on the desk. She had no idea what to do.

***

The next night, Tailor was back again his skillful fingers, ready to aid her. Eileen met his stare now with empty, despondent eyes. There was no freedom coming. She'd be stuck here forever, relying on Tailor to keep her alive. Why bother keeping the deal?

Tailor cleared his throat. "Run out of gossip, have you?"

Eileen nodded. She didn't know what else to do, what else to say.

"Something has changed." Tailor waited for a moment, stroking his chin, and finally looked up at her with a little smile. "What are they offering you?"

"A position in the 'company,' I guess," she said, making air quotes. Her tone dripped with disgust.

Tailor clapped his little meaty hands. "Perfect, just perfect! I'll finish this gold today and then when you get a place in the organization, you'll use your access to eliminate King's right-hand man, eh? That will put a damper on their little schemes while I set things up!"

Eileen nodded numbly. She wasn't agreeing so much as staring blankly at him. The man was really confusing her. What was he going to do with the information she was feeding him? Why did he even care?

***

When she awoke, Tailor was gone once again. Aldaric came earlier than usual, summoning King, and the process repeated itself. *Leiter* King picked up every one of the products, looked them over, and finally she was met with a smile.

"I suppose I'll keep my end of the deal this time." He opened the door and gestured to the hall. "The position is yours. You're now free to roam the halls, but you will do exactly as we say—and don't try anything funny. There are locks and cameras everywhere."

Locks and cameras everywhere...how in the world did Tailor get in and out?

Eileen nodded and stayed in her corner, looking up at Aldaric. *Leiter* left the room without another word. Aldaric flashed her a smile, offering a hand.

"I'll take you on a tour." His grip was firm but gentle.

Eileen took his hand, guilt and hope filling her in a mix of contradictions. If she went along with Tailor's plan, Aldaric wouldn't be here tomorrow.

***

"And this is the *Kaserne*. This is where you sleep if you don't have an outside home or if you're a recruited prisoner that hasn't yet earned trust."

Aldaric gestured grandly towards the huge padlocked door. Eileen didn't bother covering her little chuckle, which seemed to make him brighten a bit. "Do you want to go inside?"

Eileen studied the door for a moment before nodding. Aldaric swiftly entered in the combination and tugged the massive hunk of iron. Eileen stepped in and looked around in awe. The *Kaserne* consisted of a long, narrow hallway, which branched off into dozens of rooms. A soft carpet stretched down the length of the corridor.

"Impressive, isn't it?" Aldaric stepped up next to her.

She nodded and a little smile stretched across his face. "Do you know anyone in here?"

"Every one of them," Aldaric chuckled. "I see them every morning and every night. I'm always the first to rise and the last one to go to my room."

"Your room?" Eileen's brows furrowed and Aldaric scratched the back of his neck. "Yeah. I...live here. Have since I was ten."

"Ten?" Eileen gaped at him. "You were so young, Aldaric. What happened?"

He looked down at her and sighed heavily.

"It's a long story." He scanned the hallway before pulling Eileen off towards the end of the hall. "Come on. We're going to my room."

***

Aldaric's room looked like all the others from the outside. The inside was a different story. The room wasn't huge, but it was well decorated. A television was mounted on the wall, a comfy-looking bed in front of it. A sizeable desk covered in details sat in the corner, a cushioned chair in front of the black wooden counter.

A laptop, along with plenty of binders and clipboards decorated the surface. Aldaric didn't have a window, but they had to descend a rather long flight of stairs to get to his room, so it was likely below ground. His black dresser was small and neat, and a compact sofa took up the corner adjacent to it.

He motioned for her to sit on the couch and she obliged, reveling in how soft it was. Much better than the hard corner she'd called home for the last few days.

Aldaric took his place at the foot of his bed, facing her, and cleared his throat.

"A long time ago…"

***

The little boy stared at the tall lady's face. She was trying to tell him something, but it fell upon deaf ears. The last thing he remembered hearing was, "I'm sorry, your mother is gone."

He put a hand to his face and wiped away his tears. Mom had said never to cry. She told him to always smile, to find happiness in all things. She needed him to be her ray of sunshine, she'd said. His mother swore that his light helped give her strength, back when his father left, and all throughout her cancer.

He snarled at the little smear of water clinging to his fingers. His light hadn't been bright enough to save her though. With all his efforts, his mother still had been taken from him. It was his fault. It had to be.

The woman looked almost bored, as if she'd seen this scenario play out a billion times before. His eyes took on a steely gleam. She was no better than the insufferable doctors, sending them bills much too large for his mother's bank account. She didn't care about him or his loss. The woman reached out a hand to take hold of his wrist.

"Child, you listen to me. Self-pity will not make the situation any better." She squared her shoulders and looked down her nose at him. "The best thing you can do at this point is to try your best to move on. Now, come with me. We can find you a home to stay in. An orphanage."

"Don't touch me." His young voice cut over hers, ripe with anger. He pulled his wrist from her grip. *Run.*

RUN. GET OUT.

The boy tore away and sprinted down the hallways. His ten-year-old legs were shorter than hers, but he had more energy. More practice. He ran and ran, rushing frantically toward the exit he knew was coming. He knew the layout of the hospital by heart now (at least the floor his mother was on). That bright red door that led to the fire escape on the side of the building gleamed ahead.

He ran for it.

His little arms struggled with the door for a minute before finally wrenching it open. Heavy footsteps echoed from behind and reminded him of games of tag he'd play at recess. Those last few moments of dread before the hand pushed into his back…

No. She wouldn't catch him.

He threw himself through the open door, but she had already caught up. He barely felt the sun on his face when her hands clamped down on him. She held him in place by his wrists.

"Don't run away from me again, understand, child?" she hissed down at him.

Aldaric understood. He simply didn't care.

He sank his teeth into her arm and he kicked backwards. She let out a yelp and struck him out of instinct. Aldaric barely felt it. He pushed away and darted for the fire escape again. She cut him off, blocking the doorway.

"You can't run away from what's real, child." She glared at him with misplaced hatred. "This isn't a video game. You must listen to me. I know what's best for you."

"One, I've never played a video game in my life," he scoffed, spitting at her. "Two, I'm not going to do what you say just because you're bigger than me."

Aldaric dove forward, sliding beneath the woman's legs and out onto the fire escape. He climbed onto the railing and looked down. His stomach dropped at the sight of the street below. He was so, so high up.

"Get back here, boy!" The woman screamed at him as she nervously stepped out onto the metal landing.

"Not a chance." Aldaric decided he liked the possibility of falling better.

He flipped over the railing, mimicking the spies he'd seen in late night movies. He caught his sneakers on the very edge of the landing, gripped tightly to the outside of the bars, and carefully lowered himself until he was dangling precariously above the pavement.

He must climb down.

Out of reach.

His young muscles ached, protesting at the strange actions, and began to shake. His small arms were threatening to drop him onto the street. But still Aldaric kept on, his mind determined to get away. He was mere inches from placing a foot on the lower platform's edge when his fingers slipped.

His scream echoed through the alley. The wind pressed against his back as he scrunched his eyes. He left his stomach somewhere near the platform. He braced himself for the impact that was sure to come, for the pain. His eyes scanned fruitlessly for something to grab on to.

Instead, he felt strong arms scoop up under him. It knocked his breath out and sent pain up his spine. He panted for a few moments, struggling to right himself before opening his eyes.

Faces, two of them. A man and a woman.

"Oh dear, what've you gotten yourself into?" the woman asked, looking up at the angry woman screaming from the fire escape.

Her eyes were as bright as sapphires. Delicate blonde hair framed her soft features. The man who had caught him held him firmly, the faintest hint of a smile on his clean-shaven face. A strange X-shaped tattoo was inked on his neck.

"M...my momma…" Aldaric croaked out. Normally, he wouldn't have screamed or cried. But now...he didn't care. All he could think about was the body lying in the cold, bleak hospital room. He didn't dare think about his other family. He knew just what they thought about him. "She's dead. There's...no one..."

"That's horrible. You poor thing." The woman bit her lip. "What about your father?"

Aldaric's jaw tightened. "Gone."

"Oh my." The lady looked up at Aldaric's savior, concern welling in her eyes.

"Joachim, we can't just leave him here. They'll drop him at the orphanage," she pleaded with the man. She sounded...oh, she sounded so much like a mother.

His mother.

Fresh tears sprang to his eyes.

"Can we keep him, love?" She smiled.

"Keep him? He's not a lost kitten, Adine." The man glanced down at Aldaric, then back to the woman. "What would we gain from having him around?"

"He's obviously athletic." The woman's mouth curved upwards in a smile. "We could very easily train him. He would be a good asset in around six or seven years. Wouldn't you, child?"

Aldaric had no idea what he was agreeing to, but he nodded. He saw nothing but love in the woman's eyes. Whatever it was she was offering had to be better than the orphanage. They would take him away from this. From all of it.

"Very well," the man sighed and shook his head as he set the boy on his feet.

"Good, good," the woman smiled and extended her hand. "I am Adine Kronf. What is your name?"

"I'm Aldaric," the boy squared his shoulders and shook Adine's hand. "Aldaric Vrosk."

***

"You lost both of your parents?" Eileen saw pain in Aldaric's brown eyes.

"I lost my mother." Aldaric shrugged. "My father abandoned us."

"Still a loss," she countered.

Aldaric's brown eyes hardened.

"Not when you have a father like him," he sighed, rubbing the bridge of his nose. His father's fist had broken it when he was just eight years old. "But that doesn't matter anymore."

"It does matter," Eileen touched his hand. "It's part of you."

"Perhaps, but I can't change it, so I've learned to accept it." Aldaric sighed heavily. "Not all things can be changed, but some can. I want to be a good man, Eileen. A kind man. I wouldn't be alive without Adine's kindness."

"And King's?" Eileen looked skeptical.

"Perhaps once, but he's changed. Corrupted. Adine's death hardened him. He's...not a good person anymore," Aldaric huffed. "Then again, I don't suppose he was ever the perfect role model."

"Clearly," Eileen sighed.

"He...*we* make money through illegal sales, kidnapping, and other questionable means." He looked pointedly at Eileen. "It was never something to be proud of, but now? *Leiter* has allowed, even *encouraged*, us to generate blood money. Assassinating high political figures and other influential leaders."

Eileen reclined back in her seat. "That's terrible."

"I don't want to be a part of this anymore," Aldaric frowned, staring down at his feet. "But what I want doesn't matter. I'm stuck, same as you, Eileen."

Aldaric shrugged, but Eileen couldn't forget his words from earlier. *Redemption.* He looked as though he'd lost all hope.

"And I thought my life was grim," she muttered to herself.

All this time, Eileen had just assumed Aldaric was exactly where he wanted to be. That he was just some idiot, roaming the halls of this cursed place, more than happy to do the *Leiter*'s bidding. But he was a prisoner too.

"Your life before was unhappy?" Aldaric lifted a brow.

"My dad was a soldier before he got lung cancer. He got really sick. One night, he was having a tough time breathing. We were all driving him to the hospital when it happened." Eileen's throat constricted. "We were in a car crash, and... only me and Dad got out of it."

Aldaric frowned. "I'm so sorry."

"It's not your fault. I blame cancer." Eileen made herself smile. "Cancer deserves a baseball bat to the mouth."

She got a little grin in return. "Something we agree on."

***

That night when Tailor arrived, he was angry that Eileen had not held up her end of the deal. She averted her eyes for a moment, scanning the room, which was now properly furnished since she was technically no longer a prisoner.

"I asked you for one simple payment," he said with cold calm.

"Please," Eileen begged. "Anything but Aldaric. I couldn't...I couldn't betray him like that. Not now."

Tailor let out a bit of a growl, which caught her off guard. That wasn't like him.

"Think about what you are saying," he sneered, "You've *already* betrayed him."

Eileen glared at him. "I haven't."

"Oh, but you have." Tailor gave her a smirk. "You betrayed everyone here with your spying, girl. There's nothing you can say to make that untrue. Now we know who we are hunting. The minute we have their citizen I.D.s, this whole place will be torn apart. I'll find them, uncover all their dark little secrets, and destroy them all. I couldn't have done this without your help."

Eileen's eyes welled with tears and her throat clenched, begging her to allow the sobs. But she wouldn't.

Stay smart. Stay strong.

"If you're capable of such things, why don't you just take care of the *Leiter* and his men yourself, right now?" Eileen squared her shoulders. "Why don't you just go shoot up the whole place instead of wasting your time here with me?"

"You're more naive than I thought, little oath breaker." Tailor laughed at her. "One cannot simply take what is rightfully mine and walk away unharmed. There are consequences to actions, something you have yet to learn."

"And I suppose you'll teach me?" Eileen's chest swelled with anger. She turned her back on the evil little man.

"Perhaps," he chuckled at her. "You have three days' time to guess my real name. If you succeed, I will leave you in peace. If you do not…"

"If I don't, what?" She spun on him.

Eileen's question fell on deaf ears. Tailor had vanished. She stared after him in confusion. She hadn't even heard him leave. And why did she have to guess his name? What kind of a challenge was that supposed to be?

And what would happen if she failed?

***

Eileen spent the next three days in serious distress. Tailor appeared to her briefly each night to retrieve her guesses. Each guess earned an amused "no." When she ran out of names, Tailor would laugh at her and make a swift departure. She'd gone through the entire alphabet of names. Eileen was running out of ideas and was nearly out of time.

Every time she looked at Aldaric she fought the urge to apologize. As if saying sorry could ever make up for giving his life away without consent. She was beginning to lose hope. What could it be? Would his mother really be cruel enough to name him something so bizarre that he thought she'd never guess it?

On the third day, an idea occurred to her.

That afternoon after they walked the garden path, she asked Aldaric if she could tour the top floor.

The security offices and her last hope for an answer were on that level. Not wanting to deny her exploration, Aldaric agreed and accompanied her.

"The gardens I understood, but why this?" Aldaric smiled at her as they rode the elevator up.

"You think I want to be stuck at a sewing machine my whole life?" Eileen smirked.

With some clever truth bending, she managed to convince him that she was interested in moving up in the company. Perhaps someday she might wish to run the security team. She wanted to see what happened behind the scenes; maybe she could watch some old tapes, listen to the footage through headphones.

Though he still had questions, Aldaric made it happen for her and even left her alone so she could explore the security workings on her own. Ten minutes. That's what the security team had agreed to. Eileen had ten minutes to make magic happen.

She scrolled through the security logs and started from the day she'd arrived in this horrid place. She watched as King's men carried her into that dank, dark room. Eileen shivered at the sight. She had looked so helpless, so pathetic, just hanging limp from someone else's grip.

She sped through the footage until she saw the thick iron door opened by its own accord. It was the day Tailor made his final proposition. She rewound the video and turned the volume up, pressing the headphones to her ears.

A disembodied voice cut through the ambient static and right to Eileen.

"He messed with the wrong man when he stole Adine from my dungeons." Tailor muttered. "No matter, I'll have my revenge soon enough. He took my Goldweaver. I shall have his."

"What the--?" Eileen pressed the headphones closer to her ears.

"She'll never guess Rumpelstiltskin." Tailor's voice whispered. "This blasted name will be good for something."

Jackpot, little man.

Eileen walked out of the security room with her head held high. Aldaric stared at her sideways, but he said nothing.

***

When the foul, little man came that night, Eileen stood at the ready.

"How many guesses will it be tonight?" he mocked, rubbing his hands together.

"Just one," Eileen smiled back. The man raised a furry brow.

"How sad," he feigned a frown. "Given up then?"

"Your name is…"

"Yes, girl?" He waved her on, unimpressed.

"Rumpelstiltskin." Eileen smiled and crossed her arms.

"No!" His eyes widened and his face turned a light shade of puce. "I've *never* been found out! My name is never spoken. How could you possibly know that?"

Eileen smiled. "Same way magicians make their living."

"Foul girl," Rumpelstiltskin snarled, raising his gun.

Instinct kicked in and Eileen dropped to the floor, narrowly dodging the bullet. Or perhaps he missed on purpose. He seemed the type to drag out his revenge.

"You've cheated!" He pursued her.

"S-stop!" She scrambled away from him. "You never told me any rules!"

He stomped over to her, his stocky build suddenly seeming imposing. "You never cheat, that shouldn't have to be said."

"How do you even break the rules when there are none?" Eileen cried. "Please stop."

Rumpelstiltskin didn't answer. He let loose a feral growl and stalked at her, his hands raking forth. He didn't seem human anymore. His face contorted into an evil sneer as he stared at her with those beady eyes. A screech echoed throughout the room.

A gunshot rang out and Eileen slammed hard to the floor.

***

"Eileen? Eileen, answer me!" Aldaric exclaimed, heaving Rumpelstiltskin's limp form off her. She stared up into those brown eyes, speechless. She couldn't understand him through her ringing ears, but he'd just saved her life.

Aldaric's brows furrowed at her lack of response. He gently reached down to help her up. She took his hand, in a daze. She'd just witnessed *death*.

Again.

She glanced over to Rumpelstiltskin, lying limp and cold on the floor, motionless.

"I came as fast as I could when I heard the gunshot." Aldaric raked his hair away from his face. "Idiot! I've seen him snooping around outside before, but I never thought...Eileen?"

She must've looked as pale and feverish as she felt because he cut his explanation off and pulled her close to him.

"Come on, we're getting you out of here," he declared, leading her out of the room.

She didn't speak as he led her down the hallway. They sped past the *Kaserne,* the restrooms, and the string of endless prisoner cells and interrogation chambers. In no time, they burst through the rear exit of the compound and out into the chilly night air.

Eileen felt the breeze against her skin for the first time in a week. She gulped in the air hungrily, the crispness of it snapping out of her daze. She was outside.

Outside.

"Your school is less than a mile away. Straight down this road," Aldaric pointed to the empty street. "I think you know where to go from there."

Eileen looked up at him, her face tightening with confusion. Aldaric was smiling. It curved up the slightest bit on the left, making a little dimple she hadn't noticed before. The world was crashing down around them but for the first time since they'd met, he looked genuinely happy.

More than that, he looked determined. He clutched the handle and pulled the door open.

"Aldaric don't, *Leiter* will find out what you've done." Eileen sucked on her teeth. "He'll punish you and then he'll come after me."

"I won't give him the chance." Aldaric brushed his hand along Eileen's cheek. "I'm going to set things right, Eileen. Now go. Your father needs you."

She turned toward home, a hollow pit forming in her gut.

"Aldaric, I…" Eileen looked back over her shoulder.

He was already gone.

"Aldaric, no!" Eileen pounded on the door, yelling at the top of her lungs.

Drawing attention to herself was stupid and dangerous, but she couldn't just leave him like that. He'd saved her life. He'd risked everything to get her out of that horrid place. Now, he was rushing into danger head on and there was little she could do to help him. She screamed and cried, but no one answered the door.

Aldaric didn't come. No one came.

***

Eileen curled up on her sofa and read the next chapter in this week's book to her dad. They'd started the tradition after his surgery a few weeks ago. Now that he was in remission, Eileen's dad was desperate to spend as much time as he could with anyone who wasn't in the medical profession. Mostly though, he was paranoid that he might lose his daughter again. The police, convinced Eileen had simply run away from home, had been absolutely no help. Her father had been alone in his efforts to find her. The time he'd spent worrying over her disappearance had reminded him just how precious every moment together was.

It had been hard for Eileen to explain to her father what had happened to her, but she'd somehow managed it. She'd left out a few key details (especially Rumpelstiltskin and his unsavory death), but after a few long, painful hours she managed to convince her dad not to call the police. The last thing either of them needed was further dealings with "the company."

That didn't stop him from wanting to jump up from his wheelchair, grab the rifle from his gun cabinet, and show those fools exactly how he felt about what they'd put his daughter through.

"Ready dad?" Eileen smiled over at him, cracking the book open to the page she had marked.

"Let's do this," he said, locking his fingers behind his head.

"Okay, so we left off at chapter—" Eileen began, but they were interrupted by a soft knock on the door. "Hang on, dad. Be right back."

Eileen set her book down on the couch and trudged over to the door. She grabbed the baseball bat they now kept propped in the entryway, prepared to send away whatever random stranger had mistakenly come calling. They knocked again and Eileen rolled her eyes.

"Hang on, jeez," Eileen grouched through the door. "What do you—?"

Eileen's words evaporated into nothing and her bat clattered to the floor.

"Hello, Eileen." A pair of earthy brown eyes bore into hers.

Eileen's jaw dropped.

Aldaric stood there on her doorstep, a single red rose in his hand. He offered her the flower with a dramatic bow, smirking up at her from beneath his thick lashes. She accepted the gorgeous bloom with numb fingers while she drank in the sight of him.

He looked the same, but so very different.

His hair was trimmed and smooth and he was dressed in black from head to toe. His suit elaborately tailored and made of the finest pinstriped silk. Black ink peeked out just above his collar. A thick XI. He watched as Eileen's eyes landed on the new marking on his neck, then smirked and grabbed her hand.

"May I come in, Eileen?" The light danced playfully in his dark eyes. "I have a very important question to ask you."

Alex J. Clark

Author of The Goldweaver

Alex is 13 years old and lives on a mountain with her parents, sister, and two dogs. Alex has always had her feet planted firmly on the ground but she reaches her head into the clouds from time to time. This is where she hears the voices—and when she gets back down, she puts them on paper, creating stories like "The Goldweaver."

She enjoys drawing just as much, if not more than writing. You will more than likely find her drawing or playing *Legend of Zelda* or *Minecraft* on any given occasion. She has a love of small children, animals, and seafood.

Frozen Beauty

Lauren Frick

I no longer recognize the person staring back at me in the mirror. I am haunted by the ghost of who I used to be. To be honest, I never saw myself as beautiful before all this. Looking back, I realize how blind I was. I would give anything to look the way I did a year ago.

Back then, my long golden hair trailed down my back to my waist. My features were petite and delicate. My lips were a gorgeous shade of peach and my cheeks were always rosy. I was fit from my years of playing on the volleyball team and running track. My biggest stresses in life were midterms, boy drama, and maintaining my calorie intake for the day.

Now an intruder inhabits my mirror, wearing the mask of a disease that is slowly destroying my body. My scalp is bare and irritated, exposing my oddly shaped skull. My face and limbs are swollen and the tip of my nose is an angry shade of red. My lips are drained of their color and my cheeks are indefinitely sunken beneath my sallow skin. I am shapeless and wasting away. I haven't been to school in months, boys are afraid of me, and calories are obsolete.

My only concern is survival.

My sixteenth birthday is approaching quickly. I don't know if I'll see it.

"Sweet sixteen," I chuckle and shake my head in disbelief. How ironic would it be if I died on my birthday, a day meant to celebrate life?

Truthfully, I'm already gone. I'm only hanging on for my mom. She tries to be strong, but she has been slowly falling apart since the doctor delivered my death sentence last year. It only got worse when my dad left. Apparently, he couldn't handle it, so he left us to face this on our own.

She fought hard and worked harder, but the financial strain of my medical expenses was too much for her to handle on her own. We lost the house six months ago and ended up in this crappy apartment. My mom has been dealt with more heartbreak in the twelve months than most people deal with in a lifetime

She does her best to hide her sorrow when she is around me, but I can see the signs. Her red nose, her bloodshot swollen eyes, and the muffled crying I hear coming from her room every night. The walls of our twenty-third story walk up are incredibly thin.

"No parent should outlive their child," she mutters. She sobs into her pillow, a failed attempt to swallow up the noise. She'll pray for hours on end, hoping it will fix me.

It won't.

My cancer support group leader Deirdre says that everyone deals with these things in their own way. Deirdre is a breast cancer survivor and much too peppy for my taste.

"The only thing you have is your faith," she always tells us. "If you give up on that, if you lose hope, you're already dead."

I guess I'm already dead.

The sound of the key scraping against the front door rouses me from my dreary thoughts. My mom is struggling with the old, tarnished door lock. Once again, she's forgotten you need to push the knob in when you turn the key.

I make my way to the door, careful not to move too quickly. When I do, my vision blurs and the room starts to spin. Occasionally, I'll wake up on the floor in a pool of my own vomit…which is about as enjoyable as it sounds.

She's swearing at the door now. Frustrated by my body's limitations, I brush my imaginary hair behind my ear as I stumble through our flat. It's an annoying habit I haven't been able to break. I really should try harder though. Every time my fingertips graze the side of my naked scalp, I feel self-conscious and exposed.

"Stupid door," my mom grunts.

"Hi, mom," I chuckle as I twist the lock and yank the door open.

Mom jumps back, the shock on her face is momentary and soon replaced by a look of pity. Or maybe sadness.

"I would've gotten it eventually, Aurora," she says, shuffling into the living room.

"You say that every time." I roll my eyes at her. "When was the last time you successfully opened that door?"

"When was the last time you opened it for me without making a snarky comment?" She dramatically mimics my eye roll and we both laugh.

"Seriously though." My vision darkens at the edges. Laughter takes a lot out of me, so I lean against the wall for support. "How will you ever get into the apartment after I'm gone?"

Her face falls and I immediately regret my callous joke. I never think about what I say. I swear, I open my mouth and words just fall out. I'd love to blame the chemo or the drugs but I've always been this way. Unfortunately, my mom is too fragile for my sarcasm.

She is crumbling before me.

I see it in her eyes first, the shadow that dulls her bright blues whenever she thinks about losing me. Her hands shake so violently she drops her purse on the floor and the loose contents scatter around us. She sinks into a heap on the ground.

"Mom, please." My lip quivers as I kneel at her side.

She can't speak. Her only response is a series of body-wracking sobs. Deirdre always tells us it's important to let your loved ones feel what they are feeling. I sit there in silence, rubbing circles on her back like she did for me when I was a kid.

After a few minutes of watching my mother suffer, I can't take it anymore. I have to do something, anything, to make her feel better. But what? There's nothing that can fix what she is feeling.

"Mom, will you come to group with me?" I blurt.

"Really?" She raises her head off the carpet and sniffles loudly. "You really want to go? And you want me to come with you?"

"It helps," I lie, nodding enthusiastically. "It'd mean a lot to me if you came with."

"It's really making you feel better?" Her swollen eyes flood with hope.

No, it makes me feel more depressed than ever.

"Yes." I hold a hand out to her. "Wanna be my plus one?"

A sad smile spreads across her face and she slides her hand into mine. It is still wet with tears. Tears I caused. "You really don't have to do this, sweetie."

"I know, mom. I want to," I say.

"I love you, Rory." She squeezes my hand and grabs her keys from the pile surrounding us.

"I'm just going to grab my phone." I head toward my room.

When I get there, I close my door and lean against it. Now it is my turn to cry. They aren't tears of sadness or despair. I've already accepted that I am going to die sooner than I am supposed to.

My tears are for my mother. She loves me with every beat of her healthy heart. She's my rock and my best friend. She didn't leave when things got hard. She's doing everything she can to protect me. I am beyond lucky to have her.

Even if it won't be forever.

***

"Here we are, honey," Mom said, pulling into the parking spot closest to the entrance.

"Ready?"

"Totally." I force a smile. "Let's do this."

I am not looking forward to another depression session, but I put on a good show. My mom is happier than I've seen her in months. I'll play along, for her. I hook my arm through hers and we head toward to rundown building. Some of the letters have vanished from the sign outside. I'd guess that is the work of teenage delinquents, since sign at the Washington Community Center now says WASH----- ---M----- -E----.

The Community Center has been struggling to keep their doors open to the public for quite some time. The place is falling apart, inside and out, but there are no funds to maintain the facility, let alone make improvements. I'm pretty sure Deirdre pays for our sad spread of refreshments (generic fruit punch and dollar store cookies) out of her own pocket. Word on the street is they'll be closing their doors within the year. I'm not terribly concerned about that, as I'm confident I won't be around long enough to see it happen.

In a twisted way, I sort of appreciate the irony of it all.

The Center, the group, and I; we're all dying together.

"This way," I say, tugging my mom down the hallway. Once we reach the door, I wave my arms flamboyantly and usher her in ahead of me. "Here we are. Room 101, where all the magic happens,"

"I thought you said the meeting hall was a dump, Aurora." My mom stares wide-eyed ahead of her.

"It is. The place is falling ap-" I stop abruptly two steps inside the doorway and my jaw drops. "Whoa."

The once dimly lit room is now awash in a warm white glow. The blinking fluorescents, most of which were burnt out or shattered, are gone. Chic, chrome lighting fixtures dangle from stark, new ceiling tiles.

The walls are freshly painted in a soothing shade of lavender. There's an intricate silver vine mural twisting its way around the perimeter at eye level. The wobbly and mismatched plastic chairs have been replaced with plush, contemporary seating.

There's a table across the room draped in crisp, white linens with a silver runner. It is stacked high with fresh cupcakes, cookies, and other decadent treats and stretches the full length of the back wall. A woman in a crisp white chef's uniform passes out divine-looking confections to anyone within arm's reach. She does so with a smile on her face.

Deirdre walks to the front of the room, taps on a shiny new podium, and smiles down at us. Though our surroundings have changed, her demeanor has not. She still manages to address us like a kindergarten class gathered for story time.

"Please, take your seats." She gestures to the cluster of chairs in front of the podium.

"Come on, Rory." My mom leads me over and we sit down.

"Good afternoon, everyone," Dierdre chirps. "I'm sure you have all noticed there have been a few changes around here."

She applauds excitedly, waiting for us to join in. When all she receives are skeptical stares, she smiles and continues.

"The WCC has recently received a sizable donation toward the improvement of our facility. Thanks to the generosity of the Glacio Corporation, we will be undergoing a massive restoration in the coming months." Dierdre is positively giddy. "It looks as though our prayers have been answered. We will be able to continue helping people just like all of you for many years to come!"

My mom smiles and starts clapping. The rest of us join in, but our hearts aren't in it. It has to be the most awkward and pathetic round of applause in the history of time.

A handsome man steps toward the podium, beaming proudly. There's something in his smile that I can't quite place. His eyes are bright and mischievous. There's no trace of pity there. This is something I'm not accustomed to and I'm not sure how to feel about it.

He's probably in his late forties or early fifties. Despite the gray at his temples, his features are youthful and bright. His blue eyes shine behind a modern pair of thick-framed, black glasses. He's wearing dark jeans and a blazer over a Batman t-shirt.

I'm tempted to like him.

"Everyone, I'm honored to introduce to you our generous benefactor, Wil... Wilhe—" Deirdre squints down at a card in her hands, shakes her head, and glances over at the man.

"Wilhelm Fleischer," the man interjects enthusiastically. "Thank you for the warm introduction, Deirdre, but there is no need for formalities. I have a feeling we're all about to become friends. Just call me Wil. Hey guys."

Wil seems unfazed by the group's baffled expressions. His smile broadens as he looks around the room and digests our various stages of morbidity. Why is he smiling like that? Everyone in this room is either dying or watching someone they love die, and he's up there grinning like he wants to sell us a timeshare in Barbados.

"Okay, then, *Wil*. The floor is all yours," Deirdre beams at him and tosses her hair over her shoulder as she heads towards the door. She winks at Wil and waves to the group. "I'll see the rest of you next week!"

"Thank you," Wil waves at her then turns to the group. "How's everyone doing tonight?"

Stupidest. Question. Ever.

"Really?" I mutter to myself, rolling my eyes.

"Rory, hush," my mom frowns.

"I'm sure you are all wondering why I am here." Wil claps his hands together and rests them on the podium.

"You think?" One of our group, a boy around my age named Gabe, blurts out.

"As a matter of fact, I am a thinker," he winks at Gabe. "That's why I'm here."

"Awesome. Any chance you could skip the small talk and get to the point?" Gabe quips. "It's not like we have all the time in the world here."

"Fair enough," Wil chuckles heartily. "I understand that each of you has been diagnosed with a serious illness."

"It's called cancer, man," Gabe says. "And in case you're wondering, it sucks."

He looks at his dad, who sits next to him, but the man doesn't react. He fidgets with his cell phone, his expression blank. I know that look. He's already given up.

"Cancer does suck," Wil nods and clears his throat. "Believe me when I say, I truly understand. You have all been through the wringer with your treatments, I'm sure. Chemotherapy, radiation, countless surgeries, and medications? The side effects are often worse than the illness itself. Sadly, none of that pain guarantees that you won't…"

His cheerful smile fades to a grim line.

"Die?" Gabe crosses his arms. The track marks from countless IVs shine like beacons against his pale skin. "It's going to happen whether you have the guts to say it out loud or not. We all have expiration dates. Ours are just sooner than they should be."

My mother frowns and shifts uncomfortably in her seat. I catch Gabe's eye and smile warmly at him. He smirks and rolls his eyes toward Wil. His expression screams, *can you believe this guy?* I've never had an actual conversation with Gabe, but after this, I think I'd like to.

"Being given an…" Wil uses air quotes, "*expiration date,* doesn't mean death is your only option."

We all collectively sigh. Was this guy here to sell us cemetery plots or tell us about the financial benefits of cremation? Wil strolls toward the smart board and presses a button on a small device in his hand.

"Here we go," Gabe groans. His dad sits silently by, scrolling through Facebook on his phone.

"Just, hear me out," Wil says, his hands raised in surrender.

A presentation labeled *Cryogenic Freezing: Claim Your Future* pops onto the screen. I raise an eyebrow and tilt my head. My mother crosses her arms over her chest, a troubled look on her face.

"Who here knows what cryogenic freezing is?" We all raise our hands. Wil calls on me.

"That's where you make some guy into a human popsicle and thaw him out like a million years later, right?" I'm intrigued, but not impressed. "That stuff is science fiction."

"You're half right." He chuckles and jabs a finger in my direction. "Cryogenics involves the flash freezing of biological entities. I assure you, young lady, it is very much a reality."

"We should go," my mother says, grasping my hand in hers.

"Wait, mom." I mutter and hold firm in my seat, my eyes boring into Wil's. "What's the point?"

"Survival." Wil squares his shoulders and meets my gaze with equal intensity. "With our current technology, we are able to take living bodies of the elderly and the terminally ill and freeze them in time. This buys us and the patient, time."

"Time for what?" Gabe leans forward.

"Research and development, scientific breakthrough, and eventually a cure." Wil says.

"What does this have to do with us?" Gabe asks.

"Everything," Wil's features soften. "The last two decades of my life have been dedicated solely to the study of cryogenics. Unfortunately, the algorithms were imperfect, and our results were unpredictable, at best. Six years ago, we had a major breakthrough and all of that changed."

"Aurora, this isn't right," my mom pleads. "We should go."

"Just wait, mom," I urge.

He presses his button and a new slide pops up. It's a picture of a large, vertical tube surrounded by wires and dials. It's filled to the brim with a murky grey liquid.

"This is a cryochamber." Wil smiles. "We fit each patient with monitors to track their vitals, a nourishment line, and sedation feed. The cryo-fluid is pumped in through these hoses."

He points to the black tubes leading into the top of the chamber. "Once the chamber in full, we gradually begin the freezing process."

My stomach flips and my weak heart beats in my ears.

"Once the patient is sedated, we'll slowly lower the temperature." Wil's eyes are intense. "When the fluid hits negative two hundred thirty-eight degrees Fahrenheit, the process is complete. The individual inside is essentially frozen in time."

"Cool," Gabe's eyes widen. "It's like the Matrix or something."

"Or something," Wil laughs.

With the click of a button, a new photo pops up. It shows a young man's face frozen behind the foggy glass of a cryochamber. His skin is sallow and his cheeks are gaunt. He looks, well, dead.

"This is Matt," Wil smiles. "Five years ago, Matt was diagnosed with a rare form of blood cancer. He fought hard, but his disease progressed so quickly that his treatments weren't enough. When Matt came to us, he was on life support. His organs were failing. He was on a ventilator and couldn't breathe on his own. He had only days left. His parents came to Glacio with a plea. They knew that the science was only experimental, but it was also their son's only chance."

"Aurora, please." Mom's hand was shaking in mine.

"Six months ago, the medical science community discovered a cure for Matt's cancer." Wil whistles, turns to the door and it opens. "Ladies and gentlemen, I'd like to introduce you all to my dear friend, Matt."

A very healthy, very much alive, Matt walks through the door and I nearly jump out of my skin. My mom gasps, her mouth gaping in shock.

"It's nice to meet all of you." Matt smiles sheepishly and walks to the front of the room.

"No way," Gabe says. "It's the popsicle!"

His dad is definitely paying attention now.

"I know what you are all thinking." Matt smiles. "This is insane. It must be a trick, right? Wrong. What Wil is doing at Glacio is one hundred percent real. I am living proof that this man is a miracle worker. I was on the brink of death when Wil and his people took me in. Yet here I am today, standing in front of you, completely cancer free."

"I'm starting college in a few months and I plan to study medicine. Heck, I even have a girlfriend." He laughs. "When I closed my eyes five years ago, I was sure I'd never have any of those things. I thought death was my only option. I was wrong. There's another way and Wil can give it to you."

For the first time in our group's history, we all rise up and applaud in earnest. Charles, a kid who has blood cancer, whistles and pumps his fist into the air. Cheers fill the room.

We had all been given a death sentence. Was it possible that we could get a pardon?

"What's the catch?" Gabe asks and his dad nods. "I mean, this is probably going to cost my family a million bucks that we don't have."

"There's no catch," Wil smiles sincerely. "All I need from you is your bravery." "Meaning what?" I ask him.

"Meaning, I make no guarantees, other than a *chance* of survival and an opportunity to claim your future." Wil turns to me. "I am offering each of you a slot in the second round of our clinical trials. If you accept, you will be entered into cryostasis until a viable treatment or a cure for your disease is discovered. We will do so at no cost to you. What's more, we cover any living expenses for your immediate family members for the full length of your cryoterm. Our financial department will establish a trust in each of your names that will more than sustain you when it's time for you to wake up."

My breath hitches. My mom could see my sixteenth birthday. *I* could my sixteenth birthday. The room erupts in excited chatter and everyone is on their feet. People swarm Wil and Matt. Questions are being hurled at them like bouncy balls ricocheting around the room.

"This is crazy." My mother frowns and gathers her things. "Let's go, Aurora."

"No, mom." I stand my ground. "Think it through. This is literally our only chance to be together."

"Aurora, no," she says. "We don't know anything about this man and his company or what they're really involved in. I'm not going to sign your life away on a whim and a promise of money."

"What life, mom?" I sigh.

"You can't think like that, baby girl," my mom chides, tears welling up in her eyes.

"It's *all* I can think about." My chin quivers. "I'm tired, mom. I've been holding on for you. Not for me, for you. I know that you don't want to hear this and I'm sorry for hurting you, but. . . Mom, I can't do it anymore. I don't have any fight left in me."

"Aurora," her voice catches.

"Mom, please," I plead. "Will you at least think about it?"

Her brows knit, but she looks in my eyes and I know she sees it. Something she hasn't seen there for a long time.

Hope.

"I'll think about it," she relents.

***

"Are you sure about this?" My mom asks.

"Positive," I smile weakly.

My mouth is dry, my hands are sweating, and my heart beats wildly in my chest. I am completely terrified but I haven't felt this alive in almost a year.

"Okay," my mom sighs and grabs onto my hand as we stand in front of the giant glass doors at Glacio.

"I'm going to miss you, mom," I squeeze her hand.

"I'll miss you more," she says.

I don't argue with her.

"Together forever?" I lace my pinky through hers, a promise we haven't spoken aloud since I was a child.

"Forever and always," she nods.

"Mom?" I turn to her.

"Yes, baby?" She looks nervous.

"Promise you'll keep my room exactly the same."

She laughs and wraps me in a tight hug. "I swear I won't such your ugly posters, dust your knickknacks, pick up your dirty laundry, or peek in your diary."

"Hey." I pull back from the hug in mock disgust. "Those posters are not ugly, they're iconic!"

"Whatever you say, Aurora," she kisses the fuzz on top of my head.

I close my eyes and bask in the warm afternoon for just a moment longer. I have no idea when I will see the sun again. My legs shake beneath me. My strength is fading fast. My mom drapes her arm around my slender frame and helps me through the doors.

This could be the last time she hugs me for what may be years.

"I love you," I tell her as I lean into her shoulder.

"I love you, too," she chokes.

***

"Aurora, nice to see you," Wil smiles at me as he walks past.

The white gown they've given me is paper-thin and I'm already cold. I stand in a stark white room surrounded by the rest of my support group.

"Are you ready to claim your future?" Wil smiles serenely.

No one speaks.

A nurse ushers each of us into the tube chambers. It's padded but not enough to be comfortable. The hydraulic door closes slowly and for a moment, I panic. It feels like a coffin.

Gabe's tube is across from mine. I smile at him weakly and he waves. His expression mirrors my own; a mixture of fear and hope. A cloud of fine mist fills the tube and leaves goosebumps on the surface of my skin. My breathing begins to slow and I feel light. A sense of calm washes over me. My mom stands outside my chamber. She presses her hand against the glass. I match mine up with hers.

She will wait for me while they find my cure. There's no doubt in my mind.

"I'm scared," I whisper through the glass that separates us.

She starts to sing.

"Mmmm-hmmm, I want to linger." It's the lullaby my mom used to sing to me when I woke up from a nightmare. Identical tears stream down our faces.

"Mmmm-hmmm, a little longer," I join in softly singing. "A little longer here with you.

Mmmm-hmmm, it is the perfect night.

Mmmm-hmmm, it doesn't seem quite right.

Mmmm-hmmm, that it should be my last with you.

Mmmm-hmmm, and as the days go by.

Mmmm-hmmm, I'll think of you and sigh.

Mmmm-hmmm, this is goodnight and not goodbye."

"I love y—" My words trail off. My eyelids feel so heavy, I rest my eyes for a second, but I can't seem to make them open.

There's water pooling around me. It's cold. So cold.

My mother's voice fades away.

Everything goes dark.

***

Everything hurts. My arms and legs are stiff and heavy. I'm so tired.

"Aurora?"

"Five more minutes, mom." I grumble.

"Aurora, open your eyes."

"I'm so tired," I groan as I pry my eyes open. "Mom, can I please…"

A frumpy woman in a white lab coat stares down at me. She is definitely not my mom. Her mousy brown hair is pinned to the top of her head. Her features are sharp and she looks bored. Her nose is weighed down by circular glasses with thick lenses.

A blanket is draped across my lower body. It scratches against my skin. Machines beep and buzz all around me. The lights are too bright.

"Do you know where you are, Aurora?" She stares at her clipboard. Her voice is annoyingly high pitched.

"A hospital?" My voice cracks. I look around anxiously. "Where's my mom?"

"We'll get to that."

She flips through the papers on her clipboard. She still hasn't looked me in the eye. She sets her clipboard on the table and helps me sit up. "You appear to be responding well to the treatments. Your white counts get higher every day and you've put on almost five pounds."

"Wait…what?" I'm completely lost. "My treatment?"

"Yes, Aurora," she says dismissively as she pushes a wheelchair over to my bed. "We pulled you out nearly a month ago."

"What? No. Where is my mom?" I press.

"Let's get you into the chair, shall we?" She walks toward me, her gaze focused on my feet. "They are waiting for you down in radiology. When we are done there, we'll to run a series of neurological tests to—"

"I'm not going anywhere until I see my mom."

"I'm afraid that's simply not possible," she sighs. Her eyes finally meet mine. My stomach drops.

"What do you mean?"

"Your mother is in at Mercy General on the other side of town," she says. "It's against protocol for a patient to exit the facility before they've passed all post-cryo examinations."

"I don't care about your protocol!" Tears flood my eyes. "I'm not doing any tests until I see my mom."

***

A burly security guard sits next to me in the waiting room at Mercy General. The building is bright and clean. Monitors made of thin glass adorn the walls depicting various works of art. The images change every few minutes. A young woman with dark hair and pretty eyes walks toward us.

"Aurora?" She stares down at her small tablet computer.

I stand too quickly and my head spins. The guard catches me at my elbow and steadies me.

"That's me. I'm Aurora." I wring my hands together.

"This way." The nurse looks up and her eyes are sad.

She motions for me to follow. When we reach the end of the hallway, she pauses by a heavy gray door and gently lays her hand on my shoulder.

"I'm so sorry," she says.

There's pity in her eyes, but it's different from what I'm used to. She opens the door and stands aside. The guard shifts nervously on the balls of his feet and averts his gaze.

"I'll wait out here," he says. "You know, give you some space."

I nod and cautiously step through the doorway. I keep my eyes on the floor as I chew on my fingernails. The lights are dim and the room is uncomfortably warm.

"Aurora?" It's but a whisper, but the voice is familiar.

"Mom?" I narrow my eyes and approach the bed.

An old woman, frail and feeble, reaches a withered hand out to me. Her arm trembles and falls back to her lap. This can't possibly be my mother. I look around the room waiting for the cameramen to jump out and tell me this is all some sick joke.

"Aurora, come closer." There are dark circles under the old woman's eyes and her skin is paper-thin. Monitors and tubes run in all directions beeping steadily. She squints her tired eyes. "Come over here, Rory. Let me see you."

I inch closer to her. "Mom?"

She smiles and I know in my heart that it's really her. That smile kept me going long after I had wanted to give up. I clutch her hand in mine. Her eyes as soft and as loving as they always were.

"Oh, Mom," I choke as I drop onto the bed and press my head to her chest and hug her gently. Tears stream down my face as I listen to her heartbeat.

"Thank you, baby girl." She smiles and closes her eyes.

"For what?" My body shakes.

"For granting an old woman her last wish," she chuckles softly.

"Mom, don't talk like that," I sob. The beeping monitor slows. "They found a cure for me and they can find one for you."

"Aurora." my mom laughs weakly. She gently pats my hand. "A lot has changed since you went to sleep, but they still don't have a cure for old age."

"Please, don't go." I squeeze her hands and a hiccup escapes my lips.

"It will be okay." Her hand begins to relax in mine. The beeping slows to a crawl and I feel like the world is crumbling around me. "I'm going to miss you, baby girl."

"I'll miss you more," I say as tears roll down my face.

She doesn't argue with me.

"Goodnight, baby girl." She sighs and her hand goes limp in mine. The beeping stops and a flat line rolls across the screen. I lean down and kiss her forehead, then stand beside her bed. My voice shakes as I sing.

"Mmmm-hmmm, I want to linger.

Mmmm-hmmm, a little longer.

Mmmm-hmmm, a little longer here with you.

Mmmm-hmmm, it is the perfect night.

Mmmm-hmmm, it doesn't seem quite right.

Mmmm-hmmm, that it should be my last with you.

Mmmm-hmmm, and as the days go by.

Mmmm-hmmm, I'll think of you and sigh.

Mmmm-hmmm, this is goodnight and not goodbye."

I hear footsteps in the hallway as nurses and doctors rush toward my mother's room. I don't know why they are in a hurry. There's nothing more they can do.

I close my eyes and try to remember my mom as she was before. The way she laughed, the way she loved, and the life we shared before cancer tore through it all like a tornado.

Things were so hard for her after I got sick but she never once gave up on me. She wanted me to live a long and happy life. I owe her that, I decide.

It's time to claim my future.

"Goodnight, mom." I say, smiling down at her. "I love you. Always and forever."

Lauren Frick

Author of Frozen Beauty

Lauren Frick is currently a sophomore in high school. She is an ardent reader and passionate writer. When she has time outside of school and her many extra-curricular activities, she spends it with her family and friends, enjoying the outdoors, or travelling to another world through a great book. Some of her favorite things include cats (among other animals), Polar Pops, bonfires, and making memories with people who matter.

BEAST

Emily Lorenzen

The glass fogged under Daniel's breath as he stared out into the night sky. Rain fell in sheets making it difficult see much beyond his window. Lightning flashed, slicing the darkness and washing the street in an eerie white light before quickly being sucked back into the sky.

An enormous clap of thunder shook the small house on its foundation, rattling the old windows and knocking a picture, the only one in existence of Daniel and his father, from the wall. The glass shattered at his feet, sending his heart farther into his throat. With a frustrated sigh, he knelt and carefully picked up the broken pieces.

"Figures," Daniel shook his head and glared down at his father's smiling face. He'd been picking up the pieces since the man had left him behind to take care of his mother six years ago.

Another blast of thunder cracked outside and the lights began to flicker.

"Daniel!" His mother shrieked from the kitchen down the hall. "Daniel, get my Bible, quickly."

Daniel's shoulders slumped. His mother's *illness* was always worse on nights like this. At least he didn't have school the next day. Thank God for small favors.

Static electricity filled the air as the power surged once more. The tiny hairs on Daniel's arms stood on end. The bare bulb that dangled from his ceiling glowed a hot white, and then burst above him showering him in tiny bits of glass.

"Daniel," his mother moaned as a metal pan clattered to the floor.

"I'm coming, mom. Stay where you are," Daniel yelled back, scooping his phone from his pocket.

He flipped on his flashlight app as he stepped out into the hallway and grabbed his mother's Bible from a table littered with their old family photos. His eyes flicked around the dark house as he shuffled toward the kitchen to rescue his mother from whatever invisible terrors that happened to be haunting her on this particular stormy night.

"They're coming, Daniel," she sobbed, banging into things as she stumbled around their small galley kitchen. "Hurry, please, before—eep."

Daniel's mother squeaked, running right into him in her haste to escape the shadows lurking in the kitchen. He juggled his phone trying desperately not to drop it or his mother's precious book. The beam from the flashlight cut into his eyes, but he managed to save both from falling to the floor.

"Whoa, easy, mom." Daniel said, holding out the Bible. "It's just me. It's Daniel."

"The Devil's minions take on many forms." She narrowed her eyes at him and swiped the frayed book from his hands. "How do I know you're truly my Daniel?"

"For Christ's sake, Mom, really?" Daniel gaped at her.

"Using the Lord's name in vain?" She clutched the Bible tighter to her chest. She huffed, a clear sign of her disapproval, and then blew her bangs away from her face. "I guess it really is you."

"Obviously," Daniel said, a little harsher than he'd intended.

"I'm sorry honey," she said dismissively as she grabbed her son's hand and pulled him toward the table. "I thought they'd finally come for me. I thought perhaps today was the day I'd finally be called to judgment for my sins."

"Mom, did you take your meds today?" Daniel asked as he joined her at the squat dinette in the corner.

"You know as well as I do that thunder is the sound of the gates slamming as a demon escapes Hell." His mother said ignoring his question as she franticly flipped through the vellum pages. "Beware, Daniel. The gates beckon and those who sin against faith will be led astray by beasts disguised as angels."

"I know, mom," Daniel sighed, raking his hair back. "I know."

After nearly an hour of fervent prayer, Daniel's mother finally began to relax. A bit of coaxing, and a solemn vow to keep watch later, he'd convinced her to lay down on the couch where she eventually fell into a fitful slumber.

Daniel was exhausted, in every sense of the word, but he was too on edge to sleep. Instead, he curled up in his dad's old lounge chair and scrolled aimlessly through his newsfeed. His mind wandered and his eyes drooped, but sleep evaded him. Every time the lightning filled the house, he found his gaze drawn to the big picture window in the living room.

Thunder crashed and before he knew it, he was on his feet, his hands braced on the cold pane of glass. Lightning flashed across the sky, silhouetting a hooded figure standing in the middle of his front yard. Everything went silent for a moment. Daniel blinked and the mysterious figure was gone. He rubbed at his tired eyes and laughed quietly to himself. He was obviously so exhausted that he was seeing things. This both amused and worried him.

He had just covered his mother with a blanket and turned toward his bedroom when there was a knock at the door. Daniel jumped, his heart leaping into his throat. A quick glance confirmed that his mother was still asleep, so he tentatively approached the door and peered out through the diamond-shaped glass at the top.

There, on his small front stoop, stood a girl. She was soaking wet, from her mangy, over-sized sweatshirt to her tattered old boots. She cowered, shaking on his front steps, her arms crossed protectively over her chest. Her long blonde hair hung in dripping ringlets from beneath her large hood.

"Oh man," Daniel cursed, slowly opening the door. It was too dark to see her face.

"H-hello," the girl said, her voice as tiny as her stature. He didn't feel threatened by her, but the way she kept looking over her shoulder set Daniel's nerves on edge. "Can you help me?"

Daniel froze, staring down at her. The girl couldn't have been much older than Daniel. She looked so frail and shaken. What on Earth was she doing out this late at night in the middle of a storm?

"Please," she looked behind her again, her thin fingers trembling as she clutched herself in a protective hug. "Please, I…"

"Ummm," he stammered.

"I'm so sorry. It's okay," the girl shifted her feet nervously, her face still hidden. She sounded frightened, lonely. "I'll just go. I didn't mean to bother you."

She turned to leave, her body quaking beneath the onslaught of the torrential downpour.

"Wait," Daniel blurted, grabbing her hand. "Hang on. Just let me get you a towel, okay? My mom will lose it if we trash the floor. Please, just stay right there."

The girl's hand tightened in his, but she didn't pull away. She nodded meekly. Daniel turned on his heel and headed to the bathroom. He grabbed the last two clean towels from the linen shelf and rushed back to where she stood, shivering in the doorway.

"Who's at the door at this hour," his mother called after him, scrambling from the couch as he ran past. He could hear the anxiety rising in her voice and he didn't have the energy to deal with it.

He tossed a towel to the floor and motioned for the girl to come inside. She cautiously stepped onto the terry cloth and stood there dripping onto the towel at her feet.

"Daniel?" His mother tiptoed toward him, the Bible clutched at her chest. "Daniel, answer me. Who is--?"

"It's...my friend," Daniel lied, cutting her off as he wrapped the other towel around the strange girl's shoulders.

"Elizabeth," she whispered.

"It's Elizabeth, from school," Daniel said, trying his best to sound reassuring. "Her car broke down. She's going to call her parents and wait here for them to pick her up."

Daniel motioned for her to follow him to the kitchen. He searched her face, but she kept it trained on her feet. He didn't know this girl, but somewhere, deep in the pit of his stomach, he felt the need to protect her. It was strange and exhilarating.

"Thank you, umm..." she trailed off.

"Daniel."

"Thank you, Daniel." She wiped at her face with the towel.

"No problem." Daniel said softly, ushering her through the doorway and away from his mother's prying eyes. The second they sat at the table, words shot from his mouth. "Are you okay? What were you doing out there in this horrible storm? Where are your parents? Do you live around here?"

"You ask a lot of questions," the girl let out a small laugh.

"Right, sorry," Daniel said, blushing. Everything about this girl intrigued him and he had yet to even see her face.

"Don't apologize," she said, finally lifting her hood with a smile. "I kinda like it."

"Cool," Daniel smirked. "So, umm, what were you doing out in this crazy weather at one in the morning, Elizabeth?"

"I got into a huge fight with my dad." Her tone was flat.

"Parental drama," Daniel muttered. "I so get that."

"Anyway, he bailed for a, ummm, business trip, after it all went down. He won't be back until tomorrow, so I took advantage and snuck out," she shrugged. "I just wanted to go for a walk and clear my head, you know? This storm hit out of nowhere and by then I was too far from home."

"That sucks," Daniel said lamely. He wasn't sure what else to say.

"You have no idea how much it sucks," she said, sighing heavily. "If my Dad's goons figure out I'm gone, they'll call him home. If that happens, I'm dead."

"Well, I guess we'll just have to make sure you don't get caught then, won't we?" Daniel smiled. He leaned in and whispered. "My mom is a bit…strict, so I'm rather adept at parental espionage. I can help you."

"Really?" Elizabeth perked up and pulled her hood away from her face.

Daniel's breath hitched when the sodden gray fabric fell away. The right side of Elizabeth's face was bruised and battered to the point that her eye had swollen shut. Her lip was split, and an angry red welt was forming beneath it. Elizabeth read the shock on Daniel's face and her smile faded. She quickly pulled her hood back up and lowered her eyes once more.

"Maybe I should go," her voice caught.

"No, please," Daniel said. He gently laid his hand on hers. "I'm sorry. I didn't mean to stare, I just…are you okay? That looks painful. I could get you some ice if you'd like."

"What, this?" Her hand slid into her hood, touching the side of her face as Daniel stood and reached into the freezer. "It's nothing, really. I promise you, it looks worse than it is. I'll be good as new in a couple days. Always am. I've had much worse."

"Worse?" Daniel swallowed back the fire in his gut and calmly handed the girl an icepack. "Who did this to you, Elizabeth? Who hurt you?"

"I can't." Her head drooped and she sank further into her massive hood.

"You don't have to hide from me, Elizabeth," he said. "You can tell me anything."

"I don't even know you," she whispered, shaking her head.

"Exactly," Daniel said, smiling at her. "You *don't* know me, so you have nothing to lose. I promise, I won't judge you, and even if I did, when the storm lets up you can just go home and forget I ever existed."

"I suppose that's true," she said, her voice brightening a bit. "And as long as I'm home before my father returns tomorrow evening, he'll never know I was gone."

The timer on the microwave beeped, the lights flickered, and all at once, the power came back on. The dryer started back up and the television in the living room blasted through the house at full volume with yet another infomercial about a magic mop. With any luck, his mother would lose herself in the endless drudgery of late night television and fall back asleep.

Elizabeth pushed her hood away from her face, but didn't remove it completely. Her bruises were visible, but this time he made a conscious effort not to stare. Her shoes squeaked against the floor as she shifted nervously in her seat. That's when Daniel noticed her hair and clothes were plastered to her small frame.

"Let me get you some dry clothes," Daniel shot from his seat. "You're soaked to the bone. You must be freezing."

"It's kind of nice, actually. Where I'm from, it's always hot." Elizabeth muttered as Daniel walked out of the room.

As soon as he passed through the kitchen doorway into the hall, he felt himself being pulled the opposite direction. His mother's small hand was clamped around his upper arm dragging Daniel toward her room with strength he had no idea she possessed. Once they reached her corner bedroom, she slammed the door behind them and spun on her son.

"What the hell is wrong with you?" Daniel's mother hissed. Her eyes looked frantic.

"What, mom?" Daniel put his hands on his hips.

"What were you thinking letting that…that thing into our house?" She hugged her Bible close and wagged a finger at Daniel.

"She's not a *thing*, mom," Daniel scowled. "Her name is Elizabeth. We go to school together. She just--."

"Don't." She narrowed her muddy brown eyes in disbelief. "You are a horrible liar, Daniel. Just like your father. You don't know this girl. You don't know anything about her. There's something not right about her. She's not who she says she is."

"You know what?" Daniel had had enough. "You're right, mom. I don't know her, but by the time this storm passes, I will. That's how the world is supposed to work. You of all people should know that if you give people a chance and have a little bit of faith, you'll be able to see the good in everyone."

"You're naïve," she snapped, caressing the cross that hung at her neck. "That girl is a demon, Daniel. I can feel it in my bones. Get rid of it."

"No." Daniel squared his shoulders. For years, his mother had been demonizing everything Daniel cared about.

When his father left, his mother refused to acknowledge her part in it. Instead, she convinced herself the man had been tempted by the devil. Lacy, Daniel's homecoming date his freshman year, had apparently been a minion sent by Satan to tempt Daniel into a life of sin. To this day, Lacy still wouldn't speak to him. Who could blame her after the incident with his mother and the holy water? And now this.

This poor girl was little more than skin and bones. She was battered and bruised, running from an abusive situation, and his mother wanted to turn her away. She would have Daniel send Elizabeth back into the arms of whomever had hurt her in the middle of the worst storm they'd seen in years.

"No?" Daniel's mother looked taken aback. "I'm your mother."

"You haven't been my mother for a very long time," Daniel spat, and all the things he'd been holding in since his father left came rushing out all at once. "I do the cooking, the cleaning, and the grocery shopping. I am the one who makes sure you get to your appointments and that you are taking your meds. I make sure the rent is paid and the lights stay on. I fix the furnace when it locks up and unclog the sink when you forget we don't have a disposal and throw a whole meatloaf into it."

"Daniel," his mother gasped with tears in her eyes. "That girl is—"

"No," Daniel held his hand up to stop her from speaking. "Mom, I love you, but you can't keep doing this. Elizabeth is not a demon. She's just a girl, a girl who needs my help. I am not going to turn her away because of some paranoid fantasy you have about the Devil."

"Daniel, please," his mother pleaded. "She's dangerous. You have to believe me."

"Take your meds and go to bed, mom," Daniel sighed, the fight leaving his body. "I'm going out. I'll be back later. Don't wait up."

"For the love of God, Daniel," his mother said.

"Goodnight mom." Daniel walked out of her room and closed the door behind him.

On his way to the kitchen, Daniel stopped in the laundry room. He dug through the dryer and grabbed a pair of sweatpants, a T-shirt, some socks, and a nice, warm towel. When he returned to the kitchen, Elizabeth was standing at the sink wringing out her honey-colored hair.

"Everything okay?" She asked her bright blue eyes alight with concern.

"No more or less than usual," Daniel shrugged as he laid the fresh clothes on the table in front of her. "Here you go. How about you change and we'll go for a ride? The bathroom is just down the hall on the left. The white door."

"Sure, why not?" A smile lit up her face. Despite the bruises, the girl was quite beautiful.

While Elizabeth slipped into something dry, Daniel threw his phone charger, a couple sodas, and some snacks into a small bag. He busied himself in the kitchen and thought about the fight he'd just had with his mother. He had never yelled at her before. He hadn't even wanted to, really, it had all just spilled out of him. It had erupted, unchecked, from his heart. In a weird way, he felt good about that. She finally knew how he felt.

"Thanks for the clothes," Elizabeth said, patting her hair with a towel as she walked back into the kitchen. Her eyes looked brighter already and it was as if her bruises were fading right before his eyes. He could see nothing beyond that smile of hers.

"Let's go," he grabbed her hand and scooped the keys off the counter as they headed toward the back door.

***

Daniel and Elizabeth drove aimlessly around town for some time before either of them had the courage to speak. After nearly an hour of awkward side-glances and nervous laughter, the silence became unbearable. They both reached for the radio at the same time, their hands colliding just shy of the buttons.

"So do you listen to music?" Daniel asked his knuckles white against the steering wheel.

"Who doesn't listen to music?" Elizabeth giggled softly.

"Right," Daniel's face heated. He was so not good at talking to girls. "Of course. That was a stupid question. I'm sorry. Apparently, I've forgotten how to have a conversation with a sane person."

"It's fine, really. I think I am a little rusty at being a person too." Elizabeth smiled sympathetically, and then winked at him. "Besides, who says I'm sane?"

Daniel chuckled and soon enough Elizabeth joined in. Her laughter was like music and her smile illuminated the space around her. Her eyes seemed to have a light of their own.

"Okay, let's start small, shall we?" Elizabeth cleared her throat. "What's your all-time favorite song?"

"You'll laugh." Daniel blew his dark hair away from his eyes. "It's pretty old school."

"I won't. I swear," she said, making an 'x' over her heart. She leaned closer and smiled up at him. Her hair had begun to dry and was curling up on the ends. "Please, tell me."

"Suspicious Minds by Elvis Presley." Daniel blurted.

He took a deep breath, pressed the play button on his CD player, and stared straight out the windshield. The CD skipped and scratched for a few seconds, a flaw in the disc from overplaying, before the lilting melody blasted through the car's worn out speakers.

"We're caught in trap…" Elizabeth sang. "I can't walk out."

Daniel's eyes shot wide and he smiled over at her. She sang the entire song, his song, without missing a single word. When the song was over, Daniel hit repeat and cranked up the volume. "One more time?"

"Only if I have backup," she smirked.

Daniel nodded, cleared his throat dramatically, and belted out the melody along with his new friend. The song played over and over as they drove in the dark. They sang until their voices grew hoarse and the CD refused to play anymore. The silence that followed was companionable and soon Daniel and Elizabeth were talking like old friends. They let down their guard and confided in one another.

Elizabeth's father was some sort of bigwig corporate headhunter. His job took him all over the world. Though Elizabeth was dragged along with him, her father kept her under lock and key and she rarely saw much of the world. The man was a tyrant and he was hell-bent on Elizabeth following in his footsteps.

"Last night I told him I wanted my freedom," Elizabeth gingerly touched her bruised cheek as she spoke. "As you can see, it didn't go well. He told me I was defiant and that I'd never see the light of day unless it was from his shadow."

"So he just expects you to follow in his footsteps?" Daniel's brows furrowed.

"If I want any kind of freedom, yes," she frowned. "The problem is, once I commit to his work there's no backing out. I'll be stuck for life. I honestly don't know if I'm even capable of doing what he does."

"I have a feeling you are capable of just about anything," Daniel grinned at her.

"Enough about my problems," she swatted her hand. "What about you? What's your story, Daniel? And what's the deal with your mom?"

"It's complicated," Daniel said.

"Uncomplicate it," she shrugged with a smile.

So he did. He started talking, like he had when he'd argued with his mother, he just let the words flow from him. Daniel told her all about his mother's battle with mental illness and his father leaving. He admitted how exhausted he was with all of it and how he sometimes wished there was a way out.

After some time discussing their mutual disgust for the hand life had dealt them, the conversation shifted and the two of them spent hours laughing. When the sun began to rise, it was Elizabeth who suggested they pull over. They sat together in a large wooded park, on the hood of his mom's old car, and stared up into the sky as the warm pink and orange glow washed over the storm-drenched hills.

"Thank you," Elizabeth said softly, wrapping her arms around Daniel's and resting her head against his shoulder.

"For what?" Daniel smiled.

"For, I don't know, everything," she shrugged, then sighed heavily. "I'd forgotten what freedom felt like. I don't want to go back yet."

"So, don't," Daniel said sliding off the car. He held out his hand. "Let's take a walk for a bit first, okay? Where would you like to go Elizabeth?"

"Surprise me," she said, taking his hand.

Daniel smiled to himself. It was nice being able to make someone happy for a change. He pushed his other hand into his pocket and walked with Elizabeth toward a faded path that led into the woods. Neither of them spoke. Birds sang and flitted from to tree to tree. They ran their fingers over the thick moss growing on the statues in the middle of the park.

When Elizabeth saw the weather-beaten red bench overlooking a bluff, she pulled Daniel toward it.

As they walked, he bent and picked up sharp stick. A single orange leaf dangled from the end. When they were seated, he stared down at it intently. The leaf was tattered and bruised from being blown around in the storm. Water dripped from its sharp edges but the saturation made the warm autumn colors even more vibrant. Its flaws made it more beautiful.

"Pretty," Elizabeth said, trailing a finger along the frayed edges.

"It reminds me of you," Daniel said placing it gently in her hand.

"You're so sweet." She peered up at him, her hair dancing in the wind. She turned her head so the breeze tickled her face. "This has been the best night of my life. I really don't want to go back and deal with my father."

The smell of the flowers drifted on the breeze. Daniel let out a slow breath, his eyes meeting hers. The sun hit her face, making it glow with an almost ethereal light. Her flushed cheeks made the bruises that rested there seem unimportant. He took a deep breath and summoned his courage.

"You're so beautiful, Elizabeth," Daniel said, lifting her chin with his fingertips and turning her face toward him.

"But I'm not." She dropped her chin. "I'm a monster."

"Elizabeth," Daniel pressed. "I told you last night you don't have to hide from me, and I meant it. There's nothing monstrous about you. I know we just met, but I truly believe you are meant for great things. And maybe I am too. We just have to decide what we want out of life and make it happen."

"It's not that simple, Daniel," she said.

"It can be," Daniel replied, pulling Elizabeth to her feet. "I'll help you, if you'll let me."

Elizabeth took a deep breath and let it out slowly. "Yes."

Her eyes met his and something flashed in them. She cocked her head to the side, studying him. Daniel leaned in and gently pressed his lips to hers. Electricity shot through him, his mind swirled, and every cell in his body tingled. He pulled away and slowly opened his eyes.

Elizabeth was smiling, the bright amber sky reflected in her eyes making them look a brilliant red.

"I-I want..." she stuttered.

"Yes?" Daniel stepped closer.

"I want..." her breath quickened.

"What is it?" Daniel insisted. "Stop hiding, Elizabeth. Face what's in your heart. What do you truly want?"

"Freedom," Elizabeth said firmly.

"What will you do to get it?" Daniel leaned in again.

"Whatever it takes," Elizabeth breathed against his mouth.

Fire ripped through Daniel's body and he stumbled backward, his eyes wide in shock. The stick he had given Elizabeth protruded from his chest. The bright orange leaf fell from the end and drifted to the ground. He coughed and blood splattered across Elizabeth's face.

"Why?" Daniel choked out as he sank to his knees.

She smiled down at him and affectionately lay her hand on his cheek. Her face twisted and warped, her eyes began glowing red in earnest. Black tendrils of smoke swirled, writhing like snakes as great black wings spread wide behind her. The sky darkened and rain began falling once more. Thunder rolled and lightning tore open the sky. The edges of Daniel's vision darkened as Elizabeth moved closer. He sank to the ground, no longer able to hold up his body.

The girl stood over him, watching him with rapt fascination as the life drained from him. He could no longer speak. The pain began to fade and he felt his limbs lighten.

Elizabeth knelt at Daniel's side, shielded him with her massive onyx wings, and pressed a gentle kiss to his lips.

"I've never claimed a soul before, Daniel. I'm so glad you were my first," she whispered, her lips brushing against his cheek. "And now, we can *both* be free."

Emily Lorenzen

Author of Beast

Emily Lorenzen lives in a small town in Illinois. She is a big fan of the *Teenage Mutant Ninja Turtles* and *The Walking Dead*. When Emily is not at school, she uses her free time on her two favorite activities; writing and drawing. By her own admission, Emily is really into all things creepy…she just wouldn't want to experience them in person.

Cindergirl

Madeleine Harris

A small orange flame opens up in the palm of my hand like a flower in springtime, like a glimmer of hope in the dark. I lazily twiddle my fingers around and the flame grows, higher and higher, twisting and turning, until it forms a little red blossom at the top. It's just opening up when the shrill squeaks of a mouse pierce the silence and break my concentration.

"C'mon, Gus, I was just getting it this time!" A fat, brown field mouse sits on my desk, squeaking indignantly. He pokes me with his nose and makes what I assume is supposed to be an angry glare, which he can't pull off very well because he's so darn cute.

"I *know* you're hungry," I say, rolling my eyes. "You're *always* hungry."

My name is Ella Cosgrove and I guess you could call me a superhero.

I have the best elemental power, fire. I can manipulate it to appear in the palm of my hand, I can start it or stop it anywhere I want, and I can control it if it already exists. It's not just normal fire, its magic fire, which means I can make it float and form shapes. It's a huge responsibility (let's just say that my bed didn't use to have that big black mark and leave it at that), but it's also fun in its own crazy way.

Lately I've been practicing flowers. Big ones, small ones, and ones that actually bloom like the one I was working on before my greedy little mouse interrupted me.

Gus is sort of my sidekick and good friend when he's not being annoying. He's small but intelligent and learns quickly. It has only been a few months but I've taught him to pick locks, chew through ropes, and retrieve small objects. He's super sneaky and I can conveniently carry him around in my pocket. Unlike the people in my life, Gus is faithful, understanding, and never leaves my side.

"Let's try this again." I begin to re-bloom the fire flower when I am interrupted once again.

"Ella! Get down here right now," my stepmother howls from a floor below. "Come quick, the girls need you. It's an emergency!"

"Oh no, I wonder if they'll survive," I mutter. Gus squeaks and I laugh as I imagine him rolling his eyes.

Deborah and her daughters have been plaguing me since the day they took over my family. After my mother passed away, she charmed my father into marrying her. And when I say charmed, I don't mean buying him flowers and going out with him and all that stuff. I mean real, actual magic.

Seriously. I'm not kidding.

He knew the woman *two days* before he proposed. Not long after they officially tied the knot, my father was gone. The police pronounced his death a tragic accident, but they only got it half-right. I know the truth. Not that it changes anything. Either way, the last piece of whatever family I had was gone and I was left to face the world alone.

I know exactly what my stepmother is and I've made it my mission to stop her, because I'm telling you, that woman is pure evil!

By day, she plays the role of the charming widow Deborah Hunnings, grieving countess of Nightshade Manor. She wears posh clothes and fake sadness as she smiles behind her mourning veil and spends the piles of money she stole from my family. She'd pulled out thousands before I even stopped crying over the loss of my father, spending the money on clothes, shoes, makeup, a new car, and those cushy, quilted toilet paper rolls.

But when no one is looking, she shows her true form—the foul, loathsome sorceress Mistress Dark. Her features harden, her powers vibrate around her, and her cruelty knows no bounds. You can't blame me for wanting her vanquished.

Anna and Drew, her daughters, are just as bad. They're superficial, spiteful girls. They spend most of their time obsessing over hair and makeup and begging their *mommy* for expensive presents. Chances are if they aren't screaming at me, they're screaming at each other, locked in a permanent battle over which one of them will marry Justin Bieber. Meanwhile, I'm living in squalor with rags for clothes in the attic of my own home.

Harsh, right?

Unfortunately, that's my new reality. They day my father died, I was demoted to servant girl.

"Ella!" Deborah shouts, banging on the ceiling.

"I'm coming, I'm coming," I grumble as I run down the stairs for the millionth time to see what the 'emergency' is.

"Took you long enough." Deborah scowls at me as I reach the bottom of the steps. She crosses her arms over her chest and sighs. "They're in their room. Go on. Do your job." I grit my teeth and clench my fists as I stomp off down the hall.

"What is it this time?" I groan as I fling open the door to their bedroom (formerly *my* bedroom).

I walk in to an explosion of designer clothes, most of which still have tags on them, piles of makeup, broken headphones, stilettos, and all the trappings of spoiled teenage girls. The whole room smells as if they've emptied an entire bottle of perfume on the floor. Anna is lying in the middle of the mess, looking distraught. Drew is sitting on her top bunk, scarfing down spicy chips and spewing a tremendous amount of gossip on her phone.

"My favorite blouse is ripped!" Anna holds up a purple top I've literally never seen her wear.

"And?"

"*And* you can fix it. You have to sew up that nasty rag of yours all the time!" she wrinkles her nose at my tattered gray dress and then throws the blouse in my face. "Fix it, Ella! Fix it or I'll tell mother!" she whines.

How can one person be so spoiled? I sigh and grab the blouse from her outstretched hand.

"And be quick about it!" she snaps as the door closes. I snag a half-eaten chocolate bar out of the trash on the way up the stairs, grab the sewing supplies, and plop down on my cot. Squeaking, Gus nudges my arm and looks up at me expectantly.

"Yes, Gus, I've got some food for you," I toss him the candy bar and he munches on it gratefully. I sigh again as I examine the blouse.

"What do you say, Gus, should I incinerate the thing or just toss it out the window?"

He nods vigorously. I laugh and begin threading the needle, but before I could push the needle through, Deborah's voice echoes through the attic vent. I can't hear exactly what she's saying, but it sounds important. Her voice is frantic and unnecessarily chipper.

I scoop up Gus and sneak downstairs, avoiding the squeaky floorboards. When I reach the end of the hall, I peek around the corner.

There she is, Mistress Dark, in all her evil glory. Her cell phone is pressed to her ear. All her fake grief had melted away. Her midnight black hair is done up in a bun and she'd swapped her widow's uniform for a form-fitting, olive green dress and a pair of heels that are so high, I'm surprised she can even stand up.

"Yes, counselor, I know." Her voice is dripping in syrup, but she rolls her eyes. "I am well-versed in the rules of succession."

What is she up to?

"I understand. Well, I do hope you find the prince," she sneers, "If the boy is not there by midnight for the coronation, the crown falls to the next in line. Since Prince Chad has no living relatives…"

"No!" I breathe and lean closer, my foot landing on a loose floorboard. I recoil at the resounding squeak.

"You stay right there, young lady." Her voice pierces my ears like a thousand icy needles. "Ta-ta, then. See you at the coronation! Oh, and by the way, I ordered sapphire and emerald jewelry, in case you forgot. And make sure my dresses are black and green." The fake smile drops off her lips the second she hangs up. "Ella?"

"Y-yes, Miss Hunnings?" I stutter, fearing the worst. She narrows her eyes at me and my heart drops into my stomach. She is just about to speak when her phone chimes and her attention is drawn away from me.

"I'm famished. Get into the kitchen and make me something grand. Something befitting a queen," she smirks. I breathe a sigh of relief.

"Yes, ma'am." I say as I rush into the kitchen.

After nearly an hour cooking, dinner is ready. All I get to eat are some of the meager scraps my 'family' leaves behind. I eat it quickly and dash up to my room, taking the stairs two at a time. I slam my door and press my ear up to it, listening to the Hunnings argues with one another as they rush around preparing for the coronation.

After a while, the front door opened and closed, banging loudly. The second I hear them leave, I throw on my fireproof suit and gather up my reddish hair into a ponytail. Things are going to get messy.

"C'mon, buddy." I scoop up Gus and throw open the window to climb out.

Suddenly, the door bursts open and I am in the presence of the evil Mistress Dark. Her long black dress flows out behind her into waves that melt into the shadows.

I gasp.

"Foolish scum," she hisses. "Did you really think I didn't know?"

"Know…w-what," I stammer. Playing dumb may not have been the best option. She rolls her eyes and strides towards me, eyes as black as the night sky.

"*Everything.*" She sneers. I summon up my courage.

"Stop!" I try to make a fireball, but all that comes out are a few feeble, little flames.

"You're kidding."

"You can't do this!" I cry, "I won't let you!"

"There is nothing you can do to stop me." She cackles and snaps her fingers. My little flame is extinguished. "Your sorry excuse for a defense is nothing compared to my powers. You are no more than a filthy little louse. Always have been, always will be."

I back away, but she glides across the floor and before I can blink, she has her hand on my arm. I try to make another flame, but my powers seem to have been cut off. I shudder and writhe. It feels like my limbs have been plunged into a bucket of ice water.

"Quit struggling," she sneers. "You're coming with me."

I freeze. My mind is screaming for me to run, but my body will not obey. By the time I regained control it was too late. My hands were bound and I was dragged to the basement and tossed on the cold, hard floor.

"It's too bad you're going to miss the coronation, honey," she snickers. "You see, royal law states that our kingdom cannot go without a ruler for more than thirty days. It's been twenty-nine since the king died in a tragic hunting accident. The council must crown a new ruler by the stroke of midnight. If they do not, they'll be in violation of kingdom law. And of course, we can't have that."

She laughs and rolls her eyes. "Since Prince Chad has gone missing, I will graciously accept the crown in his place."

"No!" I choke out, "You can't be queen!"

"Oh, but if no blood heir appears by midnight, I will be. Goodnight, Ella." She flicked her wrist and the light fizzled out. "Or should I say *Cindergirl*?"

The door slammed, firmly locked, and I am left in the dark.

***

"I have to get out of here!" I struggle to pick myself up off the floor without success. My eyes strain against the darkness. My lip is bleeding, my head spins, and a nasty bruise is forming on my elbow.

Mistress Dark and her two daughters were long gone by the time I came to. With the prince missing and Mistress Dark in control, the kingdom will fall to chaos and well, darkness. I just have to find the prince. I struggle some more when a confused squeak pierces the silence.

"Gus! Hi, buddy." I grin as the rodent tumbles out of my pocket. I was glad to have someone to keep me company.

"If I were a loathsome, evil wretch that just kidnapped a prince, where would I keep him?" I speak aloud.

I squint down at Gus and he squeaks at me. I suddenly remember I can remove the shadows. The moment a flame sparked to life on my palm, it hit me.

"The hideout!" I cry, "Of course! Gus, we have to get out of here."

I need to get to Mistress Dark's hideout in the woods and rescue the prince before midnight. But how am I going to escape? I study my hands. They are tied up with a huge chain and padlock. I hadn't learned to melt through metal yet. Hot tears of frustration sting my eyes and drip onto my hand where they evaporate on the spot. How was I ever going to get out? I slide down farther onto the cold, stony floor.

"No." I squirm to the wall and push myself onto my feet. I wasn't going to sit around crying, waiting for some magic fairy to make everything okay.

"Gus, the lock!" I shout. He looks up at me quizzically. "Pick the lock, buddy."

He squeaks in response and begins to pick the lock on the chains that bind my hands. A few minutes later, they fall to my feet. I pick up Gus, run up the stairs, and burst out the front door.

DONG! DONG! DONG! The grandfather clock in the hall announced that it was already eleven o'clock. I only had one hour to get to the forest, rescue the prince, and get him to the palace.

No pressure.

I run out to the garage to look for a weapon and see a big tarp over… something. I yank it off and gasp at the sight.

My dad's old dirt bike.

I'd forgotten about that bright orange beauty. Memories flood my mind of the hours we'd spent in the woods, going for rides and picnicking. He even taught me how to ride it. It had been sitting here collecting dust since he died. It had been pure luck Mistress Dark hadn't found it and sold it like she did with so many other things we used to own.

I round the bike, smiling at the fancy lettering on the tank. I had given it the name 'Pumpkin' when I was only four years old.

How cool. Pumpkin matches my outfit!

She is old and poorly maintained but the rusty engine starts right up. It sputters a little, so I blast the spark plug with some flames, fill the tank with gas, and she's ready to go. I pull on the red helmet hanging on the handlebars and jump on.

My pocket wiggles and I look down. Gus is squeaking frantically.

"I do *too* know how to drive it. We're wasting time." I pat him down into my pocket and take off into the dark, ominous woods.

The bright headlights only go so far. They throw dark shadows around, making the woods around me seem even scarier. The wind lashes at me like a lion tamer's whip and there seems to be a tree everywhere I swerve. There are only forty minutes until midnight and I still haven't found that stupid hideout. All of a sudden—

SKRRRRT! I squeeze the handbrakes and skid in the dirt.

Right there in front of me is a metal trapdoor. It had Mistress Dark's mark on it, along with 'Anna was here' and 'Drew rules.' I hop off the bike and kick the stand down. I leave my helmet on because it's freezing and there isn't really time to mess with it. Just thirty minutes until midnight. I circle the trapdoor over and over, but I'm not finding a way in.

I guess random passwords. I scream Mistress Dark's name. I try burning it. Nothing works. In a huff, I kick that the door as hard as I can. The lock beeps and it opens.

"Really?" I roll my eyes and climb into the darkness.

It is a downward sloping cavern. I set my hand aflame and hold it in front of me. Down, down, down it goes. I brush cobwebs out of the way and forge on. The darkness itself is palpable, as if I could reach out and touch it. I shiver at the very thought and turn the corner at the end of the steep cavern.

"Help me! Please!" A scratchy voice echoes through the lair, muffled some. I run down the rest of the cavern to a thick wooden door with a barred window next to it. I peer in to see a bedraggled young man, a few years older than me huddled in a corner, with ratty clothes and black hair. His hands are chained to the stone wall.

"Oh, thank God," he groans. "Are you here to rescue me?"

"No, I'm here to ask your hand in marriage." I chuckle and shake my head. "Now, back up and hold on to your butt because things are about to heat up."

I crack my knuckles, open my palms, and cook up the biggest fireball I've ever managed. I toss it forward, leaving a huge hole in the door. As I study the wreckage, I notice that not only had my fireball blasted through the door, the chains had melted too. I had finally accomplished metal melting. I climb through the wreckage and awkwardly help the prince to his feet.

"Hi."

"What the…" the prince looks terrified, but there is no time to explain, we have to move.

Gus jimmied the lock on the chains around the prince's wrists and we were off. I run up the cavern, dragging Prince Chad behind me. I jump onto the dirt bike and rev up the engine.

"Get on! We have to get you to the palace!" I yell, patting the seat. He nods, hesitantly climbing up. The moment his butt touched the leather, I let go of the brakes and we tore off through the forest.

'Could we maybe slow down a bit?" He shouts against the wind.

"Nope!" I smirk and press the throttle. We shoot out of the woods like a bullet and hit the city streets. I swerve down alleyways and around street corners, nearly knocking over pedestrians. Finally, I see the palace. I squeeze the brakes and hop off in a puff of exhaust and fire. Prince Chad stumbles off the bike. I whip off my helmet.

"You're a… girl?" He stares at me, dumbfounded.

"C'mon, we're running out of time!" I drag him to the gates. A palace guard stands at the gate, permanently at attention.

"Stop right there!" He unholsters his weapon.

"Stand aside." I say, lighting my hand aflame.

I have never seen an adult, let alone a stoic palace guard, wet their pants before. What can I say? Today is a day of many firsts. Unsure of where to go, I turn to the prince. "You wanna help me out here?"

"This way," he smirks.

This time I'm being dragged. His grip on my hand is steady as we rush through the palace to the main hall doors. The crown was just inches from Mistress Dark's head when we burst in.

"Stop!" I yell, pushing Prince Chad forward. "The prince has returned!"

"No!" Mistress Dark screeches. "It's too late!"

"The clock has not struck the midnight hour." Prince Chad squares his shoulders and approaches the throne. He steps onto the platform, grabs the crown from the councilman's hand, and places it on his head. "I am the rightful heir to the throne. Despite your efforts to the contrary, the crown belongs to me."

"Praise be the king," the counsel declares as King Chad's praises echo through the grand hall.

"No!" My stepmother growls. She raises her hands at her sides, summoning her magic and rushes toward King Chad. Her dark powers coil around her.

"Don't even think about it," I leap in front of the King, my hands bursting into flames.

I've had enough. I am done standing idly by as Mistress Dark destroys all that is good in this world. As I walk toward her, the air heats around me. I can feel my powers swelling in my chest, begging to be set free. Flames lick up my arms and swirl around my shoulders. As my fire grows, light fills the space between us and the shadowy tendrils of her charm begin to fade.

"Impossible." Mistress Dark's eyes go wide as she stares down at her dwindling spell.

"Surprise." I sneer at her, throwing my arms wide until my flames completely devour her darkness.

"Guards, this woman is guilty of kidnapping and treason," King Chad roars over the chaos.

"And murder," I glare at her through the warm orange glow that surrounds me.

"Seize her!" the councilman bellows.

The guards press at my back, arming themselves as we make our way toward the evil woman hovering at the throne.

"You fools!" Mistress Dark backs away, seething with pure anger. "You're going to regret this!"

"Not as much as you will." I say, gently nudging my pocket. "You might want to bail out for this one, buddy. I have a feeling it's gonna get real hot in here."

Gus pokes his head out and twitches his nose at me, then scurries down my leg and scampers off toward the exit. I raise my hands in front of me and sculpt a massive ball of fire between them. She recoils in shock, pressing her back to the huge, stained glass window behind the throne. I launch the fireball directly at her. She tosses her inky cape around her body and evaporates into a black cloud of darkness and evil. My fireball sailed through the space where she had been standing and melted a hole straight through the rainbow-colored plate glass.

The black cloud that had been my stepmother blew out the opening like a wisp on the wind. Her shrill voice echoed through the hall.

"This isn't overrrrr!" She disappears.

"No, stepmother," I nod, staring out into the night sky. "It certainly isn't."

"Um, excuse me?" I whip around to see the king standing behind me. He points at me and grins. "Would you mind turning the heat down a bit?"

"Shoot, sorry." I say, laughing as I extinguish my flames.

"Don't apologize," he smiles and shakes his head. "You just saved my life and stopped an evil witch from taking over the entire kingdom."

"True," I say brushing a stray hair out of my face.

"Besides, you look good in flames," he whispers.

"Thanks," I say, my face heating warmer than the fire inside me.

"Seriously, though. That was, by far, the coolest thing I've ever seen." He tilts his head and steps toward me. "Who taught you how to do that?"

"No one," I shrug. "I was born this way."

"Natural-born hero, huh?" Chad raises a brow. "The kingdom could use a champion. Any chance you'd be interested?"

"Maybe," I smile, brushing past him. Gus squeaks at me from his perch near the door. I scoop him into my pocket and step out into the corridor. "See you around...*King* Chad."

As soon as I round the corner, I take off at a dead run. Adrenaline and pride fuel me. My feet don't stop moving until I am free of the castle. I burst into the crisp night air. Pumpkin is there, waiting patiently right where I left her.

"Wait!" I'd just reached for the ignition when the King Chad's voice floats down at me. His face appears in the gaping hole I've created in the window. "I never caught your name."

"Call me Cindergirl," I smile up at him as I turned the key and rev Pumpkin to life.

Together, we disappear into the night. There is no doubt in my mind that Mistress Dark will return. The kingdom will need my help again and soon, but that is fine by me. Turns out, I kind of like this whole hero thing...even if it is a big responsibility.

Madeleine Harris
Author of Cindergirl

Madeleine Harris is a major nerd and she is quite proud of it. Her *greatest passions* include reading and rereading books like *Harry Potter*, doodling pictures of cats, acting, and writing. She loves to write stories about magic, animals, kids with cool powers or anything that includes at least a little bit of humor. This is the first time she's had her work published, but it's hopefully not the last! Madeleine currently attends a performing arts school. Her major is acting, though this doesn't prevent her from liking to write. She's been in one short film called *Girl in the Trunk*, which according to her was "delightfully bloody." She lives with her parents and a dog, cat, and mutant monster (also known as a little brother). She has almost no social media, but if you ever want to discuss her creations, you will likely find her up in a tree.

Gabriel and Cosette

Polaris Jimenez

Ravens Valley was a quaint little village set deep in the forests just outside of The Great City. It was a picturesque and close-knit community; one of those places where everyone knew everyone, your family name was your status, and no one had the luxury of secrets. There was, however, one exception.

Ryan, the purveyor of the town's one and only auto shop, was the closest thing Ravens Valley had to a mystery. Aside from his skills with all things mechanical, very little was known about the man or his family. Rumors circulated that Ryan had lost his wife and immediately remarried, but the hearsay stopped there. None knew of his children, Gabriel and Cosette. Over the years, Ryan had gone to great lengths to make sure their existence remained a secret. His intention was only to shield the children from the evils and temptations of this lower world.

The evils that had taken his sweet Ariana from him.

Though he'd only recently learned his current trade, Ryan excelled at it. He took to it with unparalleled determination and learned quickly, as he did in all things. He had been an artisan for thousands of years and had mastered a great many things since he was wrongfully banished to the world beneath the clouds so long ago.

Outwardly, Ryan was a beautiful man. One might guess him to be in his early forties, though his features held a smoothness unbefitting his perceived age.

He was strong and energetic with piercing brown eyes. His dirty blond hair hung down past his broad, muscular shoulders…all the better to hold his massive golden wings.

Ryan was working in his shop one day, hunched over the engine of an old pickup. He'd been given very little time to complete the project, just two days in fact, but his family was in desperate need so he had worked very hard at it. He'd toiled beneath the open hood for hours and finally finished with minutes to spare. He smiled down at his latest accomplishment, letting his fingers slide over the brand new, specially enhanced engine he had just placed in the truck.

"Thanks to you, my beauty, I will provide for my family." Ryan placed his hands on his hips and puffed out his chest. His pride let slip his great, golden wings and they stretched out wide behind him, no longer hidden by his spell. "Today my children shall feast."

His loud voice echoed through the shop. Beneath the boom of it, he heard a soft shuffle behind him. In an instant, his brilliant feathers disappeared beneath the ink of the wings tattooed on his back. This was, quite possibly, the most valuable skill Ryan had learned in all his time on Earth.

"Talking to that hideous machine again?" Elizabeth scoffed, her arms folding.

The moment he heard his wife's lilting voice, a calm washed over him and his wings drifted back out. Ryan had met Elizabeth just six short months ago. From the moment she said hello, she'd had this effect on him. It didn't matter what the woman said to him, her voice was pure magic.

"This machine, my dearest wife, shall fetch us a good price." He rested his hands on his hips. "We can finally fill our cupboards."

"You said as much the last time," she rolled her eyes and frowned, "and that man paid you in chickens."

"He had fallen on hard times, my love," Ryan smiled at her, "and those chickens were quite delicious, as I recall."

"You are too soft, husband." She shook her head. "You have your own debts to worry about or have you forgotten that you still owe the butcher, the grocer, and of course, my dressmaker."

Despite the scowl she wore, Elizabeth was undeniably beautiful. Her shape flowed like the ocean. She had long, wavy hair the color of the night sky and flawless sun-kissed skin. She wore an elaborate white dress that hugged her shape and a bejeweled pair of white sandals. This latest ensemble had cost Ryan nearly a week's pay. In that moment, he decided it had been worth it. Ryan drank in the sight of her and his smile lit up his face. Elizabeth's emerald green eyes softened a bit and her downy purple wings snapped high behind her.

"You've been at it for days," Elizabeth cooed, swaying toward him. Her bottom lip jutted out as she lay her hands on her husband's chest. "It's unfair that I must deal with those wretched *children* while you tinker about with your toys, my love. You've promised me a kingdom fit for a queen. Where is my crown?"

"I'm so sorry, my sweet," Ryan said, his head buzzing as Elizabeth ran her finger across his wing. "I was trying to…"

Ryan's pride dissipated and his shoulders fell. Suddenly he felt like the most selfish being on Earth. His poor wife deserved to be pampered and lavished with beautiful gifts. He would make it up to her. He had to.

"I shall buy you fine jewels and we will feast on the most elegant meal your beautiful eyes have ever seen!" His voice was full of excitement.

"Yes," she narrowed her eyes with a twisted grin. "That is more like it."

A twig snapped outside.

"He's here."

Ryan's eyes lit up as their wings retracted. He grabbed the truck keys from his workbench and clutched them tightly. "It's time to get what is owed to me."

"Money this time, Ryan, not chickens," Elizabeth muttered.

A haughty young man stood before him, his face dull and unshaven. His name was Joel, and he was not a very pleasant human being. He was, in fact, rather arrogant. In his many years in this realm, Ryan had learned this to be a common side effect of immense wealth. As such, the boy's rudeness encouraged him. After all, he'd done thousands of dollars-worth of work on this machine. His compensation was eminent.

"Wow. You've actually managed to finish." Joel's lips pressed thin. He seemed almost disappointed.

"Yes, sir. I have." Ryan turned to Elizabeth with pride in his eyes. "Oh, I'm sorry. Where are my manners? Joel, this is Eliza—."

"Let me stop you there. I'm not interested in meeting the help." Joel held his hand up cutting Ryan short. "I just want my truck."

"The *help*?" Elizabeth's eyes flashed red and her arms started twitching.

Ryan felt a wave of rage roll off his wife and sensed her wings at the ready. He shook his head at her, his eyes pleading. She huffed and stomped back into the house, slamming every door along the way. He turned back to Joel and led him over to the truck.

"Have a look," Ryan said, leaning on the truck.

"Hmm," Joel rested his hand on the ridge of the extended hood and sighed.

"As you can see, I've completely restored the engine and installed each of the special modifications you requested. It was a lot of work and some of the parts were hard to come by, but she runs beautifully!" Ryan smiled proudly and patted the engine block as if it were a puppy.

"Whatever," Joel shrugged and flung down the hood.

Ryan had barely enough time to pull his hand out of the way before it slammed shut. He stood there in shock as Joel snatched the keys from him and climbed into the driver's seat.

"Later," the kid said as he cranked the engine to life.

"Excuse me," Ryan walked over to the window and held out his hand. "You'll need to pay before you can take the truck."

"Right, sure," Joel reached out and placed a single coin onto his palm. He smirked up at Ryan unapologetically. "Here you go."

"What is this," Ryan glared at the rusty penny in his palm.

"My mother said to tell you she'd take it off your tab," Joel laughed. "Don't get too excited. You still owe her for five dresses after this."

He settled into his seat, geared the engine, and drove out of the shop.

"Ryan," Elizabeth stood in the doorway, a strange smile on her face. His heart was beating so loudly in his ears he hadn't even heard her approach.

"I'm so sorry," his head fell. "He didn't pay and likely never will. The debts are piling up and I have only a meager savings left. I simply can't afford to feed and care for my children *and* give you the life you deserve."

"I know, dear." Elizabeth swallowed her disgust and embraced her husband.

"I don't know what to do." Ryan sobbed into her shoulder. "I've run out of ideas and my heart is heavy with worry."

"You needn't trouble yourself, my love," Elizabeth said softly, running her fingers through his blond mane. "I know exactly how to fix our little problem…or should I say *problems*."

***

"I miss mother," Cosette whispered.

"Shhh," Gabriel held a finger to his lips and pulled her in closer as they listened through the crack in the shop door. Their wings bobbed nervously about as they strained to hear the hushed conversation between their father and Elizabeth.

Gabriel, the older of the two, was tall and strong with shaggy brown hair and tanned skin. His wings, though much smaller than his father's, were the same brilliant gold. Cosette was much younger and a full foot shorter than her brother. She had her father's blonde hair and her mother's fair skin and rose-colored wings.

"We can't keep them anymore," Elizabeth crossed her arms.

"They're my children, Elizabeth, not stray dogs." Ryan's eyes narrowed. "I can't just toss them out with the rubbish and hope they disappear."

"Children disappear every day, my love," Elizabeth ran her finger down his face, leaving a trail of shadow in its wake.

"She's doing it again," Gabriel hissed to his sister. "He's such a fool."

"It's the charm, Gabriel," Cosette sighed. "It's not his fault. He's grieving and blinded by her dark magic."

"Think about it," Elizabeth sang. "The town knows nothing about them. Their mother is gone. No one would even notice. We could rid ourselves of them easily and finally be happy together. Maybe even earn a place back in the skies."

"Above the clouds?" Ryan's eyes got that glassy look.

"Yes, my love," she smiled. "Above."

"Fight it, father," Cosette cheered quietly from behind the door.

"I…No." Ryan shook the fog from his head. "Elizabeth, listen to yourself. You are suggesting I abandon my children, my flesh and blood."

"Flesh and blood are fleeting and easily dealt with, husband," Elizabeth's wings began to glow and darkness swirled around them. "We will never be truly happy while they are weighing us down."

"I…I can't," Ryan said, but his voice faltered and his eyes glazed over.

"He wouldn't." Gabriel frowned and placed a hand on Cosette's shoulder.

"You can and you *will*, Ryan." Elizabeth's eyes flashed and her voice echoed through the shop. "Get rid of them or I will do it for you, and I promise you, I will not be nearly as kind."

"But, how?" Ryan droned, the spell settling in deep.

"Figure it out," his wife said her eyes boring into his. "Sell them, give them away, or bury them in the woods. I don't care how you do it, just get them out of my sight."

"Of course, my queen." Ryan sank to his knees.

"Good." With a triumphant smile, Elizabeth stalked out of the shop.

"Hide!" Gabriel said.

He and Cosette scrambled to their feet and pressed their backs to the wall behind the door as it was pushed open. Elizabeth stomped past them and down the hallway toward her lavish bedroom. A few steps from the door Cosette released the breath she'd been holding. Elizabeth turned on her heel and glared at the children.

"You sneaky little insects!" She wheeled on them and sent a blast of dark energy toward where they hid.

Gabriel stepped in front of his sister and spread his wings shielding her from the beast's blast.

The shadow bounced off his wings and evaporated in a pathetic puff of smoke. Gabriel and his sister were completely unharmed. "Whoa!" Gabriel smiled and squared his shoulders. "Looks like your magic doesn't work on me, demon."

"No matter," Elizabeth scoffed at him. "It works on your father plenty."

She laughed deep in her chest and stomped to her bedroom, slamming the door shut behind her. Moments later, their father entered the house. His shoulders were heavy and he looked defeated. When his children met his gaze, something in his eyes changed. He looked angry. *Angry at them.*

"Why are you children lurking about," Ryan asked.

"We were, umm." Cosette stammered.

"We were listening," Gabriel squared his shoulders and took a deep breath. "We heard the two of you talking. That woman is cruel and you can't see it."

"Father, Elizabeth is—" Cosette began.

"Enough," Ryan held his hand up to his daughter's face. His voice was mechanical and hollow. "Elizabeth is the love of my life. She only wants what is best for me and I'll not have the two of you getting in the way. You mustn't speak such hatred toward your mother."

"She's *not* our mother," Gabriel growled.

"Go to your room, now. Both of you!" Ryan yelled, his glassy eyes determined.

"Father, please." Cosette's eyes filled with tears.

When his daughter began to sob, his tone softened a fraction and his shoulders relaxed. "Fear not, my child. You must rest, for tomorrow we will go to the forest to hunt. It will be an adventure. I promise."

"An adventure?" Cosette looked confused.

"Take your sister and go to bed," Ryan waved dismissively at Gabriel.

"Of course," Gabriel glared at his father but relented. He folded his wings and tugged Cosette towards their room.

"I am afraid, brother," Cosette said as she sank onto her warm but meager cot. "What if father really does send us away?"

"I will not let that happen, Cosette." Gabriel sat at her side and hugged her. "This is our home. No matter what, we will always find a way back."

"You will?" his sister asked through tears.

"Always," Gabriel promised. "We are special Cosette. We are from above the clouds. More than that, we are family and family sticks together."

"I love you, brother," she whispered, yawning.

"Rest your eyes, Cosette, for tomorrow is sure to be a trying day." He kissed her forehead gently and sat with her, stroking her soft hair until she fell asleep.

When all was quiet in the house, Gabriel crept out of bed and slid into his ratty old shoes. His wings pressed against his back as he crept through the hallway, careful to be especially quiet as he passed his father and Elizabeth's room.

Once he was safely outside, the boy grabbed his mother's bow and her quiver of arrows from its hiding place beneath the back porch. When he was sure no one could see him, Gabriel let loose his golden wings and rose up into the dark night sky. He soared above the trees that surrounded Ravens Valley and looked out across the hills and fields.

From up in the sky, The Great City seemed much closer than he'd been led to believe. In fact, it was probably no more than ten miles from his father's shop. The bright lights beckoned like a cluster of stars.

His father had always said Great City was a dangerous wasteland. When Gabriel had asked if they could see it, his father had told him it was not possible. The Great City was too far away for even his father's enormous wings to carry him.

"More lies," Gabriel shook his head, his small wings fighting hard to keep him in the air.

That was a worry for another day. Tonight, he must mark a trail through the woods that would bring him and his sister back to their home.

***

The next morning, when the sun kissed the mountains, Gabriel's head finally hit his pillow. His eyes had only just closed when the bedroom door swung open.

"It is time to go," his father said as he stormed into the room. He grabbed Gabriel's arm and tugged him towards the hallway. Gabriel pulled away from his grip.

"I need to use the bathroom first," Gabriel lied. He scooped Cosette's shoes from the floor and pushed her towards their father.

"Fine," Ryan sighed. "But be quick about it."

"Follow, father, Cosette. I'll be right behind you." He pulled on his shoes and watched his father drag his sister out of the room. The second he disappeared from sight, Gabriel dug his weapon out from under the bed and hid it beneath his wings.

Farther and farther Ryan led them into the woods. He didn't speak or even acknowledge their presence. He walked as if in a trance. His children followed in much the same state. Gabriel was determined to keep his sister safe. Cosette's hand never left his. They walked for what seemed like hours.

Cosette was small and tired quickly. Gabriel scooped the girl up onto his back and carried her through the jagged trees. His legs began to ache but he was determined to continue. Their father remained silent, a faint trail of dark magic surrounding him. The only sounds they heard were the animals scampering along the trees and their own labored breathing. Three separate times, they stumbled across a fat doe or buck, their footsteps sending it running off as they approached.

"What are we doing father?" Cosette finally broke the silence.

"We are hunting." Ryan sighed flatly. His eyes were blank. "If only there were deer close by. A deer would make an excellent feast for our family."

Gabriel and Cosette looked at each other in confusion. Their father really wasn't *there*.

"Oh, no," Ryan gasped suddenly. "I've forgotten my spear. We cannot very well kill our dinner without a spear, can we?"

"Father?" Gabriel narrowed his eyes.

"I will go get my spear," he said.

"We'll come with you," Cosette said, following him.

"No!" Ryan spat, then quickly smiled and changed his tone. "You children just wait here. It'll be faster if I go myself. I'll be right back."

Before they could protest, Ryan opened his wings, pushed off the ground, and disappeared into the night sky. The force of his takeoff left a crater in the ground. After a couple moments of silence, Cosette dropped to the dirt and began to weep.

"He's not coming back, is he?"

"It's going to be okay, Cosette," Gabriel hugged his sister close. "We'll get home, no matter what. We stick together, right?"

"Right," Cosette sniffled. "But can we give him a chance? Can we wait and see if he comes back for us?"

"Cosette, no." Gabriel shook his head. "He's not coming."

"Please, brother." Cosette begged. "He's our father. He deserves a chance to redeem himself. Can we wait for a bit, please?"

"Fine, but just a short while," Gabriel frowned.

The children sat together on a hollowed-out log and watched the sky lose all color. Gabriel hadn't realized how cold it had gotten until he felt his sister shivering at his side. Her teeth chattered as she looked up at him, her eyes sad.

"Let your wings warm you," Gabriel said, releasing his.

"We're not supposed to." Cosette shook her head. "Father said."

"Father is not here." Gabriel stretched out his golden wings and curled them around him, forming a warm cocoon. Cosette mimicked him and soon the chattering stopped. Gabriel's warmth enveloped him and his eyes grew heavy.

"Rest your eyes, sister," he told Cosette.

Gabriel closed his eyes for just a moment to gather his thoughts. When he opened them again, it was daylight. A tear trickled down his cheek. He swiped it away quickly and a gush of anger washed over him. Their father had not come back for them. Not that Gabriel had believed he would. "Wake up, Cosette." He said, shaking her. "It's time to go home."

Her eyes filled with tears. "Where's father?"

"He didn't come." Gabriel jutted his chin. "That doesn't matter. We don't need him."

"But how will we find our way?" Cosette choked out.

"With these," he pulled an arrow from the quiver strapped to his back. Cosette looked confused. "I've left us a trail high up in the trees that will lead us straight back home."

Hand in hand, the two of them took to the skies, no longer concerned with the prying eyes of the humans down below.

They followed the trail of treetop arrows all the way back to their ramshackle home and then slowly drifted to the ground just outside their fence line.

"You did it, Gabriel." Cosette whispered. "You got us home!"

"No, Cosette. *We* did it." He smiled at his sister. Together the two crept back into their home and curled up in their warm beds.

***

Later that morning, Elizabeth burst into the children's room with an arm full of fabrics and design books. She had her back to them at first.

"It's going to be wonderful," she sang to herself as she spun in a circle. "I can put my scarves on one wall, oh, and my wardrobe with all of my fine dresses here and—what are *you* doing here?"

"Good morning, *mother*," Gabriel smirked and waved at her.

"Ryan!" Elizabeth yelled, dropping her things as she stormed from the room.

Ryan rushed into their room a second later, his face wrought with confusion. Cosette would not look at him. Gabriel only glared.

"Father," he said sharply and Ryan's eyes filled with regret.

"Oh god," he whispered as his chin trembled; he turned and left the room.

Elizabeth strode to the room with a toothy grin. Her slinky red dress hung to the floor, but did little to hide her evil. "My dear children, you've returned. I was so worried about you."

Gabriel could hear the annoyance in her voice. The way the lies slipped past her lips was like nails scratching a chalkboard.

"Right," Gabriel huffed.

"I'll bring you a bite," she said, her voice lilting. "You should rest. It seems you've had a long night."

"You could say that," Gabriel said, hatred dripping from every word. "The journey was long, but we found our way. We always will."

"We shall see." She sneered at them as she closed the door.

Gabriel heard the jingle of keys and the turn of a lock. He got up and raced towards the door. He wiggled the handle, but it did not budge. He peered through the peephole and found Elizabeth staring back at him, her smile victorious. Defeated, he turned and slumped against the marred wood surface of their bedroom door.

"Gabriel, this is bad." Cosette sat up in her bed. "They will send us away again, I just know it. What are we to do, brother?"

"I don't know." Gabriel muttered.

His eyes scanned the room, desperately searching for something, anything, to get them out of this mess. He was tired and angry, his thoughts a jumbled mess. The edge of his mother's bow stuck out from beneath his bed, beckoning to him. His tired expression lightened and a smile pulled across his face.

"What is it?" Cosette asked, tilting her head in confusion. "Why are you smiling?"

Gabriel moved over to his bed and reached beneath the frame. He slid an arrow from the quiver and gently placed it in his sister's small hand. He ruffled her locks and sat at her side.

"They can send us away every day for the rest of time, dear sister, but mother will always lead us home." Gabriel squared his shoulders. "We must ready ourselves."

He grabbed his sister's shoes from the floor and slipped them onto her feet then dug their hand-me-down jackets out of the closet. Cosette's had belonged to Elizabeth at one time.

Gabriel had scavenged it from the trash months ago, since the woman refused to buy one for his sister. It would be far too big for her, but infinitely better than nearly freezing to death as they had the night before.

They sat together in silence anxiously waiting for whatever happened next. Finally, the lock turned and Elizabeth strode into the room. A sickeningly sweet smile tugged at the corners of her mouth.

"Here you go, children," she said dropping a crumb of bread into each of their hands. "I've brought you a bite, as promised."

"Pass." He swatted it from Cosette's hand and crossed his arms.

"Excuse me?" She had the gall to look offended. "I was merely trying to help."

"Help *yourself*." Gabriel glared at Elizabeth beneath dark lashes.

"You ungrateful little wretch!" Her hands clenched in tight fists. "I have just given you food from my own table and this is how you repay me?"

"Repay you? We owe you nothing," Gabriel stomped. His wings flew above his head as he ground the meager crumbs into the carpet.

"I will get what I deserve," Elizabeth growled and the air began to vibrate around them. "My magic can do a great many things, children. You've only seen the tip of the iceberg."

She slammed the door and twisted the lock once more.

***

When darkness fell, their father burst into the room.

"It's time to go," Ryan said.

His eyes were black and his expression hard. All traces of the father they'd once loved, the father who'd once loved them, were gone. He grabbed his children by the wrists and dragged them outside. He shoved them toward the woods and pressed at their backs.

They walked for what felt like ages. Cosette cried softly, her legs barely able to carry her. Gabriel squeezed her hand and shot a glance upward to where one of his mother's arrows gleamed in the moonlight. He nodded at Cosette and they continued walking.

The journey continued until their surroundings became unfamiliar. The trees twisted and the shadows seemed to move. Even the stars looked different in this part of the forest. They'd just crossed a downed tree that bridged a wide river when Ryan stopped dead in his tracks.

"Goodbye, children," he said flatly. With a swoosh of his great golden wings, their father took to the skies.

He didn't look back.

This time the children didn't wait. Their father was not going to come for them. They would find their way home on their own, as they had the night before.

"Where are they?" Gabriel groaned from high above the trees. After hours of searching for his mother's arrows, his tired wings were barely able to hold him. He drifted to the ground slowly and landed on shaky legs. "He's taken us too far, Cosette. I cannot find the trail."

"You promised," Cosette wept. "You said we'd always find our way."

"We will, sister," whispered Gabriel putting his hand on her shoulder. "We just have to find another path. Mother will protect us."

"How Gabriel?" She looked up at him through tears. "She's gone from this Earth."

"The same as she always has," Gabriel hugged her tight and sheltered her with his wings. "We just have to have faith. Mother always said, out of struggle comes strength."

"That's true," Cosette smiled sadly. "I hope she was right."

"Come, sister. We have a long journey ahead." Gabriel squared his shoulders.

"But where will we go?" Cosette sighed.

"There," Gabriel pointed. The Great City glowed high above the treetops.

***

"It's so loud, Gabriel. And smelly." Cosette wrinkled her nose and shuffled closer to her brother's side. Her wings were vibrating with anxiety. "I don't like it here."

"We aren't staying long," Gabriel said, looking over his shoulder as he led Cosette through the bustling streets. He couldn't shake the feeling that they were being followed.

The Great City was a chaotic symphony of noise and excitement. Even now, at such a late hour, people littered the streets and alleys. Music boomed from behind closed doors. Dogs barked and rats scurried along the sewer trenches. There were buildings tall enough to reach the sky and bright yellow cars that sped about like cockroaches under a streetlight.

"I'm hungry," Cosette grumbled as they passed a bakery window, "and so, so tired."

"Me, too," Gabriel said eying the tasty sweets behind the glass.

The children had no destination and no idea where to go. They wandered aimlessly for some time before stumbling across a sign that read, *room and board offered in exchange for labor*.

The arrow on the sign pointed down an alley. They stopped for a moment, unsure if they should proceed. The hairs on the back of Gabriel's neck stood on end and he shot a look over his shoulder again. Exhausted and out of options, they headed down the dark stretch of pavement. If nothing else, they might be able to find shelter for the night.

They were both worn out and frustrated, but Gabriel worried most for his sister. She was struggling to keep her glamour in place and her wings hidden, but there was something more. A new energy vibrated around her. He couldn't place it, but it felt familiar somehow.

"Are you children all alone?" a ragged voice echoed from behind them.

A woman dressed in black stood at the mouth of the alleyway, blocking them in. She was haggard and unkempt, her face sleepless. Dark circles hung beneath under her eyes and her hands shook.

"No," Cosette squeaked and pointed down the alley. "Our parents are waiting for us."

"I doubt that very much, little girl," the woman sneered rubbing her hands together as she stalked toward them. "Perhaps you should come with me."

"No, thank you," Gabriel muttered stepping in front of his sister.

"Awe, c'mon, pretty boy. I don't bite…hard." She laughed, her yellow-toothed grin beaming beneath the alley's dim light. "Come here."

"We don't want any trouble." Gabriel grabbed Cosette's hand and led her toward the entrance to the alley. He gave the woman a wide berth. "We'll just be on our way."

With a speed he hadn't expected, the woman shot in front of Gabriel. She tilted her head and hissed at them. "I'm afraid that isn't possible…*Gabriel*."

"How do you know my name?" Gabriel narrowed his eyes at the woman.

"Haven't you figured it out?" She laughed.

His teeth ground together as realization struck. "*Elizabeth.*"

"Please," Cosette begged, stepping out from behind her brother. "Just let us pass."

"No can do, sweetie. I've got a job to do," the woman shrugged. "If I don't deliver, I don't get paid. Don't worry, I'll make it quick and painless."

"Stay back." Gabriel shook as he desperately struggled to knock an arrow.

The woman reached him first, her fist connecting with the boy's jaw. Unprepared for the attack, he crumbled to the street in a heap. The assassin pulled a blade from her hip and hovered over Gabriel.

"Stop!" Cosette shrieked and her glamour fell. Her delicate pink wings flew wide behind her and her eyes began to glow.

The woman dropped her knife and stumbled backward falling to the ground. "Holy hell!"

"Stay away from my brother," Cosette hissed. Her shoulders heaved fast and heavy, a low growl emanating from the girl's chest. Her face twisted and her body began to shake violently. She crumbled to the ground, her wings draped around her. Her rosy feathers began to fade, now jet as a raven.

"Cosette?" Gabriel spat blood onto the pavement and struggled to his feet. He let loose his wings, his bow aimed at the woman on the ground. Cosette howled, writhing beneath her shifting wings. "Cosette?"

The girl roared and threw back her dark wings to reveal a massive grey wolf. Its teeth were easily the size of Gabriel's thumb. It growled and shook out its fur as it slowly rose up from the ground.

"Cosette?" Gabriel gaped up at the beast. The wolf nodded and folded her wings against her back.

"W-what are you?" the woman cried as she scrambled away from the children.

"I am *Justice*," Cosette roared.

"Please, don't hurt me," the woman whimpered, shielding herself behind her quivering hands. The wolf ignored the woman's plea, her teeth frothing as she stalked toward her.

"You must pay." Cosette hissed, spittle flying onto the woman's twisted face.

"Cosette, please!" Gabriel cried, He rushed to his sister's side and tussled the fur atop her head. "This isn't you, sister."

The wolf snorted, and shook its head.

"This woman is a pawn," Gabriel urged. "Justice is best served to another."

"Elizabeth," Cosette's voice rumbled low. A siren roared in the distance and footsteps rushed toward the alley.

"We must go," Gabriel begged.

The wolf nodded then turned to the woman cowering at her feet.

"Go." Cosette narrowed her bright blue eyes at their would-be killer. "Repent or I shall find you once more."

"Y-yes. I will," the woman stammered. She crawled to her feet and sprinted from the alley out of sight.

"Cosette!" Gabriel shouted, His wings splayed as he dug through his pack and pulled out Elizabeth's old coat. "Do you think you could find her?" Cosette sniffed at it then bared her fangs.

"Follow me," Cosette growled as her paws lifted from the ground.

They soared above the city and flew as fast as they could towards the forest. Gabriel followed in his sister's wake, desperately trying to process what was happening to her. Though he'd never seen his sister take this form, something felt right about it.

***

"What have I done?" Ryan cried.

When the fog had finally cleared from his mind, anger took its place. His knuckles were bloodied and bruised. Fist-shaped holes marred the walls of his home. Eventually, his strength faded leaving nothing but confusion and guilt. He couldn't remember why he'd abandoned his children only that he had.

He'd searched for them all through the forest and found nothing but a pale, pink feather stuck in the muddy banks of the river. The trail had gone cold after that and Ryan was beginning to lose hope. His thoughts swirled and his chest ached at their loss.

His blond hair drooped around his sallow face and his golden wings were shedding their feathers. His tears fell fast, echoing the storm that brewed outside his window. Lightning flashed, drawing his gaze to the tree line. A great winged wolf stepped out from the brush and into the pale moonlight.

"Ariana?" Ryan narrowed his eyes.

Was he so far gone that he was seeing the ghost of his late wife? He tore off through the house and out into the thunderous night air. Rain soaked him to the bone, but he didn't care.

"Ariana, is that you?" He stepped toward the wolf.

"Once again, father, you are blinded," the beast snarled.

"Cosette?" Ryan's eyes widened. A smile spread across his face and he ran to her.

"Stay back." Gabriel stepped out from behind his sister, an arrow pointed at his father's chest. "This ends tonight."

Cosette snarled and slashed at the muddy ground with her great paws. She spread her dark wings and howled. A flash of lightning filled the sky blinding Ryan where he stood. When his vision returned a moment later, Gabriel and the wolf were gone. Had they been there at all?

"I am going mad!" Ryan shrieked, spinning in a circle.

A loud crash sounded from inside the house. Elizabeth screamed and Ryan sped toward the open door. Broken glass littered the floor. The walls shook and a growl echoed down the hall. Ryan followed the sounds of struggle toward the back of the house. Gabriel stood in Ryan's bedroom, the great hulking wolf at his side.

"Stay back, beast," Elizabeth shouted, her hands held out in front of her. Dark shadows swirled around her, following the movement of her raking fingers. "I've vanquished an avenging angel before. I will gladly do it again."

"You are evil," Gabriel spat at her.

"Your mother said the same thing before I struck her down, boy," Elizabeth laughed.

A ball of dark energy flew from her hands toward the children. Ryan moved toward it, but an invisible force blocked him from crossing the threshold. He needn't have worried though. Gabriel threw his wings out and blocked the magic easily. It rebounded, knocking Elizabeth against the wall.

"Nice try, demon," Gabriel said.

"Foul creatures!" Elizabeth hissed as she struggled to climb to her feet. Her eyes were dark and menacing. Her beauty was gone.

It was as if Ryan was seeing her for the first time.

"She is all yours, sister," Gabriel said.

"Get him out of here." Cosette turned toward her father. "Justice is ugly. He doesn't need to see this."

Gabriel waved his hand and the invisible barrier fell. He lunged at Ryan and dragged him away down the hall.

"Go, father," Gabriel pleaded. "Please."

Ryan let his son lead him away. They burst through the open door and out into the night together. A battle raged at their backs. Rain poured down around them and the sky churned. The house shook before them and stone crumbled to the ground.

A scream shattered the night and all went silent. Ryan felt a weight being lifted from his soul. A darkness he hadn't realized was there dissipated and all became clear. He threw his arms around Gabriel and held him close. "I'm so sorry, son."

"Don't." Gabriel sobbed, returning his father's embrace. "It's okay. You didn't see."

"My sweet girl." Ryan whispered as the wolf stepped out into the garden. Red fabric dangled between her teeth. Cosette spat it onto the ground and walked toward her father. Ryan held his hand out and slowly approached her. "All is well. Let go, Cosette. I'm here."

He ran his hand along the wolf's neck and pressed his forehead to hers. She sank to the ground. Ryan cradled her in his arms and comforted her as she shifted back into her true form. Her pink wings shook and tears streamed down her face.

Soon, the clouds faded away and sun kissed their skin. With renewed hope, Ryan and his children set off, hand-in-hand, and headed for a new beginning.

Their home was destroyed and their life was in ruins, but their family had survived. Their father loved them and stood by their side. For Gabriel and Cosette, that was all the happily ever after they'd ever wanted.

"She was right, Gabriel," Cosette whispered to her brother as they walked on.

"Who was right?" Gabriel asked.

"Elizabeth," Cosette smiled wryly. "She said she would get what she deserved."

Polaris Jimenez

Author of Gabriel and Cosette

Polaris Jimenez is the fourteen-year-old author of the short story "Gabriel and Cosette." She is a huge fan of *The Lord of the Rings* and *The Chronicles of Narnia*. She is an enthusiastic fantasy lover and finds great enjoyment in writing about her very detailed dreams. Polaris is a regular teenage girl. She deals with her bad hair days and rocks her favorite pair of mismatched Chucks while grabbing people's attention with the stories she's created.

Snowe's Homecoming Demons

J.M. Bach

Part 1

(Ruby)

"Sit still, Hothead," Snowe laughed as I blew a strand of red hair away from my face.

"Are you almost finished," I groaned, fidgeting in my seat. My stomach had been twisted in a knot all day. The longer I sat there, the worse it got.

"You can't rush art, little sister." She twisted the offending hair it into a braid and tucked it in with the rest, forming a crown around my head. "I think I've outdone myself this time."

I certainly hoped so, since I'd been sitting in that chair for over an hour. My older sister loved styling hair and the Homecoming dance was the perfect excuse to go crazy. Snowe's hair was already done and plastered firmly in place with a generous amount of hairspray. Her long, dark hair always looked beautiful, but today she'd gone above and beyond. Part of it was swirled in a fancy bun atop her head while the rest was curled and pinned in an intricate system of draping loops that wound around it.

My curly, copper hair was much less cooperative so her options were limited, but she somehow managed to force my wayward locks into submission. I had to admit, it actually looked pretty.

When she was finally done fiddling with it, I teleported out of the chair and into my own room. Luckily, they were on the same floor, otherwise, it would've been hard to do. I was fairly new at teleportation and traveling long distances was still out of my skillset.

Snowe and I each had control over two of the elements. Well, I guess it was more like two and half, but we'll get to that.

My sister could manipulate water and air. Her namesake was a fitting tribute to her passion. She could manifest a fresh blanket of white snow, quite literally, out of thin air. It was actually pretty impressive to watch. Unfortunately, after a *certain movie* came out, her special talent earned her months of teasing at school.

Snowe was strong though, and never let it get to her. I admired that about her. Instead of feeling sorry for herself, she found ways to use her skills to make others happy. She was the one that suggested this year's homecoming theme be "Winter Wonderland." She was also the one who volunteered both of us to show up early to help decorate for the dance.

Sure, my sister's powers are cool, but the learning curve is definitely skewed in her favor. I mean, what's the worst that could happen if she screwed up and accidentally created a blizzard…an extra day off school? Oh, how terrifying.

My elemental affinities were much more difficult to manage and far more destructive. You can't just move earth and stone and manipulate fire without a little collateral damage. She started calling me a hothead when I was eight years old after I accidentally set my hair on fire. I've come a long way since then, but the nickname still follows me (and gets on my nerves).

I'd rather not mess with fire if I can avoid it. Much like Snowe, I preferred to focus my elemental energy on creation.

My favorite thing in the world was the beautiful sea of red roses I'd created in our mother's garden. I'd always preferred the peace of connecting with earth to the destructive power of fire. I had enough anxiety without adding that into the mix.

As demon hunters, our powers were one of our greatest weapons…or they would be if we ever learned to use them properly. In the meantime, we'd always have our skill with a demon blade and years of martial arts training to fall back on, thanks to our parents. They had both been very hands-on when preparing us to take over the "family business."

"Get back in here," Snowe yelled down the hallway. "I'm not done with you."

"Ugh," I grabbed my earrings off my dresser, closed my eyes, and reappeared in her doorway a moment later. "I look fine."

"This is homecoming, Ruby. Fine isn't good enough," she said sliding her little snowflake dangles into her ears. She patted the back of the chair and grabbed her makeup bag. "Sit. When I'm through with you, Aaron won't be able to keep his eyes off you. We are both getting our happily ever after tonight."

"Fine," I rolled my eyes, but couldn't fight the smile that spread across my face when she said Aaron's name.

Twenty minutes later, I was standing in front of Snowe's full-length mirror gaping at my reflection in awe. She was good at this girly stuff. I barely recognized myself. The only thing familiar about my appearance was my favorite pair of earrings, delicate rose-shaped studs and the demon blade strapped to my thigh beneath my dress. Both had been gifts from my dad.

I released a heavy breath and pressed my hand to my stomach.

"What is it, Ruby?" Snowe walked toward me, her brows knit in concern.

"I'm fine," I lied.

"Try again," Snowe said, spinning me to face her. "That doesn't work with me, remember?"

This is where it gets complicated and where the "half" part of our two-and-a-half powers comes in. Snowe and I share one element.

Spirit.

We didn't acquire the link to the spirit element until after our dad passed and we'd not come anywhere near close to understanding it, let alone mastering its full potential. When it kicked in, Snowe discovered she was an empath. With the proper training, she may even be able to project feelings and influence others, according to my mom. I gained the power of psychic control (which allows me to teleport), and foresight, which is not nearly as awesome as it sounds. Spirit also enhances the connection that exists between Snowe and myself.

"Spill." Snowe crossed her arms.

"I can't explain it." I leaned back against the wall and closed my eyes. "I just have a bad feeling about tonight. I can't see it clearly though. It's like a shadow is blocking my premonitions."

"You should really talk to Mom about this, Ruby." She put a hand on my shoulder.

"It would only worry her." I shook my head and stepped away from the wall.

As if on cue, Mom walked in. She was wearing her favorite paint-splattered shirt and gardening jeans. An ancient-looking camera dangled from a strap around her neck.

"Smile, girls!" A burst of white light filled the room. She giggled and flipped a button on the top. "Whoops, forgot to turn the flash off."

"Why can't you just take pictures with your phone like a normal person?" I joked.

"Where's the fun in that?" she shrugged.

Mom beamed proudly as she snapped an endless series of pictures. Despite the uneasy feeling we shared, Snowe and I managed to smile through it all and even posed a few times. Afterwards, Mom retreated to dig up another roll of film. Snowe followed in her wake leaving me alone with my thoughts. Desperate for a distraction from my anxiety, I wandered over to my dresser and stared at the framed photos scattered across the top.

One picture in particular caught my eye. It was the last family photo mom took before dad was deployed to Iraq with his hunter unit two years ago. Six months later the doorbell rang and two men in full-dress handed my mom a folded flag. I'll never forget that day. It was the one and only time I ever saw my mother fall apart.

"You look so much like him." My mom gently laid her hand on my shoulder. I hadn't even heard her come in the room. "You all ready?"

"I think so," I said, plastering on a smile as I turned toward her.

"I have a surprise for you." She handed me a small trinket box. "Go ahead. Open it."

I released the clasp and gasped. Inside, lying on a bed of black velvet was a gold bracelet. An intricate collection of golden charms dangled at even intervals around its length; roses alternating with snowflakes. At the center of the largest rose was a single red ruby.

"It's beautiful, Mom." I grinned.

"Beautiful and powerful," she said, pulling the bracelet from the box. "It's an amplification charm, Ruby."

"Wait, what?" I narrowed my eyes at her. "How did you--?"

"Your sister can't keep a secret to save her life." She laughed, placing the bracelet on my wrist.

It felt warm against my skin. A feeling of calm immediately washed over me. "The charm will enhance your elemental connections and help keep you safe."

"Thanks Mom."

"Thank your father," she smiled, handing me the framed picture I'd been staring at. "He had them made for you years ago, honey. Besides, you girls get your spirit link from him. Even now, he's still protecting you."

"Thanks, daddy," I whispered, running my finger across the glass. I'd give anything to hug him one more time. With a sigh, I gently set the frame back in its place. When I turned back around, my mom had tears in her eyes. I wrapped her in a tight hug until she was ready to let go.

"Okay, that's enough of that," mom laughed, sniffling as she finally held me at arm's length. "No more tears or bad memories. Tonight, Ruby, tonight you make new memories, okay?"

"Mom, I—" My words fell short, swallowed up by the sound of the doorbell echoing through our small house.

"I'm guessing that's for you," she winked. "I'll get the door. You and your sister need to get ready for your dramatic entrance. Don't rush in though. Let them sweat for a minute, okay?"

"Okay, mom." I rolled my eyes, but a smile crept across my face.

I closed my eyes and transported myself back to Snowe's room. She spun on me the second she felt my presence and held her wrist next to mine. Her bracelet was white gold, her silvery charms mirroring my gold. A crystal-clear diamond sparkled at the center of the largest dangling snowflake.

"Wow." I stared down at it.

"Right?" She clapped excitedly.

"Girls, would you come downstairs please?" Mom yelled up at us with feigned innocence. "You have guests."

"That's our cue," Snowe giggled, hooking our arms, and dragging me toward the stairs.

"Whoa." Adam Landry stood gaping at the bottom of the staircase, his younger brother, Aaron behind him. "I mean…whoa. You look amazing, babe."

Snowe released my arm and sprinted down the last few stairs, leaping into his arms. Adam was nearly a foot taller than she was and built solid from playing football. He caught her effortlessly and swung her in a circle. Adam's dirty blond curls hung loose around his blue eyes. His suit and sky-blue tie matched perfectly with Snowe's elegant floor-length gown.

They looked perfect together, like royalty. Snow laughed from her heart and clung tightly to his shoulders. Adam's smile was sincere and doting. My mom beamed proudly from behind her camera, the shutter clicking as she immortalized Snowe's cheesy, teen-love moment on film.

Aaron shoved his hands in his pockets, smirked at me over his brother's shoulder, and shook his head. Once Adam set Snow back on her feet, his brother was finally able to move past him and get to me.

He shifted nervously on the balls of his feet and crossed his arms as he walked toward me. I could see the outline of his biceps through his sleeve and my heart skipped a beat. His caramel-colored hair was wild and spiked in all directions providing a clear view of his dark green eyes. There was something in them that intrigued me. They held strength, but there was something else, too. Mischief, maybe?

"Hey," he said, smirking as his eyes locked with mine.

"Hey," I said, nervously smoothing the non-existent wrinkles from my long, red gown. I rarely dressed up and it felt more than a little awkward.

"You look beautiful, Ruby," Aaron smiled broadly.

"You don't look so bad yourself," I said, straightening his lapels.

He laughed and took my hand. Mom made us pose for some more pictures and then finally let us leave. Adam cranked up the music and we drove off to the dance hall to work our magic and put the finishing touches on the decorations.

Speaking of magic, Aaron's was still a complete mystery to me. I opened up to spirit and tried to see into his but his power was still shrouded. It connected to nature in some way, I could tell that much due to how close I was to earth, but I knew nothing beyond that.

A few minutes later, we arrived at the school and set to work. Soon enough, there were snowflakes hovering in mid-air, fluffy drifts rolled in waves along the walls, and elaborate ice sculptures danced throughout the room.

"It's pretty, but I feel like it needs something." Snowe stood by the front entrance and looked out over the dancehall. "What do you think?"

"I've got this." I placed my hand on the wall and willed my roses to grow. They sprouted in earnest, covering the walls in a tapestry of velvety red blooms.

"Perfect," Snowe clapped as a limo full of dance guests pulled up out front. "And just in time!"

***

We stood aside and watched as couples filed into the hall, ooh-ing and ahh-ing at the beautiful decorations.

Snowe was glowing with pride, but it was tempered by my anxiety. The uneasy feeling in my gut was definitely putting a damper on her joy.

"Ladies." Drake, the new guy at our school, slithered past us.

He was not with a date, which didn't surprise me. The guy gave me the creeps. The second he walked by the uneasy feeling in the pit of my stomach multiplied. My bracelet felt hot against my skin. His eyes lingered just a bit too long on my sister and it didn't go unnoticed. Adam shot him a look and pulled Snowe closer to his side. Aaron tensed at my side, his jaw clenching, moving me closer, as well. Apparently, he could feel it too

"Let's go dance." Adam clutched Snowe's hand.

"Right behind you." She smiled gratefully and walked with him to the dance floor.

Aaron held his hand out and nodded toward the dance floor. I threaded my fingers with his and we followed in their wake, putting as much distance between Drake and us as possible. Eventually, it came time to name Homecoming King and Queen. Of course, it ended up being Snowe and Adam. Aaron and I cheered super loud and then left them to their slow dance. We danced straight through ten songs before I decided to take a break.

"I'm going to freshen up and grab some punch. Want some?" I shouted to Aaron over the music.

Aaron smiled and gave me a thumbs-up. "Yes, please."

"Be right back." I kissed his cheek and spun on my heel.

I was standing at the refreshment table, pouring Aaron and me some lemonade when my stomach clenched up on me. My head was throbbing and my hands started to shake. I set the cup down so I wouldn't spill it on my dress and steadied myself on the edge of the table.

"Hey, beautiful." Drake stepped up beside me and smiled.

"Hi." I attempted a smile, but failed.

"Where's that gorgeous sister of yours?" He asked.

There was an odd shadow to his aura and an unnatural gleam in his eyes. A darkness. He stepped closer to me and my stomach lurched. I smelled sulfur and rot. I gave him a tight smile and walked away quickly. I rushed through the crowd of moving bodies on the dance floor and lunged at my sister the second I saw her. My eyes bore into hers, our spirits linking. She understood.

"You're sure?" Her mouth was set in a grim line.

"Positive," I said, jingling the charms on my wrist. "Drake is definitely a demon."

"Wait, who's Drake again?" Adam asked.

"The creeper that was checking out your girlfriend earlier," Aaron offered, raising a brow at his brother. "I don't know him, but I've seen him around. I get a bad vibe from him."

Of course, Adam would not know who Drake is. As the captain of the football team, he existed in a closed circle. I doubt he knew half the kids we went to school with, let alone a new kid who'd mostly kept to the shadows until tonight.

"Now you know why." I shot Aaron a look and lifted the hem of my dress just high enough to slide my blade from its holster. "We have to deal with this, Snowe."

"There's a lot of kids here, Ruby," she said grabbing my wrist. "If we do this now, someone could get hurt."

"So, we get them out," I said.

"And how do we do that, exactly?" Adam took in the mass of bodies dancing. "Should we just make an announcement or something?"

"There are humans here." Aaron shook his head. "You know the rules."

"Fire alarm?" I shrugged.

"Yes," Snow shouted.

"If that doesn't work, we could always let a couple grizzly bears loose in the hall," Adam huffed and elbowed his brother.

"Grizzly bears. Really?" I raised a brow at him. "That's kind of random."

"Not really." Aaron shoved his hands in his pockets and avoided my gaze. "And I'd prefer that be a last resort."

His connection to nature, the shroud around his powers, and that extra gleam in his eyes; it all suddenly made sense. Aaron and his brother were shifters. I didn't blame him for not wanting to go down that road. From what I'd heard, the transformation process was extremely painful.

"Let's go with the fire alarm," I said, laying my hand on Aaron's shoulder. His eyes met mine and I smiled at him reassuringly.

"Fire alarm it is, then. I'll help Snowe evacuate when it's time," Adam said, clapping his brother on the back. "Aaron, you stay with Ruby."

"And do what, exactly?" Aaron narrowed his eyes at Adam.

"Whatever it takes, little brother," Adam pinned him with a hard stare. "It's time to step up, Aaron. You can't hide from this anymore. Accept what you are and *fight*."

"What about you?" Aaron glared at his brother. "Is our precious Homecoming King afraid of getting his hands dirty?"

"I think you know better," Adam's eyes flashed and a low grumble echoed in his chest. "And you know I'm right about this. It's time, Aaron."

"I know," Aaron raked his hair back and took a deep breath. "I just..."

"You've got this," Adam pounded a fist against Aaron's chest. "You are so much stronger than you give yourself credit for. Stop thinking so much, just *be*. It will make sense when the time comes."

Snowe slid her arm through Adam's elbow and nodded toward the corner where Drake had just ducked into the men's room. Aaron fell in at my side. His eyes were intense, his jaw clenched. He squared his shoulders and spoke.

"Okay, let's get this over with," he said. "What's the plan?"

"Simple is best," Snowe shouted over the music as she pulled her own demon blade from its holster. "You two wait for Drake and make sure he doesn't escape. Once the hall is clear, Ruby and I will take care of him. We'll be back on the dance floor before this song is over."

"Don't get cocky, Snowe." I frowned at her. "I don't like the way that creep was looking at you. There is something off about him."

"He's a demon, Ruby," Snowe said. "Everything is off about him."

"I'm serious, Snowe," I said. "I have a bad feeling about this one. You need to be careful."

"Right, of course," her smile faltered. Adam grabbed her hand as they turned toward the fire alarm box at the far side of the room. "I'll send a ripple down the bond when it's go-time. Be ready."

My sister's dress swirled behind her as they walked away and anger swelled in my gut. This was supposed to be her big night. Demons had already robbed us of so much.

My senses tingled and I nodded at Aaron. "Ready?"

A shrill alarm echoed through the hall, Drake stepped out of the bathroom, and all hell broke loose.

***

"Not sure I like this song," Drake sneered, his voice barely audible over the alarm, "but I'd be willing to endure it for one dance with that beautiful sister of yours. Any idea where I could find her?"

"Stay away from my sister," I hissed at him.

"Aww, don't be like that," Drake frowned. "It's just an innocent dance."

"We know what you are," I said, holding my blade in front of me. "Cut the crap, demon."

His glamour faltered for a fraction of a second and I saw his true form.

"Like I said," I smirked at him.

"Finally caught on, have you? Took you long enough," he snorted taking a step toward me. "I guess the rumors about your family's prowess were a bit exaggerated."

"Go to Hell," I glared at him.

"Been there, done that," he shrugged and took another step forward. "I'm not going anywhere until I've done what I came here to do."

"What exactly would that be?" I asked.

"It's harvest time, sweetheart." He raised his hands at his sides. "There are hundreds of human souls here, ripe for the picking. Their essence, combined with the elemental energy of a royal hunter, will make me the most powerful demon of all time!"

"You'll have to go through us first," Aaron growled and stepped closer to my side.

I could feel Snow hovering in the back of my mind. I pressed back, desperately urging her to stay away.

"If I must," Drake rolled his eyes and pushed up his sleeves.

The air around us began to vibrate and the hairs on my arm stood on end. The bracelet on my wrist began to hum against my skin. A black cloud swirled around Drake. When it dissipated, a hoard of lower demons appeared in its place.

Screams echoed in the corridors outside the dancehall. I raised a wall of fire near at entrance so no one could come back in and get caught in the crossfire. The fire department would soon be on its way, but that didn't concern me. We had allies everywhere. The supernaturals in uniform would sense the fire's magical nature and handle it accordingly.

"Get them!" Drake shouted, pointing at us.

I flung my arms in front of me on reflex and ended up throwing a psychic wall in the process. The force of it threw Drake and his army back into the bleachers. The shock cost him and his glamour, and it fell away completely.

I couldn't stop myself from laughing. He couldn't have been more than two feet tall. His belly was round, his head was too small for his body, and he only had one tooth. In short, he was ugly as hell (all puns intended).

My laughter faltered as a ball of red hellfire sailed through the air at my head. I dropped to the ground and rolled away. It narrowly missed me, obliterating a nearby ice sculpture. What had once been a massive angel was no more than a bubbling puddle on the floor. As much as I'd learned about manipulating fire, I definitely wasn't crazy enough to try to control the weaponized flames of Hell.

By the time I got back to my feet, Aaron was locked in hand-to-hand combat with a handful of demons. Drake was summoning another blast when I felt Snowe's presence behind my flame barricade. As much as I didn't want to put her in danger, we needed my sister's help.

I tore the flames from the exit and hurled them at the demons. Snowe and Adam burst into the hall and rushed into battle. Snowe froze a smaller demon in place and thrust her blade through another's neck. Drake had managed to deflect my flames. They ignited a row of tables creating a wall of fire between us.

"Gahhhh!" Aaron was growling, buried beneath a pack of attacking monsters.

"Don't fight it, Aaron," Adam shouted as he crushed the head of a demon under his boot. Fabric tore and the floor shook. "Yes, brother!"

Demons flew through the air, and thunder echoed through the room. Two hulking grizzlies growled at my side. One with dark green eyes, the other with blue.

Adam rushed to Snowe's aid, grabbed one of the beasts by its neck, and tossed it aside like a rag doll. Aaron lumbered at my side growling and baring his teeth at Drake. His fur was thick and coarse as it brushed against my arm.

"I've always wanted a bear-skin rug," Drake hissed, then looked over at Adam. "Or two."

Aaron reared up on his hind legs and roared. Demons rushed at us from all directions and the fight escalated. Aaron charged at them, his heavy paws shaking the floor. A winged monster flew at him. With a swipe of his massive paw, he sent the thing flying into the wall where it crumbled to the floor. Another lunged for his feet but he slammed down onto it and crushed the thing's head like an eggshell.

A demon galloped toward me. I had just raised my blade when a breeze swept my cheek. One of Snowe's ice arrows landed between the demon's eyes and it dropped at my feet.

"Thanks," I spat at her, slashing another beast as it ran by.

Another rushed me and I sent my dagger flying through the air. It severed the demon's head from its body and looped back, the hilt landing snuggly in the palm of my hand. His ash had barely settled before another attacked. I lost myself in the song of steel and the resistance of my blade against fetid demon flesh.

Ash fell down around me.

Aaron roared at my side, finishing off a demon of his own. Within minutes, the room was silent, the floor scattered with piles of ash. My chest rose and fell rapidly and my body hummed with the energy of my powers. Aaron nudged me toward the bleachers with his nose and snorted, pulling me back to reality.

"Snowe?" My heart shot into my throat.

"She's mine," Drake growled.

His glamour was in place once again. His hand was knotted in Snowe's hair, a black knife held to her throat. Adam was nowhere to be seen.

"No!" I took a step towards him.

"Ah-ah-ahhh," He shook his head and pressed the knife tighter against her throat. Snowe's face twisted. "Take another step and I draw blood. I think we all know how that ends."

The need to run to her was almost overwhelming but I couldn't risk Drake's retaliation. The blade he had at Snowe's throat was forged in hellfire. If it pierced her skin, the blade's dark magic would infect her. She would either die a slow and painful death or worse, become a demon. Its proximity alone meant Snowe's powers were neutralized. If I got any closer, mine would be too.

I couldn't throw my blade or use my fire without endangering my sister and teleportation was too risky. We were stuck. Impossibly stuck. I was close enough to see the plea in Snowe's eyes, but too far away to answer it. My thoughts raced and rage boiled in my gut.

I couldn't save her.

"It's okay, Ruby," Snowe said as tears sprang to her eyes.

"Drake, please." I held my hands up in surrender. "Don't hurt her."

"Oh, sweet girl. I'm not going to hurt your precious sister," Drake smiled maliciously. "I'm going to *destroy* her!"

"No!" I lunged forward, no longer able to hold myself back. My feet pounded hard and fast against the floor. I had almost reached them when they disappeared into the dark ether. My hand sailed through tainted air that lingered where they had just been standing.

"Snowe!" I screamed as I sank to my knees. Fury coiled in my gut, flames surrounded me, and everything went dark.

Part 2

(Snowe)

Drake's laughter rang in my ears as my sister called out to me. Our spirit link was weakened by the blade at my throat, but lingered at the edge of my consciousness. I reached out to her through our bond and begged her not to come after me. Darkness surrounded me and the connection between us snapped like a twig.

Sorrow washed over me and I blacked out.

I woke some time later in a dark room that reeked of burnt matches and decay. My head was pounding and my body ached. I shot to my feet and dove forward. I'd only made it a foot or two when I was jerked back, my back slamming against the rough stone surface. A searing pain engulfed my wrists and ankles.

I steadied myself against the wall, forcing myself to slow my breathing. This was not a good time for my claustrophobia to kick in. I needed to find a way out of this mess. My physical self was shackled to the wall but without the hell blade to hinder my elements my spirit was unbound. If I centered myself, I could attempt astral projection.

I eased my body down onto the floor and reached out with Spirit. Pain radiated through my limbs making it difficult to focus, but I refused to give up. If Drake succeeded, he'd destroy everything in his path. Ruby, Adam, and everyone I cared about were in danger.

Dizziness washed over me as my astral-self struggled to escape my body. The dark magic surrounding this place was powerful enough to muffle my powers, but eventually I felt the familiar tingle and let go. My soul drifted upward sailing through cold, stone caverns and rotting wood beams. It drifted past rusted pick axes, shattered crates, and busted equipment.

My projection burst out into the night sky at the mouth of the old, abandoned mine on the edge of town. It sped through the city streets, straight to the dance hall. Ruby was sitting outside on a bench with her face buried in her hands. Aaron was at her side. His clothes were torn and blood dripped from a wound on his chest. Fire trucks and ambulances littered the streets. The school was a smoldering pile of ash and soot. I hovered in the air in front of her.

"Ruby," I shouted at her. "Ruby, it's me!"

She didn't hear me. I waved my arms in front of her but she couldn't see me either. Frustrated, I dove forward and flew straight through her chest. Her hair blew back and she shot upright with a gasp. She definitely *felt* me. On a hunch, I laid my non-corporeal hand on her head and spoke to her through our bond.

"Ruby," I thought to her.

"Snowe?" Her puffy eyes darted around searching for me. "Oh my god, is that you?"

"Yes, it's me." My heart flooded with relief.

"Snowe, are you okay?" she asked. "I thought you were dead! I'm freaking out, here."

"Ruby?" Aaron was looking at Ruby like she was crazy.

"It's my sister. She's here. Well, kind of." Ruby said. "Snowe, I can't see you."

"I'm fine, okay?" I said, dismissing her concern. "Ruby you have to come get me. Drake has me locked up at the old mine. He's going to unleash something horrible. We have to stop him."

"I know. We're on our way," Ruby said, grabbing the keys out of Aaron's hand. "Snowe, is Adam okay?"

"What do you mean?" I asked my heart racing. "Isn't he with you?"

"No." Ruby's brows knit, her gaze shifting to Aaron.

"What did she say?" Aaron asked his face tight with worry. "Is my brother okay?"

"Snowe, I think this might be bigger than us," Ruby grimaced. "You need to call for reinforcements."

"Angels?" I shrieked. "Ruby, I've never called on them before. I don't even know how!"

"We don't have a choice, Snowe," she said. "Drake is too powerful for us to take on alone. There's too much at stake. As the eldest living spirit elemental in our family, you're the only one who'll be able to establish a link. It has to be you. You have to try."

"How?" I exclaimed.

"I don't know, okay," she said throwing her hands in the air as she climbed into Adam's car. "You're the smart one, Snowe. Figure it out! We'll be there soon."

***

Adam was missing.

There was no doubt in my mind it had everything to do with Drake and his hellish Napoleon complex. If that bastard hurt a single hair on Adam's beautiful head, I would vanquish him with my bare hands.

I left the gym and searched for the connection Adam and I shared. It wasn't as strong as the one I had with my sister, but I was confident I'd be able to track him. I focused on his blue eyes and his adoring smile as I floated up into the sky. I let his love call to me and my spirit followed it.

Soon enough, I was hovering above the mine. Adam was being held in the same dank prison where my body lay slumped against a wall. I should have known.

I drifted down through the cold stone caverns until the bond snapped tight in my chest. I found Adam at the end of the deepest mineshaft. Drake was hovering above him in all his demonic ugliness. His glamour was wavering, shifting in a strange mix of his human and demonic form.

As tempting as it was, I couldn't underestimate him in this form, no matter how comical he looked. As long as Drake still had power, he was a danger. I could see it flowing off him in dark waves as he chanted in ancient Demonic. Adam writhed beneath him, the pain evident in his features.

"It's almost over, boy," Drake hissed. "Sometimes the end is the greatest mercy of all."

His eyes rolled inward and he threw his head back. A black mist rushed from his mouth and into Adam.

"No!" I bellowed.

I reached for Adam then pulled back. As much as it pained me to leave him, there was nothing I could do to help him without my body. I had to get back to my physical self.

But first, I had a call to make.

I tried for a few minutes, but all I could feel was darkness. I was too close to Hell in these caverns to get a good link to the heavens, so I drifted up. Higher and higher I rose. I was above the clouds before I finally felt something. I had no idea how to summon an angel, so I did what anyone else does when they are in over their head and need help.

I prayed.

And prayed.

Then I prayed some more.

My projection was beginning to weaken when I finally heard a voice call out.

"What do you want child?" It boomed.

"Oh, thank God," I sighed. "Please, I need help!"

"Angels do not interfere in the world of men unless there is a dire need." She sounded unimpressed. "Why should we help you?"

The angel was scolding me, now? My projection was fading and my patience was officially exhausted. "Oh, I don't know. Maybe because a demon and his minions attacked my school, kidnapped me and my boyfriend, and is trying to take over Hell?" I shrieked. "If you do nothing, Drake will harvest the souls of innocents and drain my elemental powers, one of which is Spirit. If I'm not mistaken, that would give him access to Heaven, would it not?"

Silence.

"That's what I thought." I said. "If you wish to maintain the balance, you must intervene."

"Very well, young hunter," the voice continued. "I will grant your request. My name is Zadkiel, angel of freedom, benevolence, and mercy. Return to your body and I shall appear before you."

"Thank you." I smiled and let myself fall from the sky.

My projection slammed into my body violently. When I woke up, Drake was standing over me sneering.

"How was your nap, princess?" Drake laughed.

"What do you want from me?" I asked my hands chilling as I fought to freeze my chains.

"Nothing big, really," he shrugged. "I simply wish for you to use your Spirit link to cross into Hell, travel beyond the fires, and transport a demon to this plane."

"Why on Earth would I do that?" I exclaimed, pausing in my efforts for a second.

"Because you have ice powers, my dear. You are likely the only one who could survive such a journey." Drake smiled down at me. "If you deny me, I will send your sister in your place."

"Ruby," I whispered.

"I will give you some time to think about it," he said, running a claw down my cheek. I winced as blood ran down my face.

Drake licked it from his finger and walked out of the cavern. His laughter faded down the corridor and once again, I was alone. My efforts to freeze my shackles were failing miserably and my strength was fading. I closed my eyes and tried again.

"Open your eyes, child." A face both foreign and familiar stared down at me framed by an enormous set of wings.

"Zadkiel." I sighed and tried to stand up, momentarily forgetting about the chains. The metal bit into my limbs and I hissed in pain.

She tilted her head at my bindings and chanted softly. Her words, though I could not understand them, rang with power. The chains broke apart. I tried to pick one up and it turned to metal dust in my hand.

"Sana," she whispered and gently touched my face. I felt the claw marks heal. In the back of my mind, I felt my sister's presence growing steadily closer.

"We need to find Adam," I told Zadkiel.

"Ahh, yes. Your king." She smiled serenely. "Worry not, child. You'll be very happy."

Confusion flooded me as I climbed to my feet, but we didn't have time for questions.

"This way," I said, leading her toward the chamber where Adam was being held.

Three demons guarded his cell. Zadkiel held out her hand and blasted pure, heavenly light at them. The beasts collapsed into piles of ash filling the corridor with the scent of brimstone and rotting meat.

"That is vile," Zadkiel scrunched her nose. With a sweep of her wings, she cleared out the rank odor and replaced it with the smell of fresh pine. "Much better."

When we looked inside, Adam was gone. All that remained was a crumpled piece of paper with a note scrawled on it.

Your boy toy and I are outside. Come and get us.

Zadkiel looked at me in confusion. "I do not understand. How is he both a boy and a toy? Please explain."

"There's no time for that," I barked. Had the situation not been so serious, I would have laughed at her comment.

I reached out to his love and it drew me upward. They really were outside. Miles of mineshaft and a dozen or so demons later, Zadkiel and I stood at the mouth of the mine, staring out over chaos and flame.

Ruby and Aaron were already here locked in battle with an army of demons. Drake and Adam stood on the sidelines like spectators at a sporting event.

Adam had shifted, his grizzly a towering mass compared to the demon at his side.

"I shall aid your sister and her companion," Zadkiel nodded then pointed to Adam. With a wave of her hand, he sank to the ground groaning as he shifted back into his human form. "Your king needs you."

"Thank you," I spun on my heel and raced over to Adam but he beat me to the punch.

Literally.

My boyfriend's fist sailed toward my face. I would have been knocked off my feet if not for my reflexes. I dodged the blow and ducked behind a tree.

"Adam, it's me!" I shouted at him.

He spun on me, his brows furrowed. Instead of the ethereal blues I had come to love, his eyes were as red as blood.

"What did you do to him?" I shouted at Drake.

"Kill her!" Drake commanded.

"As you wish, Master," Adam said his voice hollow and robotic.

Zadkiel flew past me and tackled Drake, who let out a yelp of surprise. They exchanged blows and fire flew around them. White light clashed with darkness and the battle raged on. Adam slunk toward me with murder in his eyes. He swung at me.

"Adam, please," I begged, ducking away from him. "Honey, it's me, Snowe."

He cocked his head, but didn't stop coming at me.

"Babe, you have to fight it. I need you to come back to me." Tears welled in my eyes. "Please, I can't lose you!"

His eyes narrowed in confusion. He shook his head and lunged at me. My back slammed hard into the tree.

His hands locked around my throat, his face just inches from mine. My vision darkened at the edges and my body began to tingle.

"I…love…you." I choked out, my lips connecting with his.

When he pulled away, the red in his eyes was gone.

"Sn—Snowe?" His voice shook. "What…what happened?"

"Adam!" I crushed him with a hug.

"Snowe, you're okay," Ruby rushed to my side.

Her face was covered in ash and blood. Her eyes were glowing with power. Aaron pulled a very confused Adam into a hug and clapped him on the shoulder.

"Well done, young hunters. You've fought well," Zadkiel said, dropping a barely conscious Drake at out our feet. "I do not believe this demon is deserving of my mercy, but I will leave the choice up to you."

"Sometimes the end is the greatest mercy of all," I glared at Drake.

"No, please." Drake sputtered.

His pleas were swallowed up by a flash of white light. His ashes scattered on the breeze.

"Until we meet again," Zadkiel nodded then took off into the skies.

There was no doubt in my mind that we would.

That night we had a party at our house—after a long-winded lecture from our mom about not calling for help sooner. Ruby and Aaron were inseparable, and Adam never left my side. We talked, laughed, and danced all night long. As the clock struck midnight, I took in my family and realized that I'd had the perfect happily ever after all along.

J.M, Bach

Author of Snowe's Homecoming Demons

J.M Bach believes that home is where the heart is. She's moved six times and lived on both coasts. She now resides colorful Colorado with her parents, two sisters, three dogs, and as many books as she can find space for. She is a third-generation writer; both her mother and her mother's mother are published authors.

From an early age, J.M. believed the best stories had a bit of magic. When she's not writing, you can find her in the barn surrounded by horses. She is also an avid superhero fan and is always waiting for the next big superhero movie to debut.

Bippity, Boppity, Blood

Makayla Desmit

"Salagadoola, mechicka-boola, bippity boppity boo," I howl at the top of my lungs. "Put them together and what have you got?"

"Hold still, Cin," Tyler, the orderly, barks in my face. His meaty hand clamps onto my jaw.

"Bibbidi-bobbidi-boo." My words mash together as Tyler's hand crushes my face. It sounds funny, so I sing louder.

"Stop that dreadful noise, this instant," Doctor Lewis yells as he tightens the restraints on my wrists. "Just swallow the damn pills!"

An orderly named Tyler forces my jaw open with a tongue depressor and crams the antipsychotics into my mouth. He smiles victoriously. I gag until they come back up and spit them into his face. Acid burns my throat and my eyes water uncontrollably. The whole ordeal makes Dr. Lewis cringe.

Totally worth it.

"Better luck next time, your majesty," I laugh, blowing my hair out of my face. The king hates it when I fight.

"I don't get paid enough to put up with this," Tyler groans, wiping the moisture from his face as he storms toward the door. "Sorry Doc, I'm out."

"Of course, you are. I knew I couldn't expect much from you." Dr. Lewis turns back to me. His chubby, pale face is twisted with annoyance. Or sadness maybe? I can never tell with him. "You know, it doesn't have to be like this, Cin."

"Bippity, boppity, boo!" I thrash my head back and forth.

"See you tomorrow, Cin." He sighs then walks out of my cell.

"Farewell, my king." I shout after him.

When the door locks behind him, I scream as loud as I can for as long as I can. My throat is raw and angry and I have a bitter, metallic taste in my mouth. It coats my tongue and rests between the crevices of my teeth.

My voice falters, so I relent. My screams have painted the padded walls of my cell a beautiful shade of crimson. I like it. It's prettier than the stark white I'm so used to. I tug at my restraints, but as always, they don't budge. The leather bindings bite into my skin. It's painful, but only just.

"I'm bored," I sigh and slam my head back onto my pillow.

I start recounting the spots and stains on the ceiling tiles. There's no point. There are fifty-six thousand, two hundred and forty-seven of them. At least there were yesterday. And the day before.

This has been my world for as long as I can remember. I've been here since I was about ten. That's when stepmother had me committed. After a particularly trying day at school, I snapped and shoved a pencil through my teacher's eye. I know what you're thinking, but she deserved it.

Probably.

I think I'm a fun psychological puzzle for the doctors here. Some believe my "condition" is genetic. Others think it started when my mother died. I honestly doubt it.

I don't even remember her. How can someone who *was*, change the person you *are*? My father's death mattered, but mostly because it left me alone with *her*. And because he chose it.

I don't belong here.

Dr. Lewis disagrees.

He's not my favorite person. He's a contradiction and I don't like contradictions. He's handsome but misshapen. He has kind, blue eyes but he is always so arrogant and hostile. He smiles while he writes horrible lies about me on his stupid clipboard. He forces pills past my teeth and makes me choke them down with my own saliva. Correction. He doesn't do it himself. He's much too important for that. Instead, he orders his subjects in the gray scrubs to administer his potions. I laugh at them every time. His poison may muddle my thoughts and confuse my heart, but it will never mask the truth.

He doesn't want me sane.

He doesn't seem to know that pills cannot change my soul. Maybe someday he'll learn. Maybe I will teach him.

My loyalty to the king is conditional.

The prince, however, has my undying devotion. John Lewis Jr. is a beautiful man. His eyes, unlike his father's, hold true kindness. His voice is music and he smells like nature. At least I think that's what nature smells like. I haven't been outside in so long I can't be sure.

The prince will take over this kingdom one day. Someday soon, I hope. Sometimes he takes the king's place behind the big desk. He smiles when he talks to me about my thoughts. He doesn't look down his nose at me and he doesn't have a clipboard full of lies. He even winked at me once and slipped an extra pudding cup onto my lunch tray.

Yes, our love is truly the stuff of fairy tales. Why then, am I not his priority?

The king interferes, I think.

"My son could never be interested in someone like you," the King once told me. "He's not your true love. He's not even your friend, Cin. He's an intern and a medical professional. Nothing more."

I used to have friends, but they lived in the walls of my house. They sang me to sleep and woke me up in the morning. They told me I was beautiful. My stepmother said they didn't exist. She said the voices were just in my head, but I knew better.

I miss those days and sometimes I kind of miss my home. My wicked stepmother took that from me. She's the reason I'm in this dungeon. After my father died, she went back to school to become a therapist. When I was sixteen, she came to work for the king. She says it's because she wants to help me, so I don't end up like my father. I don't believe her.

What she wants is to be important. Or maybe she just needs the money to maintain her weird shoe fetish. Either way, I don't really blame her…not for that, at least. We all want things. Hell, *I* want things.

I will get what I want, even if people get in my way.

And they do.

The Grand Duke, for example. He follows my prince everywhere he goes. He holds the prince's hand when he thinks no one is looking and comforts him when the he gets upset. They eat together in the dining hall each day and steal away in dark halls. He guards Prince John's lips and vaults his kisses. I hate the Grand Duke. He has what I want.

Sorry, *had*.

***

"Wake up, Cin."

It's my new friend. She calls herself Patin. I'm unsure which wall she lives in. I've not had friends come to me since I came to this horrid place. It's been nearly a week since the king was able to force his dreadful potions into my belly. Patin arrived on day two. She was quiet at first, but now she screams at me. She wants to free me, she says. I don't know if I believe her, but it doesn't stop me from listening to her ideas.

"Cin, it's time."

"Go away," I moan, peeling my tired eyes open. It's dark in my cell and the halls are quiet. I was dreaming of my prince and she stole that away. We were dancing. I want to dance with him again.

"Tonight is the night, Cin," Patin persists. "Do as I say and you shall have your dance." How does she always know my thoughts? She has magic, I think.

"Did you take it?" Patin asks. "Did you take the key from the king?"

"Yes, but…" I start.

"No buts, Cin. It must be tonight. It must be *now*." Patin's voice is firm. "The prince is waiting. The royal guards are distracted. If you want your happily-ever-after, you must go now."

"But I'm shackled." I grunt at her.

"You'll find a way, clever girl," Patin laughs. "You always do."

I tug at my restraints. They scrape my skin but I don't stop. My wrists burn and I hear a crack. My right hand is free. I slam it against my bed. Another crack and I can feel my fingers once more. "Go to him, Cin." Patin purrs. "Your prince is waiting."

***

"What happened to your wrist, Cinthia?" Stepmother asks.

It took her nearly ten minutes to notice the scabs and bruises. She was too busy prattling on about her own problems to notice mine. Apparently, someone broke into her house last night. Not much was taken, she says, but it scared her. I struggle to hide my smile.

She's wearing a brand new pair of glittery, pink heels. They wrap around her feet like ballet slippers. I've not seen them before. They must be a replacement for the blue pair that disappeared from her closet last night.

"I'll have the nurse take a look at that when we're done here," she frowns.

I glare at her. She's interrupting my lunch, which annoys me. Meals are the only time my hands are not bound. Besides, I had a long night and I'm starving. She sits on the edge of my bed, blind to my hatred for her.

"Mmm," I groan happily biting into my soggy ham and cheese.

"Cinthia, have you seen Doctor Lewis today? I know you had a session scheduled." The witch looks concerned. "I can't seem to find him and he hasn't called in. I tried John Jr. as well, but…"

"Have you checked hell?" I blurt.

Food flies from my mouth and lands on her neatly pressed, pink shirt. The horrified look on her face tickles me. I erupt in laughter and launch my pudding in her direction.

"That's it!" She wipes the chocolate goop from her face and glares down at me. "I can't deal with you today."

She walks out of my cell, and lets the door slam. I am alone again.

I'm used to her locking me away.

She's been doing it since I was a child. I've only been home a handful of times since then. She locks me up there, too. Home visits mean days spent in the tiny room at the top of the house. She doesn't let me out.

That's when the voices in the walls speak the loudest. Sometimes they tell me I'm beautiful and special. They sing to me and try to lift my spirits. Sometimes they speak only evil. Both are fine with me.

It's been nearly a year since my wicked stepmother took me back to that place. I cried for three days, begging my prince to come rescue me. He didn't hear me. He didn't come. I would rather stay in the dungeon than go back there, now. At least here, I see my prince.

Sorry, *saw*.

I only have a few minutes peace before the door to my cell opens once more. Stepmother walks in with a young woman in a white coat. I've never seen her before.

"This is Dr. Karnes. She will be filling in for Dr. Lewis today," Stepmother says ushering the woman in. She's changed her blouse, but she's still wearing those stupid pink shoes. She turns to leave and shoots me a look. "I will be back shortly. Behave yourself, Cinthia."

"It's nice to meet you, Cinthia." Doctor Karnes shakes my hand, her eyes narrowing on the wounds at my wrist. "You can call me Angie, by the way."

Angie must be new. There is still hope in her eyes and her smile is genuine. She sits on the chair by my bed and sets down her bag. She apologizes for the king's absence and assures me he will return soon.

She's wrong, but I don't tell her that. Not yet.

She starts telling me about herself. I don't listen because I don't care. After today, I doubt I'll ever see her again. I stare at her blankly, replaying my magical night in my head. It's so fresh in my mind I swear I can still smell the coppery bite of it and feel the warmth on my hands. Angie coughs and it draws me back.

She's still talking.

I meet her gaze and smirk. Angie has a lazy eye. It sneaks away from her every few seconds. She thinks I'm listening. That's good. It buys me time.

I study the outline of her face until I have it memorized. I count every freckle, every blemish. There are fine hairs that poke out from her rounded nose. I note how the wrinkles fold over her face and how she tries to cover them with chalky makeup. It's a shade lighter than her skin and makes her look like a vampire.

Her bright eyeshadow competes for attention with her rosy cheeks. Her brash red lipstick has made its way to the edges of her front teeth. I should tell her, but I won't. I don't know if I like her yet.

"Anyways, enough about me," Angie laughs nervously. "We're here to talk about you."

She reaches into her bag and pulls out a clipboard. I immediately decide I hate her. The metal clasp holds a thick stack of neatly typed pages. She fumbles to find the right one.

"I guess I'll need a pen," she mutters to herself, then digs blindly through her bag. "Ouch!"

She pulls her hand back and hisses. Blood drips from the tip of her thumb and onto the floor. It's beautiful. My favorite color. I stare at the droplets on the faded vinyl floor and smile. She pulls a tissue from her pocket and scrambles to stop the bleeding.

"Sorry about that, sweetie." Angie smiles apologetically as she wraps the tissue around her wound. "Okay, so how are you feeling?"

I can't tear my eyes from the blood near her shoe. I'm transported back in time for a moment and my heart sings with joy.

"Cinthia?" Angie pats my leg gently.

My head jerks up and I lock eyes with her.

She shifts uncomfortably in her chair, dodging my stare. Then she moves her bag so it covers the red droplets. She tries to be subtle about it, but fails. "How about you tell me a little about yourself."

"Would you like to hear about the dream I had last night?" I smile sweetly at her.

"Sure," she says. Her eyes shine with renewed enthusiasm. She thinks I'm opening up to her. "Dreams are the window to the soul. That sounds like a great way to get to know you, Cinthia."

"Please, call me Cin," I say politely. She wants to believe I trust her so I let her pretend.

"Of course," she beams proudly. "Go ahead, Cin. The floor is all yours."

***

Leaves rustle across the ground as I make my way toward the castle. A cool breeze blows ruffling the edge of my blue satin gown. It matches the bejeweled mask I wear. Tonight, I really feel beautiful. I feel like a princess. Light glints off the iridescent slippers on my feet. I smile down at them. They fit as though they were made just for me. Besides, that cruel woman would never miss them.

When I reach the castle entrance, I am greeted by the sounds of music and laughter. Colorful lights flood the courtyard and fancy carriages litter the lane. Men in sleek suits and women in elaborate dresses and masks make their way toward the great hall. The kingdom is already celebrating our happily ever after, it seems.

My fairy godmother was right. Tonight is my night.

I knock on the door and take a deep breath. A moment passes before a small man answers the door. He carries a silver tray with long-stemmed glasses. He hands me one, and ushers me in. I sip on the bubbly drink and make my way through the room searching for my love.

He's not in the foyer or the sitting room. He's not in the kitchen, either. I circle back to the front of the hall and leave my empty glass on a small table. So far, I don't recognize any of the faces here except one.

The king.

He stands at the top of a grand staircase, staring down at his subjects. I meet his gaze, but he doesn't recognize me. I head up the stairs and walk right past him, or at least I attempt to. I'm not accustomed to such fine footwear. I stumble a bit as I move around him. He catches my elbow and smiles.

"Easy there," the king tilts his head. "Have we met?"

"No, sir," I smile sweetly at him. "I've never been here before."

"Well, you are quite lovely, young lady," the king says. "What is your name?"

"Duchess," I say. It's not a total lie.

"It's nice to meet you, Duchess," he shakes my hand. "My name is John and this is my home. It's no palace, but my family and I are quite happy here. Say, have you seen my art gallery?"

"No, sir," I say. "I'd like to, though."

"This way." He takes my hand and my stomach lurches. He ushers me through a door at the end of the hall and we step inside. The walls are lined with elaborate paintings and sketches. I hum my favorite tune as I marvel at the colors. "What's that song you were singing just now?"

"These are beautiful." I say, swooning a bit for good measure. I almost let him in on my secret. I must be more careful. I distract him with flattery. "You have exquisite taste, sir."

"Thank you, dear. You know, I should introduce you to my son."
The king has his back turned, his gaze focused on a watercolor hanging
above his mantle. "You'd be great together."

"We will be," I tell him, sliding one of my shoes off as I press on at
his back. "And you will not stand in our way."

I leave the gallery in search of the man with the silver tray. The
sounds of laughter fill the room. It's different from the laughter I'm used
to. It's happy without the slightest hint of mania. I don't like it. I grab
another glass of golden liquid and down it in one gulp. My face feels hot to
the touch.

I walk on in search of my prince. Instead, I find the Grand Duke.
He sits in a corner, his arms crossed. He chews his bottom lip and stares
across the room. I follow his sight line and finally find my prince.

He is surrounded by women, both fair and foul. They dote on him
and giggle sweetly. One of them kisses his cheek and my hands start to
shake. The Grand Duke stands suddenly and storms from the room. The
prince is so distracted by the attention, he doesn't notice.

Perfect.

After I've located and dispatched the Grand Duke, I return. I slip
through the crowd and walk straight up to my prince. He looks at me in
confusion but smiles politely. I lean in and whisper to him. I tell him the
Grand Duke is searching for him. That he was upset. He is waiting in the
gallery to talk. The prince looks worried and follows close at my heel.

When we reach the room with all the beautiful things, the Grand
Duke is not there. He never made it that far, but my prince doesn't know
that. He's convinced the Duke has left him forever. He blames his father.
He needn't worry about the king, though. He is sleeping in the dark corner.
He will never interfere again.

I comfort the prince. I promise to fix his wounded heart and I swear to love him more than anybody. I tell him I will dance with him forever and never let him go. He looks at me strangely then. The women must have been witches. They still have him under their spell.

He loves me. I know he does, but he's blinded.

So, I make him see.

We spend the rest of the night together. The prince never leaves my arms. I hold him and we dance alone in the dark. His skin is cool to the touch, but I know his heart is warming. I kiss his lips and stroke his hair. My hands are sticky and I've lost a slipper, but I don't care. I finally have what I want. My love sleeps next to me, his head dangling from his neck onto my shoulder.

My heart is full.

As with any fairy tale, our perfect night must end. The clock strikes midnight, light floods the room, and a woman screams. I promise my prince I will return for him once I rid the kingdom of the dark sorceress. Then, we will be together forever.

His silence tells me he knows that I speak the truth.

I escape through the window and climb down the rose trellis, dropping to the courtyard below. I run fast and scream out for a bright orange carriage as it speeds by. The man driving mutters under his breath but avoids eye contact. He must know I'll soon be royalty. He takes me back to my own kingdom, where I sneak past the guards and into my tower. Once I'm there, I hide my beautiful things and plot my revenge on the evil woman who locked me away.

Silence fills the room. Angie's face has lost all color, save for what she painted onto it.

"So, what'd you think?" I ask picking at my teeth.

She doesn't speak. She stands, grabs her things, and walks out of my cell. Seconds later, the guards rush in. They wrestle me into my jacket and I'm hugging my heart. I pretend my prince has his arms around me and it makes me smile. I feel a sharp poke in my thigh. My body tingles and night falls around me.

***

"What have you done, Cinthia," my stepmother asks as my eyes slowly drift open.

I try to lift my arms but they don't fully cooperate. They flop back down to my side, limp. I turn to my hip and wrestle my hand under my pillow. I smile at what I find there. They hadn't thought to go through my room, I guess.

"Now," Patin whispers.

"Go away," I groan. I'm too tired to deal with my fairy godmother right now.

"Cinthia, I'm not going anywhere," my stepmother says.

"Do it now," Patin urges. "It's time to finish this."

I swat in the general direction of her voice. I end up smacking myself. I laugh at the ridiculousness of it and try again. I'm able to lift my arm a bit higher this time.

"You've been given a mild paralytic," she says, her mouth set in a grim line.

I don't know what that means and I don't care. My fingers are tingling and I kind of like it. My stepmother sits on the corner of my bed, staring down her nose at me. She paints her face with fake concern.

"Cinthia, talk to me." Her voice is curt.

"About what, exactly?" I roll my eyes.

My arms are tingling now.

"Tell me what really happened," she says. "I talked to Angie, Cinthia. She told me about your dream."

"So?" I glare at her.

"I know all about your little obsession, Cinthia. It's all right here in your file," she says slapping a thick folder onto my bed. "And after what happened to Dr. Lewis and his son last night...Cin, the police are on their way. They'll want to speak with you."

"Your prince is waiting, Cin," Patin's voice booms at me, drowning out my stepmother's. "If you do not go to him now, he will think you've broken your promise. He will think you've forsaken him."

"Please, honey." My stepmother inches closer and gently touches my face. "I just want to help you. That's all I've ever wanted."

I never asked for her help. I don't need it. She's the crazy one, not me. She isn't helping me, she's the reason I'm locked away in this dungeon. Her and the king. Adrenaline burns away the last traces of numbness in my body.

"It wasn't a dream," I blurt and swat her hand away. I open my mouth and the truth falls out. "I had to get rid of the king."

"W--what?" My stepmother looks confused. Terrified.

She should be.

"He had to die, stepmother," I smile at her.

"Why?" She's frozen, unable to move.

"He was standing between me and my one true love," I say, my hand clutching the bloody, glass slipper that's hidden beneath my pillow. "And so are you."

Makayla Desmit

Author of Bippity, Boppity, Blood

Makayla Desmit is the author of the chilling piece, "Bippity, Boppity, Blood." The short story is a part of the anthology, "Twisted Fairy Tales," a book where she worked exclusively with a team of very talented teen writers. Makayla is addicted to shopping, social media, and binge watching every show on Netflix.

After high school, Makayla plans to go to college, then law school, and eventually pursue a career as a criminal investigator. Writing has always come easy to Makayla. Although her future career may not be focused on the construction of words on paper, this is not the last adventure she will create. This twisted tale is just the beginning.

Cheap Thrills

Grey Nebel

The hotel room was austere and adorned generously with the crunching corpses of roaches. The carpet was a faded brown with an assortment of unidentifiable, multicolored stains. Some were dried solid, others more recent. There was one bed. Gretel wasn't thrilled about sharing it with her brother Hansel, but she supposed that it was better than sharing with bed bugs. The shower had mold growing in the corners, but the toilet and sink seemed to be working fine.

The place was less than ideal, but it was all they could afford with the little bit of cash Gretel and her brother had pilfered from their mother's purse. And it was far better than being *out there*... especially at night.

The hotel was in the worst part of town, nestled between an adult shop, a discount liquor outlet, and a hookah bar. The hotel lobby reeked of marijuana and must, which seemed to be unnoticed by the other people in the hotel, who strutted about shamelessly in less clothing than Gretel felt comfortable wearing to bed. Armed city guards patrolled the walkways on every floor, but were greatly concentrated at ground level.

Their heavy footfalls echoed in Gretel's ears as she tried to force herself to sleep.

It was a pointless endeavor. Women screamed and babies cried. Sirens blared up and down the alleyways. The unmistakable sounds of their neighbors' alcohol-fueled quarreling burst into the kids' room through the paper-thin, gray walls.

Gretel's nerves had been on edge since they'd checked in. The man at the front desk had taken their money and asked no questions. Actually, he hadn't even looked up, just tossed them a key, grunted out their room number and pointed which way they should go. Faded graffiti covered nearly every vertical surface outside the rooms. Most of them had at least one broken window.

When they finally found their quarters, Gretel and her brother had thought themselves lucky when their room's windows were among the few still intact. That glimmer of hope was quickly squelched when they discovered the broken door handle and gaping hole where the key mechanism should be.

"More streusel, please," muttered Hansel in his sleep, flopping over onto his side. Those three garbled words had been the first break in his snoring in hours.

"How are you even sleeping right now?" Gretel smacked him with her pillow.

He snorted but otherwise didn't stir. She smiled at him, despite her frustration. Hansel may not be the smartest person she knew, but he always had her back. Even when she was being an idiot.

"Forget it," Gretel sat up, her legs dangling off the bed.

A fresh crimson stain sat right below her feet. Once again, Gretel was thankful she'd decided to wear her Converse to bed. She stepped cautiously around the spot and made her way toward the windows. She double-checked the locks (at least those still worked), then made her way over to the door. The chair she had wedged against it was still firmly in place. Just to be safe, she crammed another one in next to it and pressed her tired back against the wall.

It was going to be a long night.

Bang…bang!

A fist pounded heavily against the hollow door. Gretel held her breath and ducked behind the chair barricades. There hadn't been a moment's peace since they had arrived. A man dressed as police officer had come first, but he had been high as a kite and his pants were nowhere to be seen. Later a woman had come demanding that her two-timing boyfriend come out and face her. She threatened Gretel through the lock hole, convinced that her man had been shacking up there. If the guards hadn't happened by a few minutes into her tirade, the woman would probably still be out there.

Bang…bang-bang!

"*Hansel.*" Gretel hissed at her brother. "Hansel, wake up!"

He was sleeping so soundly he hadn't heard the ruckus outside the door, so it was no surprise he didn't hear Gretel's plea for help. Hansel was either oblivious to the troubles around him or simply too tired to care.

Bang…bang

Bang-bang-bang

"Housekeeping!" There was a hoot of laughter from outside.

"Yeah right," Gretel muttered, staring down at the pile of dead bugs near her left foot.

Bang.

Gretel moved to press her back against one of the chairs holding the other in place with her arm. She wondered where all the guards had gone. It may have been after two in the morning, but this place was more dangerous at night. After being cast out, the dregs of society had found a haven for themselves in the darkness. They'd claimed this territory as their own and Gretel had landed herself and her brother right in the middle of it.

In her short sixteen years on this planet, Gretel had never been away from her family for more than a few hours. Her only time away from home was spent at school or working her part-time job at a shop less than a block from where she lived. She desperately wanted adventure. She had fought with her mother, begging for more freedom. She was tired of being so sheltered. College was just two short years away, after all. How would she learn to fly if she was never allowed to leave the nest?

When a couple friends invited Gretel on a weekend trip to the city, she'd jumped at the opportunity and asked her mother if she could go. Gretel's mother hadn't even considered her request. She insisted her daughter wasn't ready for that kind of responsibility. The denial had struck a nerve. Gretel felt smothered and desperate to escape.

Despite her inexperience, Gretel somehow thought herself capable of surviving in the real world. It hadn't been her intention to bring Hansel along, but as soon as he'd figured out his sister's plan, the boy's bag was packed. He refused to let his sister go it alone.

It had been less than twenty-four hours since they'd run away and Gretel was already missing the comfort of her own bed and the rich smells of her mother's cooking.

After some time, the banging finally ceased, and the sudden silence brought Gretel back to reality. Heavy footsteps retreated down the walkway taking the garbled laughter with them. Gretel sank to a crouch and finally allowed herself to breathe once more.

Hansel hadn't moved an inch since the noisy ordeal had begun. He snored happily, drooling on his pillow. Exhausted, Gretel stumbled over to the small table by the window and sank into the last remaining chair. It wobbled but didn't collapse.

Water dripped in the bathroom. At some point, the neighbors' seemingly endless bickering had gone silent. Gretel was disturbed by the sudden lack of sound. Now would be the perfect time to rest, but no such luck. Thanks to the adrenaline coursing through her veins, she felt more awake than ever.

She stood up slowly, making a noise of distaste, and cracked her back as she walked toward the tiny kitchenette in the corner. She'd treat herself to a cup of bland hotel coffee as a reward for surviving this latest trial.

She loaded the filter, added the water, and stared blankly as the warm brown liquid trickled into the cracked glass pot. Once it was done, Gretel poured some into a paper cup and sank back into the wobbly chair. She was just beginning to nod off when…

Bang-Bang.

"Sweet Jesus." Gretel jumped, spilling half the lukewarm coffee onto her leg.

Gretel set her coffee down on the table and tore back the curtain in a huff, ready to berate whomever had caused the disturbance. She was tired and cold and she'd had enough.

A woman stood there, her face pressed close to the glass. Her dark hair shone an eerie blue beneath the light of the streetlamps. Her smile was cyanide-laced sugar.

Her lips were cracked and dry and her teeth chattered together. Her long, slender legs were barely covered by her short skirt and thigh-high boots. Her top was not so much a shirt as it was a pink metallic bra. Gretel suddenly felt awkward in her sweatpants and baggie hoodie.

"Let me in." The woman tapped on the glass. "It's cold out."

"Yeah, it's cold," Gretel scowled. "It's winter."

"Funny girl." The woman laughed, but the sound was sharp, dishonest. She crossed her arms over her chest and shivered, her scantily clad body shaking so hard her earrings jingled. She kept looking over her shoulder. "Let me in."

"Go away." Gretel raised her middle finger and shook her head.

The woman narrowed her eyes for a moment, and then tilted her head back as her mouth opened into a wide grin. Twisted laughter shattered the silence of the night.

Gretel sighed. This was not the first time she'd wished to be more intimidating. The woman was not the least bit deterred by Gretel's refusal and showed no signs of leaving. Anger swelled in the girl's chest as the woman continued to laugh at her. She was sick of adults not taking her seriously.

"Joke's on you lady," Gretel flipped her off again. She let the curtains fall and turned her back on the stranger outside her window. "Have a nice night."

"I'm sorry," the woman whined, her voice cracking as she tapped the glass. "I shouldn't have laughed at you. I'm just…I'm so tired and cold, I can't think straight. Please."

Gretel walked away from the window, wringing her hands. What if she had misjudged the woman outside? What if the dark-haired stranger was simply in the wrong place at the wrong time? Gretel could certainly understand that after the night she'd had.

Finally, her guilty conscience got the better of her. She stormed to the window and tore back the curtains. Sure enough, the woman was still there. Still cold. Still shivering. She pressed her palms together, begging.

"Please, just let me in for five minutes so I can warm up a bit." She looked over her shoulder once more. "I swear, I'll be a *perfect* angel."

"Five minutes," Gretel narrowed her eyes. "Then you're gone."

"Promise," the woman smiled, crossing her heart with a sharp blood-red fingernail. "You won't even know I'm here."

Gretel sighed and squared her shoulders as she walked over to the door. She slid the chairs aside and opened the door just far enough for the strange woman to squeeze through before putting them firmly back in place.

The smell of cigarettes and bad decisions swirled in a cloud around the dark-haired woman as she walked into the room. It did nothing to improve the already pungent stench of the room. Gretel coughed and covered her nose, then double-checked that her furniture barricades were firmly in place.

One shady person crossing their threshold was more than enough for the night.

"Thank you, darling," the woman purred and a chill crept up Gretel's spine.

Gretel resisted the urge to gag, immediately erasing the word darling from her vocabulary.

"I'm so cold," the woman pouted, staring at the blanket that had fallen to the floor near the end of the bed.

"Again… it's winter." Gretel rolled her eyes. She walked over to the bed, picked up the blanket and tossed it into the woman's hands. The hotel would likely have to burn the thing later.

"Such a sense of humor," the woman smiled and cocked her head to the side, circling Gretel like a cat slinking around its prey. Gretel's stomach knotted and she took a step back. "What's your name, girl?"

"Gretel." The word fell from her mouth as if on instinct. Gretel chided herself. Why had she given away her name so easily? It didn't make sense. She'd been so guarded and the creepy woman made her feel odd in the nastiest of ways.

"Miyako. Glad to meet you." The woman grabbed Gretel's hand before she could protest and shook it vigorously. Her voice had a raspy edge to it, presumably from the same vice that created the musty smell on her clothes. She spun in a circle, taking in the room. "Nice place you got here, kid."

"Yeah, it's a real palace." Gretel snapped, wiping her hand off on her pants. "Five minutes and counting."

"Of course," Miyako said as she kicked her shoes off and plopped down on the end of the bed. Hansel groaned, but didn't wake. Of course.

"Oh, who's this handsome boy?" Miyako smirked at her brother and winked at Gretel. "He the reason you are here?"

"Gross," Gretel wrinkled her nose. "That's my brother and we are here because…we just are."

"Don't you have a home?" The woman yawned.

"Don't you?" Gretel crossed her arms.

"I had a room here, but I got kicked out by a gang," she pouted. "I really need somewhere to stay."

"Uh-huh," Gretel avoided Miyako's gaze as well as her hint.

"Gretel," the woman stood and stepped toward her. "Why aren't you with your mother?"

"We ran away," Gretel's voice cracked.

"Oh honey," Miyako frowned. "You need your mother. Everyone needs a mother."

"No." Gretel flinched. "I don't."

"I wish I still had a mother." Miyako sighed and sank back onto the bed, her head resting on Hansel's legs.

Gretel had no idea what to say to that, so she said nothing. Her eyes began to feel heavy, and she wavered on her feet.

"Poor girl. You should rest," Miyako said sweetly, her words intoxicating. She got up, pulled Gretel toward the bed, and gestured for her to lay down. "How about I stay here, just for tonight. If anyone tries to get in, they'll have to go through me."

"I…" Gretel yawned.

"I will take care of you." Miyaho squared her shoulders. "I promise."

Gretel nodded slowly. She was just so tired. She didn't know why, but the raw emotion in Miyako's voice had felt honest to her. Miyako covered Gretel with the blanket and smiled down at her.

"Take the couch," Gretel said.

The directive was met with compliance. Miyako nodded and moved her willowed body to the threadbare couch. The woman's breathing fell steady and even shortly after she closed her bloodshot eyes.

Gretel breathed a sigh of relief.

Sleep had softened Miyako's painted face. She looked like a woman fully capable of scattering the stars in the sky. There was no evidence of hardship on her relaxed features. Gretel couldn't help but smile. Miyako looked at peace.

There was no danger. Hansel and Gretel were safe.

***

Gretel awoke to the smell of buttery pancakes. The sound of bacon sizzling on a hotplate beckoned her to rise. Pancakes had been her favorite as a child but when she'd hit her teen years, Gretel had lost her appreciation for a hot, homestyle breakfast. Most days she drank coffee and ate a bag of chips for breakfast.

Moves still lethargic, she blinked the sleep out of her eyes. She put on her glasses and reached out to her brother, but he was no longer by her side. The bed was cold where he had been. Panic shot through her like a bullet, the slowness from just moments prior a distant memory.

Gretel shot out of the bed and rushed toward the smell of syrup. Miyako stood by the cooktop, still in her skimpy outfit from the night before. Her hair was pulled up into a bun.

"Miyako, where is my—?"

Hansel stepped out of the bathroom, clutching a paper cup.

"Hansel!" Gretel rushed toward him.

He didn't respond. He stared at her blankly and blinked. His knuckles white and his eyes red. After a moment, he turned and walked over to the table.

Odd.

"Good morning, darling," Miyako smiled as she danced around the tiny kitchen area. "Breakfast is ready. Your brother is already on seconds."

She'd placed a small stack of pancakes on a plate in the middle of the table. Hansel stood above it, picking at a pancake saturated with syrup. He was smiling, but he had a distant look in his eyes. Something wasn't right.

"I said good morning, Gretel," Miyako pressed. "Where are your manners?"

"Umm, good morning?" Gretel narrowed her eyes.

"Wonderful," Miyako smiled. "Would you like some coffee and pancakes?"

Gretel's stomach growled as hunger overtook her good sense. "God, yes."

Gretel hadn't eaten since they'd left home and it did smell amazing. She took one of the pancakes and bit into it hesitantly. It was a little bitter so she dipped it into the syrup. Memories of Sunday morning breakfast with her family flooded her mind as the sweetness washed over her tongue. She couldn't fight her smile.

"My mom always made the best pancakes," Gretel muttered.

A cup of coffee slammed onto the table in front of her.

"I bet mine are better." Miyako's smile was a thin veneer over something more malicious. "Do you like them?"

"Yes," Gretel spat on reflex, ducking Miyako's glare.

"Drink your coffee," the woman grunted, not acknowledging Gretel's response.

Gretel did as she was told and emptied her cup. The coffee was too strong for her palate but she didn't want to make Miyako any angrier than she had. The woman's mood swing set Gretel's nerves on edge.

"Thirsty," Hansel coughed and took a sip of his water.

Hansel was tense but his eyes were glazed over. He barely blinked and kept scratching at his neck. Gretel put her pancake down and narrowed her eyes at Miyako. Miyako laughed.

"What's going on here?" Gretel pounded her fist on the table.

"I don't know what you mean," the woman shrugged. "We're just having a nice family breakfast."

"Family?" Gretel's eyes went wide.

"Eat up, young lady," Miyako pointed to Gretel's plate. "People say my cooking is just...heavenly. Isn't that right, darling?"

She ran her finger along Hansel's jaw. He nodded and smiled up at her adoringly. Gretel felt sick. She stood up too fast and yet, somehow too slow. The room spun around her as she stumbled to the bathroom. Her stomach churned and she began to sweat. Hansel was cooing.

Gretel had barely made it to the restroom before her breakfast came back up. She coughed and gagged her throat burning as acid rushed up into her mouth. Had her anxiety gotten the better of her again or was it the food? She hadn't felt sick at all before she'd eaten, but the pancake had tasted fine and Gretel didn't have any food allergies.

Gretel was hesitant to leave the restroom. She took extra time, cleaned herself up, and even wiped down the counter and cleaned the mirror. She was embarrassed, but more so confused.

A poor man's symphony echoed through the room as things crashed to the floor just beyond the door. The sound drew her out from the relative safety of the bathroom.

"It's fine. Everything is fine," Gretel chided herself as she slowly turned the knob. "Stop assuming the worst."

But the worst is exactly what she saw.

Hansel was slumped on the floor. His body was convulsing and tears streamed down his face. Miyako crouched over him, muttering in his ear. Hansel shook his head, his eyes wide. The woman rolled her eyes and leaned back in to whisper to him once more. Sobs wracked his body as his limbs twisted.

Hansel never cried.

Gretel stepped forward and the room swayed around her. The world brightened and sound amplified. Her head was pounding but she felt energized, more alive. The sky was calling her. She wanted nothing more than to fly.

Focus.

Hansel's body stilled and a smile spread across his face. Miyako smiled and patted his head gently. "There you go, spread your wings."

"Stop!" Gretel stumbled toward him. "Hansel, we have to go."

"Why?" Hansel's eyes stayed locked on the dark-haired woman at his side.

"Yes, why?" She glared up at Gretel.

"Miyako is keeping us safe," Hansel frowned. "I want to stay."

"No, Hansel," Gretel grunted, grabbing her brother's arm. "Come on. We're going home."

"You can't," breathed Miyako.

"What did you do to us?" Gretel spat at her.

"I made you better," she smiled. "Dust makes everything better."

"Dust?" Gretel hesitated. "What does that mean?"

"We're angels now," Miyako laughed.

"Angels," Hansel murmured. "I like that."

Dust.

Angels?

"Oh, God." Gretel rubbed her head trying desperately to remember what her health teacher had taught her in their unit on drugs last year. "Hansel, how many pancakes did you eat?"

Her brother shrugged, toying with the ends of the older woman's dark hair. "So pretty."

"How many, Hansel?" Gretel grabbed his collar and shook him.

"I…umm…" Hansel frowned. "Like, six."

"Get out," Gretel glared at the woman.

"No thanks." Miyako shrugged.

"Wait, what?" Hansel blinked rapidly, his pupils dilated as he clenched and unclenched his fists. He tried to stand, but his legs gave out. He slid down the wall, stifling a sob. "What is happening?"

"Get. Out." Gretel said again.

"Make me," Miyako glared at the girl and laughed.

Gretel tugged on her arm. "I let you in to save you but I'll drag you out to save *him*."

"No," Miyako yanked her arm away. "You won't."

Crack.

A flash of pain, an angry red and dismal black flashed across Gretel's vision. When she opened her eyes, Miyako was standing between her and Hansel, her hands balled into fists.

"No," she said, her chest rising and falling rapidly. "You can't leave. I'm your mother now."

"Miyako plea-" Gretel was cut off by a burst of pain in her stomach. She winced, no longer able to breathe. The floor rushed up to meet her and hit her head hard.

"Get off her," Hansel shouted. "Gret…Ugh."

There was pressure on Gretel's back. Oh, *God,* the pain.

"Apologize," the beast of a woman growled down at the girl. "Now, Gretel."

"No." Gretel closed her eyes, a last-dash attempt to fight off the onslaught of pain.

"Apologize!"

Her arms were twisted and pinned behind her back.

The pain was blinding. Gretel was sorry. She was so, so sorry. She was desperate to end the pain, but more desperate to save her brother.

If it was a fight Miyako wanted, a fight she would get.

Gretel threw her head back and bashed the woman in the face. It stunned Miyako for just a moment, but it was long enough for Gretel to work away from the force pinning her down. Before the beast could retaliate, Gretel summoned the last of her strength and thrust her fist forward into Miyako's face. Gretel heard a crack and blood rushed from the woman's nose but she barely flinched.

"Best thing about dust? No pain." Miyako cracked her neck with a bloody smirk. "Now, apologize."

"No." Gretel slowly backed toward the kitchen.

Miyako rushed at Gretel at leapt through the air with a snarl. Gretel ducked out of the way at the last second. Miyako lost her footing and fell forward into the table. The woman's head crashed into the corner of it with sickening thud. She slumped to the floor with a grunt, the plate of tainted pancakes toppling off onto her limp form. She was still lying in a heap on the floor crying out for her "children" when Gretel finally managed to drag Hansel from the dank hotel room.

***

"Wake up, Hansel," Gretel elbowed her brother. "We're home."

A taxi slowed to a stop in front of a plain white house in a safe little suburb. The sun was rising on the horizon and the birds were chirping. Gretel paid the driver with the last of the money they'd stole from their mother's bag. She and her brother, still in a drug-induced stupor, stumbled up the front walk and into the house.

"Mama?" Gretel said as she opened the door. "We're home."

"Oh dear God!" Her mother raced from the kitchen with tears streaking down her cheeks. Hard worry lines had etched themselves across the woman's face and it looked as though she hadn't slept in days. She dove at her children and wrapped her arms around their necks squeezing tightly. "It's you, it's really you. My little angels have come home."

"Home," Gretel murmured, her eyes welling with tears.

Her shoulders shook as she sobbed into her mother's arms. Despite her tears, an uncontrollable smile broke over her face. Miyako may have been completely insane, but she'd been right about one thing.

Gretel's mother might be overprotective, but she *needed* her. Gretel hadn't realized how much she loved her mom until she thought she might never see her again. Gretel sighed and sank deeper into her mom's embrace.

"What happened to you two? I've been beside myself with worry. Are you okay?" Gretel's mother asked she let her children toward the kitchen.

"We will be," Gretel sighed, clasping her mother's hand and dragging her brother along.

"Are you hungry? When was the last time you ate?" Her mother's worried hands searched for injuries she'd never be able to see.

"Hungry," Hansel finally chimed in, stumbling at his sister's side. He was still completely out of it. "Food."

"I can make you a streusel." Their mother's eyes lit up, "or perhaps some nice fluffy pancakes?"

"Mama?" Gretel stopped in her tracks.

"Yes, angel," her mother replied, her eyes hopeful.

"There is one you can do for me," Gretel said.

"Of course," her mother said, squaring her shoulders. "Name it. Anything."

"Stop calling me angel," Gretel smirked. "And please, for the love of all things holy, *do not* make pancakes. Ever again."

Grey Nebel

Author of Cheap Thrills

Grey Nebel, a young Atlanta-based writer, finds herself entirely guided by her right brain. As an actress, technical theatre worker, writer, and all-around nerd, she has enjoyed stories since she learned how to walk (hint: a long time).

She suffers from a severe tea addiction, prides herself on her knowledge of world history, and learns languages to fill her free time (what better way to improve on English than write a story, right?). Led by spontaneity, she hopes to make her dreams come true. Be it writing or climbing a mountain, Grey has hopes to do it all. After all, she only gets to live once!

The Archer

Alexander Hartman

"Breakfast is ready!" Peter's mom yelled from the bottom of the steps.

"Coming, mom," he shouted back, glancing at the clock on his desk.

It was nearly seven-thirty. His father would be home from the factory any minute. Peter needed to hurry if he had any hope of eating in peace. The smell of fried egg sandwiches and crispy bacon was calling out to him. He scooped up his backpack, tossed it over his shoulder, and took the creaky old stairs two at a time.

"Happy last day of school, honey," Peter's mom said as she flipped an egg in the skillet. "Orange juice is on the counter. Help yourself, but save some for your dad."

"Uh-huh," Peter said rolling his eyes as he dropped his backpack onto the kitchen floor and swiped a piece of toast from the plate on the table.

Peter had never been particularly close to his father, but their relationship had become more strained in the last couple of years. He couldn't really pinpoint what had caused the riff between them, but it was undeniable. It was as if Peter's existence was an inconvenience.

He used to think that his father's animosity was just a reaction to stress. After all, the man spent more hours at work than he did at home. But there seemed to be more to it than that. The man was angry…all the time and Peter had no idea why.

"I dropped your new bow off at Bob's yesterday. He said he'd have it all cleaned up and ready to go by the time you are out of school," Julianna said. "If you want to head to the range today, you can stop by and grab it on your way. Just make sure you are home in time for dinner. I'm making pork chops."

"Gotcha," Peter muttered around a mouthful of warm honey-wheat.

"Manners, Peter," she laughed, smacking his shoulder playfully with the spatula. "I swear you were born in a cave."

Julianna Sentry was the most loving, patient woman Peter had ever known. She had been a stay-at-home mom for as long as he could remember and she excelled at it. When Peter was a child, she would take him on adventures. They'd hike through the woods together while Julianna wove tales of magic and enchantment. They'd swim in Crystal Falls Lake and climb to the top of the tallest trees. She never missed a game, a doctor's appointment, or a single birthday party. That was more than he could say about his dad.

"Sorry, Mom," Peter smirked, lowering himself onto a chair.

"Eat up," she said dropping fresh bacon next to the egg sandwich on Peter's plate.

"Yes, ma'am," Peter said shoving an entire piece into his mouth.

Every year on the last day of school, Peter's mom would make him his favorite breakfast. It was meant to be a celebration of his academic accomplishments as well as the arrival of summer.

Today's meal was nothing shy of heaven. The bacon was cooked to perfection and his sandwich was warm and gooey with melted cheese oozing out the sides. He ate greedily, relishing every bite.

The front door opened and Peter's stomach lurched. His father was home and judging by his angry muttering, he'd likely had yet another epically crappy day on the job. Peter knew very little about his dad's job, but apparently, it sucked.

"Morning, Edward," Julianna smiled at her husband as she set a plate down on the table for him.

"Hi honey," Peter's dad half-smiled and kissed her on the cheek as he dropped his keys on the counter. He looked exhausted. For a moment, Peter almost felt sorry for him.

That moment passed quickly.

"What's all this?" Edward grumbled, staring down at the spread on the table.

"Last day of school." Peter stared blankly at his plate.

"And?" His father glared at him. "Somehow that warrants an entire paycheck's worth of food?"

"It's tradition," Julianna said, patting Edward's shoulder as she walked out of the kitchen. "Eat up."

"Expensive tradition," he huffed shaking his head at Peter. "Your mother coddles you."

"Whatever," Peter muttered. He wrapped his sandwich in his napkin, shouldered his backpack, and left the room.

"Have a good day, Peter," his mom yelled from down the hall. "See you after school!"

"Bye, mom," he said, slamming the front door behind him.

With any luck his father would be back at work by the time he got home. Summer was just getting started and Peter was determined to have a good day. He shook the negativity from his thoughts and began the mile long trek to school.

The smell of freshly cut grass filled Peter's nose and the sun warmed his skin. He smiled to himself and breathed in the cool spring air as he finished the last of his breakfast. Peter loved this time of year. It was as if the whole neighborhood was waking from a long hibernation. Once summer was here, the whole subdivision would be abuzz with the sounds of children at play and neighbors sharing a cool drink on a warm day.

"Hello there, Peter!" Dr. Stevens' head popped up from behind a massive rose bush. He had been Peter's pediatrician when he was little. His mom had loved that the man lived at the end of their block. She'd was so disappointed when Dr. Stevens retired last year, even though her son was much too old to be his patient anymore.

"Hey, Doc." Peter waved back. "Roses are coming along nicely, sir."

"I'm going to win the blue ribbon for this year's garden walk, for sure." Dr. Stevens winked and put his gloved hands on his hips. "I have it on good authority that Mrs. Tillman's prize-winning lilies are not looking so good this year."

"Good luck," Peter laughed and turned the corner.

Despite the early hour, landscapers and pool cleaners all over the area were hard at work sprucing and beautifying. A rainbow tapestry of blooms and blossoms lined the walks and danced around trees. The houses were all neatly painted with matching shutters and doors. Shrubs and hedges were painstakingly trimmed to exacting specifications.

Sports cars and pricey SUV's gleamed in the morning sun. The people of this neighborhood were rather well off and it showed. They took great pride in their homes and went to great lengths to keep them looking picture-perfect.

Then again, the local Home Owner's Association would stand for nothing less. Their rules, most of which made little sense to Peter, were oddly specific and strictly enforced. Peter's dad still hadn't forgiven him for the fine they got last summer when he accidentally got blue spray-paint on the driveway.

As much as Peter loved his home and most of his neighbors, he couldn't picture himself living in a place like this when he grew up. He had loftier ambitions for himself than a nine-to-five factory job, a cookie-cutter home, and micromanaging neighborhood committees. Yes, Peter was destined for greater things.

He refused to become his father.

A stick cracked behind Peter. The sound pulled him from his daydreams and launched his heart up into his throat. When he turned around, there was no one there.

Hair rose on the back of his neck and a flutter thrummed in his chest, just behind a childhood scar. He shook his head and kept walking, convinced it was all in his head. His run-in with his father must have him on edge.

Peter glanced down at his cell phone and picked up the pace. He had ten minutes before first bell. His attendance had been perfect all year. There was no way he was going to be late on the last day.

Leaves rustled at his back, though there was no hint of a breeze. Peter stopped in his tracks and spun around. He saw…something, a shadow, perhaps, disappear behind a large oak on the corner.

Tinkerbell, the Jensen's ancient Yorkshire terrier, was yipping hysterically at that same tree.

Peter had never heard Tinkerbell bark at anyone. Ever.

"Hello?" Peter inched forward.

Tinkerbell's hackles rose and she began to growl. Her eyes were locked on something, an animal maybe? Peter's phone beeped, letting him know he had five minutes to get to class. He didn't have time to figure out what had spooked the little dog, even if it'd had the same effect on him.

He turned toward school and began to run. Sweat dripped down the side of Peter's neck and saturated his collar. His breathing came in short, steady bursts as his feet pounded the pavement. He was nearly ten blocks from school but Peter had no doubt he would make it in time. Though he wasn't much into school-sponsored sports, Peter was extremely athletic.

From a very early age, Peter had spent most of his free time learning to fight. Three days a week, Peter took lessons at the local martial arts club. Over the years, he'd learned everything from basic self-defense to mixed martial arts. He loved the challenge of it all, but there was more to it than that. Peter had made many friends at the club, including his best friend, Sarah.

When Peter wasn't learning how to defend himself, he could be found at the archery range. His mother had taught him to shoot when he was little. He loved it even more than he loved karate and Taekwondo. In fact, Peter rather enjoyed all his uncommon pursuits. It wouldn't have mattered if he hadn't. His parents had never given him the option to quit.

Peter was less than a block from his destination when a gravelly voice called out to him from behind. He stopped short, his shoes skidding across the sidewalk.

"I know who you are." A man in a large black cloak stood in the middle of the sidewalk. He was less than ten feet away, but Peter hadn't even heard him approach.

"Excuse me?" Peter narrowed his eyes, but the man's face was hidden beneath the massive hood.

"Did you really think you could hide from me forever?" The man laughed and a chill raced down Peter's spine. Undaunted, the stranger took a step toward Peter. "You have something that belongs to me. I want it back."

"I think you have me confused with someone else, sir." Peter took a step back, his thumb hovering over the emergency button on the cell in his jacket pocket.

"I think not," the man huffed. He tilted his head to the side and a sliver of light crept beneath the edge of his cloak illuminating a sharply angled jaw and the hint of a graying beard. "You know, Peter, you look so much like your father when he was younger. I hope, for your sake, you are more intelligent."

"Look, I don't know what you want from me, but I really need to go." Peter's voice shook. He wanted to run, every fiber of his being was screaming at him to do just that, but his feet seemed to be glued to the pavement.

"I want only what is rightfully mine!" The man shouted and held out his hand. "Give me the charm and I will leave you in peace."

"The what?" Peter's brows furrowed. "I have no idea what you are talking about."

"Don't play the fool with me, boy. Give me the charm!" He grabbed Peter's arm and pulled him closer.

Peter's fear evaporated in an instant. Instinct and years of training took over. He clenched his hand, flung his wrist in a wide circle, and jerked it sharply toward the ground wrenching himself from of the stranger's grasp. The moment his hand was free, he thrust it forward into the man's face. It connected with a satisfying crack and the man lurched backward.

Peter didn't stick around to find out how much damage he'd done. The guy was obviously drunk or crazy and Peter had no desire to see what he would do next. He took off at a dead sprint and didn't stop until he burst through the front doors at his school.

The good news was the halls were empty so no one had seen is dramatic (and sweaty) entrance. The bad news was he was definitely going to be late for class. He stormed to his locker, swearing under his breath as his sweaty fingers struggled to enter his combination. After the third failed attempt, he pressed his head against the cold metal surface.

"Ugh," Peter sighed.

"You're never late." A hand clamped down on Peter's shoulder and he let out a yelp. When he turned around, his friend Sarah was standing there, a brow raised in amusement. "Jesus, Peter. Jumpy much?"

"Sorry," Peter sighed glancing past his friend toward the front door. "Weird morning."

"Ditto. Must be something in the air." Sarah pushed Peter aside and began twisting the dial on his locker. "Let me help you with that."

Peter's phone chimed and a notification box popped up on his screen. He had an incoming video message from his mom. Weird. His mom had literally never sent him a video before.

"Nine, eleven, twenty-two," Peter said absently while staring down at his phone. Thanks to the school's pathetic internet, it was taking forever for the message to load.

"I know," Sarah rolled her eyes. "You act like I've never had to do this before. Oh, and you should probably turn that off so you don't get busted. It would suck to get it confiscated on the last day of school."

"Right, good call." Peter powered off his phone, stashed it in his locker, and dragged himself off to receive his first-ever tardy slip.

***

Aside from the fiasco with the crazy guy that morning and Sarah's odd mood, Peter's day had gone fairly well. It was the last day of school, so most of his teachers were playing movies or letting students hang out and sign each other's yearbooks. Peter's team won capture the flag in gym class, which was a big deal since they'd defeated the seniors. The student counsel surprised everyone with pizza for lunch, instead of the mystery meat the menu had promised. Peter even managed to talk his way out of the being marked tardy. All things considered, the day had gone quite well.

When the final bell rang, the halls erupted in chaos. Papers were thrown haphazardly into the air and textbooks were left lying in piles on the floor. Kids littered the front lawn laughing and celebrating the end of another long school year. Music blasted from all sides of the parking lot. Everyone hung out just a bit longer than usual on the off chance they didn't see each other for the rest of the summer.

"Wanna hang out tonight? We can order Chinese and watch lame eighties movies on Netflix," Sarah asked Peter as they walked out into the late afternoon sun.

"Maybe," Peter shrugged. "I was thinking about going to the archery range for a bit. My mom got me a sweet new bow I've been itching to try out. I'll text you when I'm done though, okay?"

"Sounds good, Robin Hood." Sarah laughed and ran to meet her girlfriends near the edge of the lawn.

"Dork," Peter rolled his eyes and pulled his phone out of his backpack.

He had forgotten about the random video message his mom had sent him that morning. His phone had been off all day and the signal was weak so the video was still downloading. He really needed to get a better phone.

"See you around, Sentry," a friend shouted from a passing car.

Peter waved and kept walking. Once he dropped his stuff off at home, he was out of there. He couldn't wait to pick up his new bow and head to the range. He'd nearly fallen over when his mom had given him the sleek, black weapon a few days ago. It had once been her father's, Julianna had told him. He had passed it on to her and now it was his. The bow was magnificent and fit his grip perfectly.

Peter was so caught up in his excitement he nearly stepped in front of a fire truck as it rushed past. The driver laid on the horn and Peter stopped short, his heart beating wildly in his ears. Two police cars followed in the engine's wake, their sirens blazed and lights flashed.

His phone buzzed, letting him know the video had finally loaded. Peter carefully crossed the street and turned toward his neighborhood. Once he was safely on his path, he cranked up the sound and tapped on his mother's message.

"Peter, I need you to listen to me." Julianna's voice was barely a whisper. Her eyes wild and frantic. "He's here. He's found us."

Smoke billowed all around her and her face was smattered with soot. His mother looked terrified. Her eyes darted over her shoulder every few seconds as she crawled across the floor.

A wall of flames rose behind her and a beam crashed down in the background. She screamed and dropped her phone. It clattered to the ground, the camera trained on the ceiling. Peter saw nothing but fire.

"Mom!" He screamed down at his screen.

A moment later, he saw her face once more.

"I'm so sorry we didn't tell you the truth, son. Your father and I hoped you'd never have to know that world. We were fools." Julianna's voice was weak. She coughed and looked over her shoulder again. When she turned back, there were tears in her eyes. "Go to the place where all the magic lives. The truth lies behind the falls. Peter, you must—"

Her words gave way to a blood-curdling scream as a silver hook buried itself in the flesh on her shoulder. His mother's eyes shot wide as she was yanked backward. The screen went black and the message ended.

Peter ran all the way home.

***

Fire trucks and ambulances lined both sides of Peter's street. Barricades blocked each end and gawkers lurked about. Police officers wandered around shouting into their walkies and barking orders at onlookers. Dr. Stevens saw Peter coming and reached out to stop him.

"Peter, don't," he begged.

Peter dodged his grasp and shoved his way through the crowd. He ducked under the wooden roadblock and stormed toward the smoldering pile of ash that had once been his home.

"Whoa! You cannot go in there, kid." A police officer stepped in front of him. "It's too dangerous."

"This is my house!" Peter screamed in the man's face. The officer wrapped his arms around Peter and slowly pushed him back. Peter fought him but his body was too numb to put up much resistance. "Let me go."

"No can do, son," the officer said. "You need to stay back."

"You can't do this." Tears burned at Peter's eyes. "Please, I have to find my mom."

"I am sorry, kid," the police officer sounded sad, but his grip never faltered. "There's nothing left to find."

"You're wrong," Peter screamed at him. "My mom is—"

"She's gone, son," the officer frowned. "There's no way anyone could survive that blaze."

Peter's legs gave out and collapsed beneath him. The police officer caught him before he hit the ground. He steadied the boy and led him over to one of the fire engines. When they reached the other side, Peter could no longer see the burning rubble. The officer ushered him to the curb and told him to sit. Peter had no idea what else to do, so he dropped to the concrete in a heap.

Distraught and in need of comfort, Peter grabbed his cell and tried calling his father. It went straight to voicemail. He tried again. Nothing.

"Damn it." Peter mashed the end call button and dialed again. This time he left a message. "Dad, when you get this message, call me. Something bad happened. The house...it's gone. Mom's gone! Oh my God, just freaking call me, okay!"

"We'll send a unit to find your dad. It's going to be okay, son." The officer wrapped a blanket around Peter's shoulders and handed him a bottle of water.

As if a sip and a snuggle could magically erase the horrors he'd just seen.

Magic!

"That's it." Peter muttered and sent Sarah a text.

911. Be at Crystal Lake Park in 10. Bring your bow staff and wear comfortable shoes.

Peter tossed the scratchy blanket to the ground and took off running. The police officer shouted for him to come back, but Peter ignored him. His mother had left him a trail of breadcrumbs and he'd be damned if he wasn't going to follow it…right after he picked up his bow.

***

"Holy crap, Peter!" Sarah's eyes went wide as she stared down at his phone. "The fire…and your mom…. and was that a hook?"

"Yeah," Peter frowned. "And after that whole thing with the crazy guy this morning? I am kind of freaking out here."

"Jesus." Sarah raked her hair back and crossed her arms over her chest. "I thought *I* was having a bad day, but this? Peter, what are you going to do?"

"I'm going to do exactly what she told me to do," Peter said. "And I am going to find her."

"*We* will find her." Sarah grabbed Peter's hand and banged her staff on the ground. "We're a team, remember?"

"Thanks, Sarah," Peter said.

"Always." She nodded. "Wait! Peter, what about your dad?"

"I tried calling him like ten times, but it went straight to voicemail. I even tried from the land line when I stopped at Bob's to grab my bow." Peter wrung his hands. He'd never been so furious at another person in his life. "My mother was abducted by a crazy person with a hook for a hand and my jerk of a father can't even be bothered to answer his phone!"

"I'm sure he got your messages, Peter." Sarah put her hand on his shoulder. "He's probably on his way home right now."

"What's the point? There's nothing left." Peter raked his hair back. "Let's go."

Peter slung his bow and quiver over his shoulder and pulled Sarah toward a nearby hiking trail. The sun was low on the horizon and the sky had taken on a warm pink hue. Birds chirped lazily in the trees and critters scampered about in the brush. They acted as if today was any other day.

The path to the falls had long since grown over. Weeds and thorn bushes pressed in on both sides and the trail was littered with debris and broken branches. It twisted through thickets and dipped under fallen trees. Anyone else would likely have lost their way, but not Peter. Even if he hadn't known the way by heart, he had no doubt he could get to the falls.

The closer they got to Crystal Lake, the more it called to him. It pulled at him like gravity, like a chord stretched tight in his heart. As much as he'd loved this place as a child, he hadn't remembered ever feeling this way when he was here. Something was different.

Perhaps *he* was different.

Whatever truth Peter's parents had been keeping from him, the falls held the key to unlocking it. And hopefully the key to finding his mother. Peter and Sarah had walked nearly a mile in silence before Sarah finally spoke.

"I don't think I've ever been to this part of the park before." Sarah jumped over a large hole in the trail and ran to Peter's side. "Where are we going, exactly?"

"Crystal Lake," Peter said pointing ahead, "to the waterfall."

"I thought that area was blocked off," Sarah frowned. "My mom said they fenced it in before we moved here. She said there were mud slides or something?"

"Or something," Peter shook his head.

Mudslides. That *had* been the official story.

Peter had been around ten or eleven when his mother told him they would no longer be able to go on their special hikes to the falls. The city had deemed that part of the Crystal Lake Park to be unstable. It was too dangerous for hiking, she'd said. Peter had never had any reason to believe that had been anything but the truth.

Suddenly he wasn't so sure.

A rusted, chain-link fence lay ahead. Signs were posted all over it warning away hikers and trespassers alike. Danger. Caution. Do not enter. Watch for falling rocks. Unstable terrain.

"So, what happened to you this morning?" Peter looked down at Sarah as he began to climb the fence.

"Nothing." Sarah grunted. She shoved her staff through the chain link and started climbing up.

"No, this morning in the hallway, you said you'd had a weird morning, too," Peter said dropping to the ground on the other side. "And you've seemed off all day. What's up?"

"It's nothing, Peter." Sarah lowered herself to the ground and walked past him toward the sounds of rushing water. "Come on. We have to be getting close."

"Hey." Peter grabbed her hand and slowed her pace. "Are you okay?"

"I'm fine," Sarah said, but she wouldn't look at him. "Given your situation, I hardly have a reason to complain."

"Come on," Peter said. "It's going to take a bit longer to get to the falls, so you might as well just spill."

"Fine," Sarah sighed. "It's my dad."

"What about him?" Peter asked.

"He left." Sarah's voice cracked.

"What do you mean *he left*?" Peter asked his voice heavy with concern.

"I mean he's gone, Peter. He left a stupid note and just bailed." Sarah wacked a stone with the end of her staff. It bounced off a nearby tree and scared a flock of birds into the air. "I mean, he and my mom have been fighting a lot, mostly about me I think, but I didn't know it was that bad."

"Whoa," Peter said, shoving his hands in his pockets. In all the years he'd been friends with Sarah, he'd never met her father. He probably never would now. That hardly mattered though. Peter hated him for the pain he'd caused his friend. "God Sarah, that sucks. I'm sorry."

"Yeah, it's pretty crappy," Sarah said. "But like I said, it's nothing compared to what you are going through."

"That doesn't mean—ahh!"

Peter's foot caught on a branch and he lost his balance. With his hands in his pockets, he couldn't catch himself. He fell face first onto the hard ground where he tumbled down an embankment and skidded to a stop at the base of a pine tree. The world spun around him as he fought to catch his breath.

"Peter, oh my God," Sarah yelled as she ran over to him.

Peter grimaced and rolled onto his back. The side of his face was throbbing and he tasted blood. He sat up gingerly and raised a hand to his face. His eye was already swelling shut and his fingertips came away red.

"That's definitely gonna leave a mark," Peter groaned.

"Or twenty," Sarah said, shooing his hands. "Let me look at it."

"Sarah I—" Peter caught her hand as it moved toward his face.

"Don't be a baby, Peter." Sarah shook her head at him. "I just want to make sure you didn't break your face."

The moment Sarah touched Peter's face, his pain stopped. The swelling around his eye began to wane and the sick feeling in his stomach ceased. Sarah's eyes went wide as she stared at Peter's fading injuries.

"Holy crap," she said dropping to the ground at Peter's side.

"How did you—?" Peter gaped at her.

"I have no idea," Sarah stared down at her palms.

They were glowing.

***

"It's beautiful, Peter." Sarah stared wide-eyed ahead.

Crystal Lake was aptly named. The water was so clear you could see straight to the pebbled floor. A massive waterfall sliced through the side of the bluff that surrounded it. The water foamed and frothed where it spilled into the lake. A path of large, mossy stepping-stones dotted the surface of the water and disappeared beneath the falls. A soft layer of mist obscured the path from view and sliced the waning sun into a thousand tiny rainbows.

"My mom and I used to come here all the time when I was little. She told me stories about fairies, dragons, and magical gateways to enchanted lands. She always said that this place was where all the magic lived," Peter said as he carefully stepped onto the first stone. "I'm starting to think that was more than just a story."

Sarah followed Peter all the way across the lake and onto a small embankment at the base of the waterfall. The last stone was a bit of a leap for Sarah, but she managed to make it across.

"Okay, so what do we do now?" Sarah asked.

"Stay here and keep watch. If anything weird happens, yell as loud as you can and I'll come running," Peter pulled his bow off his shoulder.

"I think we're a few hours past weird, Peter," Sarah said, holding up her hands. The glow was faint now, but it was still there.

"Right," Peter smirked, then squared his shoulders and took a deep breath. "Okay, I'm going in."

"Be careful," Sarah said, gripping her staff in both hands. "And Peter? If you're not back in five minutes, I'm coming in after you."

Peter nodded and dashed through the icy water to the cave that lay beyond. Darkness washed over him as he stepped inside. It was silent, except for the sounds of water dripping and his heavy breathing. The temperature dropped significantly the moment he had crossed through the falls. It didn't help that he was now soaked from head to toe. His socks sloshed inside of his shoes with each step.

Peter pulled his cell phone out and swiped the screen. It sprang to life. With a sigh of relief, he turned on his flashlight app and swung it in a wide arc in front of him, surveying his surroundings. The pale, white light reflected off the wet surface of the rough stone cavern. Massive stalactites stabbed toward the cave floor like razor sharp dragon's teeth. Water dripped from their tips and pooled in cracks and crevices on the ground.

He stepped over the pools and carefully trudged on. An invisible force pulled him onward and deeper into the cave. He had no idea where he was going, only that he had to keep going. Forward was really his only option at this point. His heart was beating wildly in his chest and his breath formed anxious clouds in front of him. Something shuffled across the cave just beyond the reach of his flashlight. Peter froze.

"Hello?" Peter's voice was shaky. "Who's there?"

No one answered, but Peter knew someone was watching him. He could feel it. His phone vibrated in his hand, the screen went blank, and darkness surrounded him once more.

"Crap," Peter muttered. Amid all the drama, he hadn't thought to charge his phone. "Perfect."

Peter's mind raced and he started to panic. He was in the middle of a dark cave, surrounded by sharp rocks, and he had no idea where he was going. He was completely in over his head. He was just about to yell for Sarah when he heard laughter echoing around him.

"Well, well, well, the prodigal son returns." A deep voice grumbled. "Took you long enough."

Peter couldn't see two inches in front of his face, but he sensed the man inching closer. He loaded an arrow and raised his bow in front of him. The problem was, he couldn't be sure where the mysterious man was standing. The acoustics of the cave were playing tricks on him.

"Who's there?" Peter demanded, his bow swinging back and forth in the dark.

"You probably don't remember me," the man huffed. "You were just a baby when your father abandoned his post and left me to guard the Ethereal Gateway on my own."

"Ethereal Gateway?" Peter was lost, in every sense of the word.

"He didn't tell you." The voice sounded annoyed. "Of course, he didn't."

"Who didn't tell me *what*?" Peter was equally irritated now. He had no idea what was going on, but he was tired of all the cloak and dagger nonsense. "I don't know who you are or what you are talking about but I've had enough. Show yourself!"

"As you wish," the man sighed.

A rush of air blew Peter's hair from his face. It vibrated against his skin and a soft white light filled the cave. A man stood directly in front of him, just inches from the tip of his arrow. His hands were glowing. Blood dripped from a large gash in his scalp.

"Is that really necessary?" He glared down at Peter's bow.

"I don't know you," Peter said, his mouth set in a grim line.

"Perhaps not, but you know my daughter," the man smiled and looked over Peter's shoulder toward the mouth of the cave. "If I'm not mistaken, she is close by."

"Wait, you're—" Peter's eyes widened.

"Sarah's father, yes." The man bowed deeply, his hand across his chest. "Barry Bell, at your service."

His long brown hair fell forward revealing the tips of abnormally pointed ears. His clothes were plain and earthy and he had a wooden bow strapped to his back. The surface of the weapon was rough with bark and leaves sprouted from its length. The chord glistened like gold. The man rose to his full height and straightened his frock.

"Now that the formalities are out of the way, would you be so kind?" Barry gestured to the arrow pointed at his chest. He sighed when Peter didn't immediately relent. "Honestly. Why would I hurt you, boy? I've spent the last few years of my life trying to protect you. Despite your father's cowardice, I stayed true to my mission."

"My father is a great many things, but he's no coward. And you *should* be protecting your daughter," Peter frowned but lowered his bow. "Sarah thinks you abandoned her."

"Collateral damage, I'm afraid." Barry's eyes clouded and the corners of his mouth dipped down. "It took me years to track you down, child. Imagine my surprise when I found you here, in this wretched world. There's no magic here. I can't imagine how your father managed it all those years. Being so far away from the source of his power must have been excruciating for him. I sneak back into Neverland every few days to recharge and I can barely stand it here."

Peter had no idea what to say to that. He stared blankly at Barry until he continued.

"Peter, your father was a Guardian," Barry said. "He was supposed to protect the Gateway and the Charm, but abandoned his post and took it for himself. After the High Oracle's prophecy, he whisked you and your mother off and disappeared to this dreadful realm. He abandoned Neverland and left his people in the hands off that monster."

"Neverland?" Peter shook his head in disbelief. "But that's just a story."

"I assure you, Neverland is quite real." Barry said. He waved his hand toward the far end of the cave. The shadows that lingered there dissipated, revealing a large wrought-iron gate. A warm glow emanated from beyond its massive scrolling bars. "In fact, that is where you were born, Peter."

"You can't be serious," Peter said his eyes fixed on the gate.

"Oh, but I am," Barry said, lowering himself onto a rock. "After your father's betrayal, I was sent to by the Oracle to find you and retrieve the artifact. If that beast got his hands on you before you came into your power, he would be the only one in our world who could wield the Charm. With it, he would take control of the Gateway and there'd be no stopping him."

Blood poured down the side of Barry's head. He closed his eyes for a moment and wavered in place. His skin was taking on a pallid color.

"Peter, you have no idea what I have sacrificed to protect you." Barry said. "I moved the Gateway and my own family to this horrible place. My wife and daughter have been in your world for so long they've forgotten their magic."

"That's not my fault," Peter said. "I didn't choose any of this."

"Neither did I. It was my duty, not my choice, Peter." Barry shouted. "I gave up everything and put my family at risk to prevent that scourge from entering your world. I'd been quite successful until this morning when he sliced open the side of my head with his blasted hook. I have no idea how he even found the—"

"Hook?" Peter cut Barry off. His heart shot into his throat. "That's the guy who attacked me this morning. Barry, he has my mother!"

"I know," Barry sighed. "I've failed Neverland. I've failed you. I'm so sorry, Peter."

"Don't be sorry, be helpful!" Peter exclaimed. "You said it was your job to protect our family, so get up off your butt and do it."

"That is no longer my duty," Barry said. "The moment your father crossed back through the Gateway, the responsibility fell back onto his shoulders."

"My father was here?" Peter stepped forward. "When?"

"He passed through no less than an hour ago," Barry grunted.

"I'm going after them," Peter rushed forward, but Barry grabbed his arm.

"That's exactly what he wants, Peter," Barry said. "He's baiting you. If you return to Neverland, your powers will emerge. Hook will sense your presence and he will come for you."

"Let him come," Peter said squaring his shoulders.

***

"So, I'm a fairy." Sarah shook her head and stepped over a rock on the muddy path. "Guess that explains the glow-in-the-dark hands thing and the way I healed you and Peter. So, what happens now? Am I going to sprout wings and start granting wishes or something?"

"No wings, no wishes, but yes, you are Fae, Sarah." Barry said. "Your mother was once a Healer and I am a Lightkeeper. It's actually quite rare for a Fae child to inherit powers from both parents."

"You lied to us all this time, dad. You let us forget our magic." Sarah glared at her father as they made their way through Neverland's Twisted Forest. "I always felt so out of place here and now I know why. Is that why Mom drinks the way she does? Is that why she is so angry all the time? She misses her magic and she doesn't even remember it."

"Yes." Barry eyes were fixed on the path ahead, "I had no choice."

"You always had a choice," Sarah said. "You just made the wrong one."

"Speaking of choices…" Peter cleared his throat and stepped between Barry and Sarah as they walked. "Why didn't my parents just tell me the truth a long time ago?"

"When the Oracle spoke her prophecy, your father panicked. The idea that his infant son would either one day rule Neverland or die at the hands of a murderous, power-hungry psychopath was all a bit too much for him. Your mother was beside herself. Julianna wanted you to live in peace, even if it meant they could not. I suspect they were trying to shield you from it all," Barry shrugged. "You know, give you a *normal* life."

"Normal life, huh?" Peter huffed. "What could be more normal than forcing a kid to learn ten different ways to cripple a man with his bare hands before the age of ten? Or how to shoot an arrow with enough accuracy to pick a quarter out of his mother's fingertips from fifty yards away? Yup, totally normal."

"You love that stuff, Peter," Sarah said.

"That's not the point," Peter groaned. "If they were so confident they could shield me from danger, why prepare me for it?"

"They just wanted what was best for you." Barry told Peter.

"The truth would have been what's best for me," Peter frowned and slid his bow from his shoulder. "And having a father that didn't hate me would have been nice, too."

"He doesn't hate you Peter," Barry sighed. "I may not be a fan of your dad's, but I know this; he has been in pain for the last seventeen years. He couldn't go back to Neverland. Hook would have sensed him and followed him straight to you. He's been disconnected from his home and his magic for nearly two decades. A lesser man would have crumbled. My own wife did, and I know I would have."

"So he resents me then?" Peter said. "I'm the reason he had to leave."

"Fathers will do anything for their children." Barry looked past Peter at his daughter. His eyes were sad and full of regret.

The three fell silent after that. There was far more to think about than needed to be said. Even if Peter had felt like talking, he was far too overwhelmed by the day's events to put his thoughts into words that would make any sense. His entire life had been a lie.

The moment he crossed through the Ethereal Gateway, something inside of Peter had shifted. It was as if a veil had been lifted from his mind. One-winged butterflies danced circles in his stomach and his body was humming with energy. His fingers and toes were tingling and his senses were sharp. Sounds were crisp and colors more vivid. The scent of fresh, spring blooms and distant campfires drifted on the breeze. The fragrance was so dense he could taste it in the back of his throat.

Thick, mossy vines draped from one tree to another, swaying above them as they wandered through the lush forest. According to Barry, the Twisted Forest was a living creature. It formed a protective barrier around all of Neverland and kept watch on all those who passed through. Only those born in this realm could safely cross its borders and enter the kingdom. If an enemy stepped foot into the woods, the forest and all its creatures would take action eliminate the threat.

The deeper they plunged into the woods, the more Peter wanted to run. Despite having no knowledge of this place, he instinctively knew which direction he needed to go. The midday sun peeked through the edge of the tree line at the far edge of the forest.

Peter's heart started banging wildly in his chest. Darkness pulled at him from beyond the light and he knew they were getting close. Unable to hold back any longer, Peter began to run. He ducked and dodged through the maze of tall trees and leapt over a small ravine. Sarah and her father were struggling to keep up.

He burst free of the canopy and emerged out onto a large cliff overlooking the water. There, in the middle of a vast and endless sea, was a single ship. It was massive and ancient looking, with great, black sails and rough wooden surfaces. A man in a red coat and tall black boots stood at the wheel, shouting orders at the small army of men that scuttled about on the deck.

"Hook," Peter muttered, glaring at him from afar.

Barry rushed out of the trees and dragged Peter to the ground. "Stay down, boy! He'll see you."

Peter hit the ground with a thud, the force of it knocking the wind from his chest. He glared at Barry, and then turned back toward the ship just in time to see a bald man with an eye patch approach the captain. He smiled proudly and dropped a large burlap sack onto the deck at Hook's feet.

"Good on you, Patchy my old friend!" Hook shouted, clapping the man on the back with his metal hand.

Patchy winced, but said nothing of the blood that had been drawn. Instead, he wore it like a badge of honor.

With a bow, he stepped down off the platform and into the accolades of his comrades.

"Peter, look." Sarah gasped and pointed. "Your mom!"

Tied around the base of the ship's central mast, was his mother. She was crying and struggling against her ropes. With a triumphant smile, Hook nudged at the burlap with the toe of his shiny, black boot. The edge of rough, brown fabric fell away and Peter's heart dropped to his stomach. The thrumming behind his scar was unbearable.

Edward Sentry lay slumped inside that sack. Blood covered the side of his father's face. He wasn't moving. Just as Peter was about to jump to his feet, he felt the point of a blade pressed into his back. Sarah screamed and Barry grunted as a boot stomped down onto his chest. Footsteps pounded the ground as a handful of pirates surrounded them.

"Don't move, boy," the man barked down at Peter. "Cap'n Hook would be none too pleased wiff me if'n I brought you to 'im in pieces. I reckon he'd like to do that honor 'imself."

"Go to Hell," Peter coughed and the dirt swirled around him.

"Right, then. Nighty-night, hero," the man laughed. Pain flashed behind Peter's eyes, and everything went dark.

***

The world was spinning backwards and Peter's stomach lurched. Muffled voices and guttural laughter bounced all around him. Lilting fiddles and twittering flutes played a celebratory jig. Someone was crying. Peter's eyes drifted open.

"Morning," Captain Hook's face was inches from his own. His nose sat crooked and an ugly bruise surrounded his right eye. "So nice of you to stop by. And you've brought friends! How wonderful."

Hook gestured to the mast of his ship. Peter's mother, Sarah, and Barry were watching him from the helm. They were bound and gagged. Pirates surrounded them pointing blades of every shape and size at their necks. Peter struggled to sit. His vision blurred, but he managed to get himself upright.

"As you can imagine, I don't get many visitors. It's been centuries since we've had afternoon tea. Let's see." Hook clasped his hands behind his back and began pacing. "If memory serves, it's customary for the guest to bring their host a gift, is it not?"

"What do you want," Peter reached his hand behind his back and felt for his bow. It wasn't there.

"I want what I've always wanted, you silly boy," Hook laughed.

"A shower?" Peter huffed. "Maybe a toothbrush?"

"Clever." Hook smirked and nodded at the man standing behind Peter. "Brutus, if you'd be so kind."

"Aye, Cap'n." The man stepped forward and yanked Peter to his feet. It was the same one who'd knocked him out on the bluff. He held Peter's arms behind his back then leaned forward and whispered in his ear. "Thanks for the pretty bow. It'll fetch me a right fair nugget at the market, I reckon."

Peter glared over his shoulder at Brutus. The bow his mother had given him just days before, along with his quiver, were slung loosely over the man's right shoulder.

"I have nothing to give you," Peter turned back and narrowed his eyes at Hook.

"That's not entirely true, now, is it?" Hook stepped toward him. He raised a thin sword to Peter's chest and sliced down the front of Peter's shirt. He tapped the raised flesh of Peter's scar and smiled. "Ahh, yes, there it is, just as your father said. Mind you, he took some convincing, but my men can be very persuasive."

Peter looked down to where the blade touched his skin. His brows furrowed in confusion. The scar was glowing with a faint, blue light.

"I don't understand," Peter said. Julianna was fighting her gag and shouting at him but he couldn't understand what she was saying.

"See there? You've had the Charm all along, child," Hook said as the tip of his blade pierced the skin on Peter's chest.

Julianna thrashed against her ropes and Peter screamed out in pain. Hook's smile grew along with the gash near Peter's collarbone. When Hook had sliced the full length of Peter's scar, he dropped his sword to the ground. With a smile on his face, he shoved the end of his finger into Peter's open wound and pulled out a small, silver trinket on a thread-thin silver chain.

The Charm was shaped like a feather. Blood dripped from the tip but did little to dull the bright blue glow that surrounded it.

"Your father was quite clever hiding the Charm there," Hook said, staring down at it with greed in his eyes. The charm swung back and forth in front of him like a pendulum marking time. "No matter. It's mine now and there's nothing you can do to stop me."

"Why are you doing this?" Peter grunted.

"Because I can," Hook smiled.

"What shall we do with the prisoners Cap'n?" Brutus asked.

"Feed them to the sea." He clutched the Charm in his fist, grabbed up his sword, and walked to the mast. He cut the ropes that bound Sarah to the post and tossed her at one of his men. "Starting with the girl."

"No!" Peter shouted.

He threw his head back and cracked Brutus square in the chin. The man's grip faltered just long enough for Peter to drop to his knees and roll away. Another pirate rushed at him. Peter swept the man's feet out from under him with his leg, then shot to his feet and dove at Brutus.

Still dazed, Brutus swung at Peter, his blow sailing wide of the boy's face. Peter took advantage, grabbed the back of the pirate's neck and yanked downward as he thrust his knee into Brutus's chest. Brutus heaved as the air was knocked out of him and slowly fell forward.

When he hit the deck, Peter scooped his bow from the man's limp body and shoved his hand into the quiver. Most of the arrows had scattered in the chaos. Only one remained. Peter loaded it and pointed the tip directly at Captain Hook.

"Hook!" Peter shouted. "Let her go or I'll pierce your heart."

The pirate army froze where they stood, their eyes bouncing between Peter and their master. The deck of the ship fell silent, save for the sound of Captain Hook's laughter. He held Sarah in front of him, his bloody sword pressed to her throat.

"Are you really so confident?" Hook sneered.

"Let her go," Peter growled. "This is your last chance."

"Really, now." Hook raised a brow. "You haven't the upper hand, child. Think about it. If you miss, your little princess here will lose her head, you'll watch your whole family die, and I will still have the charm."

"I don't miss," Peter said, releasing the arrow.

***

"Did he hurt you?" Peter rushed to his mother's side and sliced through her ropes. "Jesus, are you okay?"

"Are *you*?" Julianna dove at her son and wrapped her arms around him.

"I'm fine, really." Peter said calming her worried hands.

All around them were pirates on bended knee, bowing to her son. Julianna stared at them with wide eyes then turned to Peter.

"Peter, I'm so sorry. We should have told you about all this, but your father and I—" Julianna froze. "Oh my God. Edward!" With tears in her eyes, she dove to the deck and clutched at her husband's arm.

"Give me a minute, Mrs. Sentry," Sarah groaned. Her hands glowed brightly as she brushed them over Edward's face. The effort took a lot out of her, especially since she'd only come into her powers a few short hours ago. Sweat rolled down her pale face and she began to shake, but soon enough Edward's eyes fluttered open.

"Julianna?" He gasped, and then turned to Peter. "Peter. You're okay. I thought—"

"I'm good," Peter smirked.

"The Charm!" Edward lurched forward, but he was still too weak. He immediately collapsed back onto the deck.

"It's safe, Dad." Peter laid his hand over his heart. "The Charm is back where it belongs."

Sarah's magic had erased both Peter's wound, as well as his scar. In their place hung a tiny silver feather. It glowed as bright as truth and held the promise of a future in a home he'd never known existed. Peter had been right all along. He *was* destined for great things.

And Neverland finally had its rightful king.

Alexander Hartman

Author of The Archer

Fifteen-year-old Alexander Hartman lives in a small town in Illinois with his parents, five brothers, and floppy-eared, four-legged sidekick. He's relatively new at this writing thing, but has won a few awards along the way. Prior to being chosen for the Twisted Fairy Tales Anthology, he'd only ever created stories for fun. His story, "The Archer," was inspired by the adventures of Peter Pan, a tale he always enjoyed as a child…perhaps because growing up seemed so incredibly overrated. In addition to writing, he enjoys golf (which he excels at), bowling, art, and hanging out with friends. Prior to this project, Alexander had no idea the amount of work that went into being a published author. Still, he enjoyed the challenge and learned a lot throughout the process. He would like to encourage other young writers out there who are thinking of publishing to shoot for the stars and take that leap. If you have a story, tell it. If you have a dream, make it a reality.

Acknowledgments

First, Alternate Ending Publications, and its fearless leader, Aria Michaels, would like to thank all of the amazing young authors who submitted their stories for consideration. Sharing your words with the world is one of the bravest things you will ever do. We commend you on taking that leap and trusting us with your word-babies.

Faith, Alex, Lauren, Emily, Madeleine, Polaris, J.M, Makayla, Grey, and Alexander were each chosen for publication for their unique vision and distinct voice. These young authors (not one of whom is over the age of seventeen, by the way) worked tirelessly for months on end to edit, refine, and perfect their stories. With the tireless support of their family, friends, and the entire support staff here at AEP, these kids have moved mountains to make their literary voices heard. We are honored to be a part of that beautiful song. Well done, Twisted Fairy Tales team. Well done!

We would also like to thank the army of indie community talent who donated their services and support to this project. Amy Manemann, when Aria came to you with an insane plan to open a publications company with the sole purpose of building a bridge between the indie book community and the young literary talent of the world, you didn't even flinch. When she told you she wanted to publish teen authors, she expected you to run. Instead, you smiled, gave her a hug, and said, "What can I do to help?" Know that she will forever be grateful for your support and your fierce friendship. #Always

Lou J Stock, we were honored to have your beautiful creation as the face of the Twisted Fairy Tales Anthology. Your generosity (and patience) will not soon be forgotten. You truly are an artistic genius and one Hell of a human being. Jordan White, we thank you for the countless hours you spent murdering comma splices, correcting our grammar, and illuminating all that was dark. Your editing genius knows no bounds. Your unique eye for plot points and shiny details has made this collection even more lustrous than it was at its conception.

To Amber Garcia, of Lady Amber's PR and Reviews, there is truly no way to express to you just how thankful we all are for the hard work you have done to put this project in the hands of so many. We are humbled and truly honored to have you as part of the team. To Katy Walker, our dedicated official blogger and social media share-master, we send you hugs and an infinite supply of gratitude. You gave these kids their first, true moment in the spotlight with your fun interviews and social media blasts. No one can ever take that experience away from them.

To Chris Philbrook, your aid in all things legal and binding was invaluable. Had it not been for your honest and generous tutelage, Aria's head may very well have exploded. To Jeff Clare, we thank you for your advice and counsel on the trials, tribulations, and subsequent victories in the world of anthology production. To Shane, for all your behind the scenes support.

To you, the reader, who spent hours of your life allowing the words of ten young authors into your hearts, thank you. You've given these kids something that will stay with them for the rest of their lives.

Impact.

Accomplishment.

A legacy.

CPSIA information can be obtained
at www.ICGtesting.com
Printed in the USA
LVOW08s0722290517
536140LV00004B/348/P

9 781545 345368